IN FORTUNE'S FOOTSTEPS

IN FORTUNE'S FOOTSTEPS

Lisa Main

CHIVERS

| British Library Cataloguing in Publication Data available |

This Large Print edition published by BBC Audiobooks Ltd, Bath, 2010.
Published by arrangement with Robert Hale Ltd.

U.K. Hardcover ISBN 978 1 408 47780 9
U.K. Softcover ISBN 978 1 408 47781 6

Printed and bound in Great Britain by
CPI Antony Rowe, Chippenham and Eastbourne

CHAPTER ONE

'Is that the lot of them?' Jake Cooper the letter carrier asked, pointing to a bundle of envelopes on the counter of Borthwick Post Office. It was the fourteenth of February and the pile was bigger than usual.

'Yes but I expect there'll be more by the end of the day.' Sarah Penghalion, the postmistress, gathered up the letters and handed them to Jake who scowled.

'Precious lot of nonsense, if you ask me. When I wanted to walk out with my Nellie I asked her straight out. I didn't waste good money on fripperies like cards to speak for me. All this does nothing but give me extra work and my legs aren't what they used to be.'

'I know, Jake.' Sarah smiled kindly. The old man had been complaining about his legs ever since she'd been a child and had started helping her grandparents to run the small shop and post office but she was fond of him despite his gloomy outlook on life. 'I'm sure there are more this year because the lads in the regiment want to be sure that their sweethearts receive a Valentine before they sail.'

'I dare say.' Jake looked slightly mollified. 'When do they march out?'

'This afternoon.' Sarah's smile faded.

1

'Papa's packing his kit now.'

'Now don't go looking so worried, Miss Sarah.' Jake gave her one of his rare smiles. 'Your Papa's a brave man and a good soldier. He'll have those savages defeated and be back here before you know it.'

'I hope so, Jake.'

The bell above the shop doorway jangled and a woman bustled in.

'You should see the clouds building up over the bay, Miss Penghalion. We'll have rain before nightfall you can be sure of it.'

'As if today wasn't hard enough already,' Jake grumbled as he slung his bag over his shoulder and headed for the door. 'I doubt any of the young ladies will appreciate that I've been soaked to the skin to make sure they get pretty words from their Valentines.'

'I often wonder how Nellie puts up with his ill humours.' As the door closed behind Jake, the woman lowered the black woollen shawl that was over her head and placed her basket on the counter in front of Sarah. 'I expect you've received more than one sweet token from gentlemen wishing to be your Valentine today.'

'Oh no, Mrs Thomas.' Sarah felt her cheeks grow hot. 'I'm sure there's no one who would wish to send me one.'

'I don't understand why not. You're every bit as pretty as your sister Lucy and, as I recall, Henry Bell couldn't wait to get her to the altar.

2

I'll take two penny stamps please.'

'Yes, Mrs Thomas.' Sarah opened the stamp book, picked up the long pair of scissors that sat beside it and began to carefully cut two stamps from a sheet of the black stamps printed with the Queen's head. She hoped Mrs Thomas would have nothing more to say on the matter of matrimony but, to her dismay, that wasn't to be the case.

'Why don't you go and visit with your brother John in Exeter? I'm sure you'd find a husband there.'

'I'm really quite happy here as I am.' Sarah carefully laid the scissors down again. 'Besides I couldn't go away and leave Grandma on her own, especially now that Papa is going overseas again.'

'Oh yes, I'd heard the regiment was to sail for Africa today.' Mrs Thomas sighed. 'Such a terrible business. I couldn't believe my ears when Frank read the newspaper report out to me. Who'd have thought the Zulus could defeat the Queen's army, and what heroes at Rorke's Drift defending the wounded the way they did. You must be very proud of your pa going out to take up the fight.'

'Yes, we all are.' Sarah lowered her eyes and hoped Mrs Thomas wouldn't notice that she wasn't being entirely truthful. She was proud of her father but she hadn't been able to help being angry when he announced his intention to sail to Africa with his regiment. After

3

almost twenty-five years' service in the Otterly Lancers, George Penghalion was due to retire from military life but had volunteered to join his comrades one last time. Sarah couldn't understand why he wanted to put himself in such danger and his family through the worry. 'Is there anything else you'd like, Mrs Thomas?'

'Yes, I'd like a pound of sugar and two bags of oatmeal please.'

When Mrs Thomas had paid for her purchases, Sarah helped her to pack them in her basket and then she drew her shawl over her head again.

'Be sure to tell your pa I sent my best wishes.'

'I will. Thank you, Mrs Thomas.'

When the door closed behind the older woman, Sarah slipped out from behind the counter and opened the door that led into her home behind the shop. At once the smell of fresh bread and cakes washed over her. Her grandmother had started baking just after dawn that morning and as she inhaled the sweet aromas of ginger fairings and apple cake, she realized just how hungry she was.

'Isaac Bell, I can see your hand creeping up onto that table and I know how many curd tarts are on that plate so think again before you try and steal one.' Sarah smiled at the sound of her grandmother's voice. She tried to sound stern but both Sarah and her sister,

Lucy, knew it was just an act. There wasn't a kinder woman in Borthwick than Anne Penghalion and she'd raised her son's family without any word of complaint after his wife had died giving birth to Sarah. Now she doted on Lucy's children, especially four-year-old Isaac, and Sarah suspected he'd be given a tart without having to resort to theft.

The kitchen of the small cottage was busier than Sarah could remember it being in a long time. Once there had been so many people living in the house that it was hard to fit everyone around the table. Then Grandpa Rufus had died, Lucy had married and John had gone to teach in Exeter. Now when Papa was away only Grandma and Sarah shared the room with Bosun, the Post Office cat, for company. Today however Lucy was there with Isaac and her new baby, Georgina, and Papa's tall frame was dwarfing everyone else as he tried to resist all the food his mother was pressing on him.

'Ma, if I eat all this I'll be too weighed down to fight and no good to anyone.'

'You need good food inside you, George.' Grandma sounded adamant. 'It's a long voyage and who knows when you'll eat again when you're in Africa.'

'We do have cooks, Ma,' Papa replied, laughing. 'But I'm prepared to concede none of them can bake as well as you. Perhaps I will find room in my pack for just one more mutton pie.'

Sarah watched her father bend to kiss his mother's cheek as he took a pie. He was already in his uniform and his white helmet was sitting on a chair beside his knapsack. For as long as she could remember Sarah had always been proud to see her papa in his bright red army jacket with its sergeant's stripes on the sleeves but today the sight of it made her feel nothing but anxiety.

'Ah Sarah lass, there you are.' Her father grinned and the ends of his thick brown moustache curled up. 'Was Jake pleased to see the extra work he had today?'

'Not in the least but he sends you his regards and so does Mrs Thomas.'

'Come and have something to eat while you've the chance, Sarah,' her grandmother said. 'There are potted meat sandwiches and the mutton pies are cooling nicely.'

'It all looks delicious.' Sarah moved towards the table, noting as she did so that Isaac did indeed have the remains of a curd tart in his hand. She picked up a sandwich and was just about to take a bite when the bell over the shop door jangled, letting her know that she had another customer. 'Unfortunately, I'll have to wait to find out how good it tastes.'

After selling Adam Kebble from the butcher's shop three penny postage envelopes, Sarah was about to return to the house when she found that her father had come out into the shop and was standing a short distance away from her.

'I was hoping to have the chance of some words with you away from all the others. I know you're not best pleased with me at the moment.'

'Papa, I—' Sarah tried to protest but found that she couldn't. She'd tried so hard to hide her feelings from her father but clearly she had failed.

'It's all right, lass, I understand why you're angry. I know I promised your grandma last time that I wouldn't go to fight again and I saw her trying to hide her tears when I told her I was going again as well as you did.' He reached out and laid a hand on her shoulder. 'I fully did intend to retire. Nothing would have made me happier than coming home to my family for good but you must understand that I can't abandon my post now. Over a thousand good men died at Isandlwana. More will die if we don't go to their assistance. I swore I would give service to my queen and country and I can't turn my back on that promise now. Do you understand, lass?'

'Yes,' Sarah said quietly. She was ashamed of her earlier resentment. She should have made more effort to understand that the army had been her father's life and that the idea of turning away from his duty when he was needed was unthinkable to him. 'I wish I could be as brave about it as you are.'

'I think you've a great deal of courage.' He smiled at her. 'I'm very proud of how you've done a grand job taking care of the business here since your grandpa died. Ma couldn't have managed without you. When I come home I'll be able to lighten your burden and then you can have a little more time to enjoy life. You more than deserve it.'

'Make sure you come home to us safely.' Sarah threw herself into his arms and buried her head against his shoulder. 'We miss you so much when you're away.'

'There now, don't take on so.' He stroked the back of her head. 'I'm relying on you to look after everyone for me while I'm gone. Will you do that for me?'

'Of course I will.' Sarah raised her head again and wiped away the tears on her cheeks.

'You see, you are brave.' Her father glanced up at the clock behind the Post Office counter and sighed. 'It's time I was heading for the barracks. We'll be marching out to Otterly and the boat soon. I'd best go and say goodbye to the others.'

At that moment the door from the house opened and Lucy appeared, looking worried.

'Is Isaac in here with you?'

'I don't believe so,' Sarah said and her father shook his head.

'He was still at the table when I came out and I closed the door behind me. He can't reach to turn the handle.'

'Oh no.' Lucy went pale. 'He's not in the house either. He must have got out and I don't know where he's gone.'

'He can't have gone far.' Sarah went to console her sister. 'Have you looked in the garden?'

'Yes and there's no sign of him. Oh Sarah, where can he be? It's not like him to run away.' Tears filled Lucy's eyes and Sarah took her hand as their father hurried across the shop and out into the street. A few seconds later he returned shaking his head.

'He's not out front either.'

'What if he's gone down to the harbour?' Lucy suddenly cried. 'He might fall off the sea wall and he can't swim.'

'I'll go and see,' her father said but Sarah shook her head.

'Let me go. You won't be able to get there and back before you're due to leave for the barracks.'

An anguished look crossed her father's face and Sarah could see he was torn between his duty and his love for his family.

'I'll likely find him before you've gone very far and we'll run down to the main road to Otterly to wave to you as you all march past.'

'At least then I'll know he's safe.' He nodded with approval at the plan but he looked no happier.

'Don't worry, Lucy. We'll be back before you know it.' Sarah gave her sister's hand one last squeeze and then ran out of the shop.

It was bitterly cold outside and the wind cut through Sarah's woollen dress as she ran down the cobbled road that led to the harbour. She heard laughter coming from The Three Bells Tavern as she passed and briefly envied the customers who would be sitting by the cosy log fire with nothing more than the price of their ale to worry them.

After the pub came the row of low-roofed, stone-built fishermen's cottages. The boats were out so there were no nets hanging out front to dry for small boys to play hide and seek in. Sarah's chest was beginning to hurt with the exertion of running but she didn't stop until she reached the small harbour. The tide was out so at least Lucy's fears of drowning were unfounded. Sarah hurried to the edge of the sea wall and looked out over the expanse of ribbed sand. There was a lone figure digging out near the shore line and, cupping her hands around her mouth, Sarah called out to him.

'Ned, have you seen Isaac.'

At first she thought the wind had drowned out her voice but then, just as she was preparing to lift her skirts and pick her way out to the old man, he slowly straightened and turned to face her.

'No.' His voice was faint and Sarah strained to make out the words. 'You're the first living soul I've seen in the hour since I came down here.'

'Thank you.' Sarah turned away. Isaac had been missing for less than an hour so she was now certain that he hadn't come this way. However, the relief that this knowledge brought her was tempered by the fact that she was still no closer to finding the little boy. She wondered if she should go back to the house and see if he had gone back of his own accord but if he hadn't and she returned without him then Lucy would be distraught.

It was then that she looked up towards the trees on the hill at the back of the village and she had a sudden inkling of where Isaac might be. Bluebell Wood was named for the thousands of lilac blooms that carpeted the ground each spring. It was still far too early in the year for the flowers to be out but Isaac liked going to play there at any time and the last time that he had walked there with Sarah he had set up camp in an old hollow tree trunk. He'd been delighted with his new find and told his aunt that he would go to live there when he was grown up. If he was going to hide anywhere it would be there. Sarah turned off the road that led back to the post office and began to hurry along the path out of the village and up towards the wood.

The track was muddy and as she strode along, Sarah looked down hoping to see a set of small footprints which would confirm she was looking in the right place. She didn't see the figure running in the opposite direction until they almost collided and they both came to an abrupt halt.

'Sorry, miss. I didn't mean to rush up on you like that. It's just that I'm going to be late if I don't hurry m'self and then I'll be up for all kinds of trouble.' Looking up, Sarah saw the speaker was wearing the uniform of the Otterly Lancers. His helmet and pack were both clutched in one hand and, from his ruddy cheeks and erratic breathing, she guessed that he'd been running for some time.

'You've left it a little late to head for the barracks.'

'I know, but there was someone I had to see before I went.' His bright blue eyes dropped. 'Only when I got to where she'd been living she weren't there. She's moved on and I don't know where she's gone now.'

'I'm so sorry.' Sarah couldn't help but feel sorry for the young soldier. He seemed so sad and he was little more than a boy—far too young to be going out to face a savage enemy in a hostile land. 'I hope you get to the barracks in time.'

'I will if I run fast enough.'

He had already begun to run again when Sarah had a sudden thought and called after him.

'Have you seen a small boy on this path?'

'Yes.' The soldier didn't stop but looked back briefly. 'He was up the hill a bit, heading into the woods.'

'Thank you and good luck.' Then she was right. Sarah turned away from the departing figure of the soldier and started walking up the hill with renewed vigour.

The wood was a dark and colourless place at this time of the year. The leaves that had fallen the previous autumn were grey and brittle beneath Sarah's feet and the trees looked stark and bare against the slate-coloured sky. Some of the more superstitious people believed the bluebells were a sign of fairy activity and that children who wandered into the wood alone might never be seen again. Sarah didn't believe the stories but today, in the cold and low cloud, it seemed a much more forbidding place.

'Isaac!' she called as she walked along the path. 'It's Aunt Sarah. Where are you?' There was no reply. She heard rustling in the leaves behind her and turned hopefully but the sound had been made by a blackbird scrabbling for food. 'Isaac, it's all right to come out. No one is cross with you.'

This time she was sure she heard a muffled sob and she moved quickly in the direction of the sound. Her nephew was sitting on a moss-covered rock with his knees pulled up against his chest and tears flowing down his dirt-streaked face.

'Oh Isaac, what's the matter?' Sarah went to crouch down beside him, pulled her handkerchief out of her sleeve and began to dab at his red and swollen eyes.

'It's not fair,' the little boy muttered tearfully. 'Grandpa said he was going to stay at home forever but now he's going away again. He told a fib.'

'He didn't mean to.' Sarah could see the same mix of hurt and anger in Isaac's expression that she'd had to battle with herself when she'd first heard the news. Now she had come to appreciate her father's position but could she make Isaac understand why his grandfather had apparently lied to him? 'Grandpa loves you very much,' she said gently. 'And he wanted to stay at home with you.'

'Then why is he going?' Isaac interrupted angrily.

'Because some other soldiers are in trouble and they need Grandpa to go and help them. It says in the Bible that we should always help other people, doesn't it?'

Isaac nodded half-heartedly and Sarah continued.

'It won't be too long until he comes home again and this time he really will stay.'

'But I want him to stay now,' Isaac protested and Sarah put her arm around him.

'I know. We all do but we must be brave and make Grandpa proud of us. Do you think you can do that?'

Isaac considered this for a moment and

then gave a solemn nod of his head.

'Good boy.' Sarah kissed the top of his head and then, conscious of passing time, rose to her feet and held her hand out to Isaac. 'Come on, let's run down to the road and watch Grandpa march past with the regiment. You can wave to him.'

'Will he wave back?' Isaac slid off the rock and put his hand into Sarah's.

'He might when no one is looking.' Sarah smiled down at her nephew and hoped that Lucy would be too relieved at his safe return to notice the bright green moss stains down the back of his trousers.

Despite being named after the larger nearby town, the Otterly Lancers were barracked closer to Borthwick. Once Sarah and Isaac reached the place where the track rejoined the main road, it only took them ten minutes to walk down to the crossroads where the soldiers would march past. Four thatched cottages stood at the roadside. Sarah made Isaac huddle up against the rough stone wall in front of them so he could have shelter from the wind and then settled down to wait for the sound of the drum that would signal the appearance of the Lancers.

'Why aren't they coming?' Isaac asked.

'They will soon.' Sarah hoped she was right. Now that she was standing still, the cold wind was even more biting. She wished she had the benefit of her coat or even a shawl to pull around herself and Isaac.

'If you're waiting to see the Lancers, you've missed 'em.' The unexpected voice came from behind them and made Sarah whirl round in surprise.

'I'm sorry.'

'I said you've missed 'em.' The speaker was an old woman who had come out of the end cottage carrying what looked like a pan of chicken grit. 'They went past here a few minutes back. I reckon they'll be half way to Otterly by now.'

Isaac's face crumpled.

'I want to see Grandpa,' he wailed, burying his face against Sarah's skirt.

'Oh there now, don't take on so.' The woman's tone softened. 'I've got treacle biscuits inside. Will one of them make you feel better?'

'No!' Isaac's head shook vigorously and, although she couldn't see his face, Sarah knew he was crying again. She frowned. If only she'd found the little boy sooner. Now not only was Isaac inconsolable but her father was marching off to war without the reassurance of knowing that his grandson was safe. There was only one thing she could do to rectify the situation.

'Come on.' She took Isaac's hand in a firm grasp. 'We're going to Otterly.'

'That's a fair walk,' the woman remarked.

'I know but it takes a good while to load the ship and we can get there before they sail. Do you want to go and see the ship, Isaac?'

'Oh yes, Aunt Sarah.' Isaac looked up and she saw determination in his eyes. 'I can walk all the way. I won't get tired.'

'All right, but first we must hurry back to let your mama know you're safe and then fetch our coats. It'll be even colder by the time we head for home tonight.'

Lucy didn't seem to know whether to be angry or relieved when Sarah took Isaac back into the house so she settled for a combination of both, hugging and scolding him all at once. Sarah left them alone and went through into the shop where her grandmother was sweeping the floor.

'I thought I'd do this now and save us a bit of time later on. It's not been too busy while you've been gone.'

'Grandma, do you think it would be all right it I took Isaac into Otterly. We missed Papa on the road so he doesn't know that Isaac's safe.'

'Of course it would.' Her grandmother nodded. 'I can manage in here for a couple of hours. Make sure you wrap up warm, mind.'

'We will and I'll try to get back in time to deal with the evening post.'

'Don't worry about that.' The old woman gently chided her. 'I was packing letter sacks before you were born. I'm sure I can still remember how to do it. Just you run along and get to Otterly before the ship sails.'

'Thank you, Grandma,' Sarah smiled and

then hurried to fetch her coat.

*　　*　　*

Lady Constance Weston had been crying ever since the carriage had started its journey in to Otterly. She knew she was behaving in a most unladylike fashion and that her mama would be appalled by her lack of dignity but she couldn't help herself. She had tried to be composed all morning but, now that the moment she had been dreading was here, she couldn't contain her grief any longer.

'Come now, Constance, it won't be as bad as you imagine.' Hugh, her husband of three weeks slipped his arm around her waist.

'It will.' She sniffed from behind her handkerchief. 'I don't want you to go. Can't you stay?'

'You know I can't, my love. I have an obligation to my regiment. Think what a poor example it would set to the men if I sought to shirk my duty simply because it happens to have cut short my honeymoon. We must be grateful I was given permission to drive to the ship rather than marching with the regiment or we wouldn't have this extra time together.'

Constance sniffed. Even though Hugh's words sounded sincere she couldn't help thinking he was in some way excited at the prospect of seeing action and that even if the chance to stay at home with her presented

18

itself he would be reluctant to abandon the chance to seek glory on the battlefield. Mama had been right. Men were often inclined to be heartless.

'I wish I could go and stay with Mama while you are away.' In the months before her marriage, Constance had become increasingly stifled by life in London with her widowed mother and had told herself that she couldn't wait to move to the country and be mistress of her own house. However, now that she was to be alone in this strange new place, she wanted nothing more than to scuttle back to the safety of her old home.

'Your mama is still in Florence,' Hugh pointed out. 'You would be alone in London, too. I'm sure you'll find plenty to occupy you around your new home in the coming weeks and you'll be able to ride again when the weather improves.'

'That won't be for weeks yet.' She became aware of sounding petulant and bit down on her lip. That wasn't a becoming attitude for a lady. It was bad enough that she probably had a red nose and swollen eyelids by now. It wasn't the image of his bride she wanted Hugh to take to war with him. She dabbed delicately at the corners of her eyes and tried to smile at her husband. 'But you are right, that will lift my spirits a little.'

'Stop!' Hugh hadn't heard her. He hadn't even seen her smile. He'd been staring out of the window until he'd suddenly leapt up and hammered on the roof of the carriage to alert the driver.

'What is it?' Constance asked as the carriage jolted to a halt.

'We just passed a young woman on the road. She was carrying a child and I thought she tried to hail us. She may need help.'

'Hugh, we can't wait or you will be late.' Constance knew she was being selfish but as far as she was concerned there were times when it was justified. These were her last few precious minutes alone with Hugh and she didn't want to share them with an interloper.

'It will take no more than a moment.' Hugh pulled down the window and stuck his head out. 'Do you need assistance?'

'Please, sir.' Although she couldn't see the speaker, Constance could hear desperation in the woman's voice. 'I must get to Otterly before the Lancers sail but my nephew is exhausted and unable to walk any further. If you're going to Otterly, please may we ride on your rear luggage board? I have a little money with me and can pay.'

'I know you.' Hugh leaned out a little further as though to take a better look at the woman. 'Aren't you Sergeant Penghalion's daughter?'

'Yes, sir. I'm Sarah. This is my sister's little boy, Isaac. I promised him we would get to the docks in time to say goodbye to his grandpa but he can't go any further.'

'Well, you can't ride on our luggage board,' Hugh said decisively. 'It's dangerous and far too cold. Come up inside with us where there is at least some comfort to be had.' Withdrawing his head from the window, Hugh swung the door open.

'Thank you, sir.' The gratitude was evident in the woman's voice.

'It's the least I can do for George Penghalion's daughter. He's a good man and has been of great service to me on more than one occasion. Here, give me the child.'

Hugh reached down and a few seconds later deposited a little boy in front of his wife. Constance stared at the child's dirty face and mud-encrusted clothes with a faint sense of horror. Just what sort of people was Hugh expecting her to travel with? Such a thing would never have happened in London. She was relieved when Sarah stepped up into the carriage and she saw that she, at least, looked more presentable.

'I am Captain Weston and this is my wife Constance. My dear, this is Sarah Penghalion. Her father has served with me for many years.'

'I'm pleased to make your acquaintance, ma'am.' Sarah had a soft Devonshire accent but she was well spoken. The plain felt hat she was wearing had fallen out of fashion some time ago but although her long brown coat was drab it was clean and something on its collar caught Constance's eye as the new passengers were settled into the seat opposite.

'What a pretty brooch.'

'It was my mother's.' Sarah's fingers strayed up to the cameo. 'It's all I have of hers.'

The carriage started to move again and Hugh took his watch out of his pocket.

'We'll make Otterly in no more than a few minutes so you will have adequate time to see your father before we sail.'

'You've been very kind.'

'Not at all. We can't have this young man missing his grandfather, can we?' Hugh sat forward to smile at Isaac but the little boy was overcome by shyness and buried his face against Sarah. She put her arm around him and smiled apologetically at Hugh.

'It's been an arduous day for him.'

'Of course.'

Sarah had heard her father speak of Captain Weston in the past but hadn't realized that he was so young. He was a striking figure in his uniform which, like those of all other officers, included spurs and a sword. No wonder his wife was looking at him with such adoration in her eyes. She seemed even younger than her husband and with her blonde hair and bright blue eyes, reminded Sarah of a doll that Lucy had once owned. Her plum velvet coat and matching feathered hat were the most splendid clothes that Sarah could recall seeing but for all her finery the girl didn't look happy. It was plain that she'd been crying. Her husband was heading to war just as Sarah's father was. Sarah could understand her grief and found that she felt sorry for Lady Constance despite her obvious wealth.

A few minutes later they reached the outskirts of Otterly and Isaac grew brave enough to sit up and look out of the window as they clattered over the cobbles around the docks.

'There's the boats.'

'Yes indeed. That one there with the tallest mast is the one your grandpapa and I will sail on.'

When the carriage stopped, Hugh got out first, then offered his hand to help down first Constance and then, to her surprise, Sarah.

'Please,' he murmured as she negotiated the step, 'will you stay with Constance until we sail? She knows no one here and is not used to going out without a companion.'

'Of course I will.'

'Thank you.' Hugh inclined his head in appreciation and then turned to swing Isaac down to the ground. 'Come along, we must find your grandpapa at once.'

*   *   *

From his vantage point a short distance away, Ewart Davenport sighed, first as he watched Hugh say goodbye to his wife and then again when he saw the badge of rank on the officer's shoulder.

'Really, brother.' The man standing beside him shook his head. 'I do not understand why you were so set on coming here. You refuse to go and wish the men farewell and have done little but indulge in doleful groans since we arrived. Why not walk over and greet your comrades?'

'You know full well that I can barely walk anywhere, Race,' Ewart muttered as he banged the stick he was using to support himself against the ground. 'No one in the Regiment wishes to be burdened with an officer who can only hobble. I see they've already promoted Weston to take my place.'

'Then that is his misfortune,' Race said with a good-humoured laugh. 'Let him go and face the spears of the enemy on your behalf while you recuperate at leisure.'

'Do you think I wish to sit idly by while others do my duty?' Ewart rounded on his brother and his eyebrows creased over his dark brown eyes. 'Sometimes I wonder if you were born with any sense of family honour. You're fit and well. Rather than spend your days endeavouring to work as little as possible you could have enlisted in the Lancers like our father and his father before him.'

'I would make a poor soldier.' Race seemed unaffected by his brother's angry outburst. 'And dodging bullets is no way to spend one's

24

life. Although I can't deny the uniform must be a boon when it comes to attracting young ladies. There are a great many pretty faces in the crowd today.'

'I doubt that's the reason these men have taken the Queen's shilling. I've been alongside them when we've been under fire and there's no thought of pretty faces then.' Ewart sighed again. 'I wish to my core I hadn't come off that horse and could be with them during these coming battles, too.'

'If it is of such consequence to you then why not sneak aboard the ship now?' Race shrugged his shoulders. 'By the time you're found it will be too late to turn back. Your leg will heal on the voyage and then you can fight to your heart's content.'

'Only you could think of such a thing.' Ewart's expression made his exasperation plain. 'No doubt that is just the plan of action you would undertake if it suited your ends but one day you will come to learn that you cannot always act in the way you wish to. I'm under orders to remain here and I will obey them no matter how painful it may be.'

'At least let us ease the pain a little.' Race shivered. 'A mug of ale and a warm fire in that inn will set us up for the journey home.'

'Go if you wish,' Ewart said. 'I'll stay here and watch them sail out.'

'Very well. You'll know where to find me when you're ready to leave.' Race looked relieved to have a chance to escape and he headed for the inn opposite the quay without looking back.

Ewart stayed where he was for some minutes more, watching as dock workers carried boxes of supplies into the ship's hold. He couldn't remember a time when he'd felt more desolate. The Lancers had been his life since he'd joined them as an eighteen-year-old subaltern. Following his father's death, that winter, he'd accepted that he would have to resign his commission in order to run the family estate but he hadn't expected fate to rob him of his final chance to serve his country. Suddenly he decided that he didn't want to watch from a distance. Even if he would no longer sail with them, he could at least go and stand with the regiment one last time.

The cold wind seemed to have insinuated itself into the depths of his wound and he winced as he put weight on the leg. He'd heard it said that pain could drive a man to madness and now he understood why. It disturbed his sleep at night and only that morning his mother had commented on the uncharacteristic shortness of his temper when he'd snapped at the maid for spilling milk at the breakfast table.

'Captain Davenport, sir. It's a pleasure to see you here.' A thin man with a grey beard and a pace stick stuck under his arm hurried across as soon as he saw Ewart.

'Thank you, Sergeant Major, though I take no pleasure in watching you sail without me.' It had been a mistake to come closer. Now that he could smell the polish coming from the buckles on the uniforms and see the eager expressions of the men as they stood in rank, he felt even more isolated. However, it would have been churlish now to walk away. Instead he made his way slowly along the line of familiar faces and acknowledged their greetings with nods.

'Grandpa!' A child suddenly ran in front of him and flung its arms round the legs of someone in the front rank.

'Isaac, you're safe, thank the Lord.'

Ewart recognized the voice of Sergeant Penghalion and then watched as the man broke out of rank and bent to pick the child up. This was a punishable offence and Ewart had no desire to see the sergeant disciplined.

'Penghalion, get back in rank!' He meant it as a warning that the sergeant major was close by but realized, too late, that his voice sounded harsh. The sergeant put the boy down and moved stiffly back into his place.

'Isaac, come here.' A dark-haired woman stepped forward and took the child's hand before casting a reproachful look at Ewart. 'It won't do to get Grandpa into any more trouble.'

Ewart's first instinct was to try and explain

27

but his leg was throbbing and he doubted he would be believed. Instead, he turned away and limped morosely in the direction of the inn.

When the ship finally slipped its moorings and began to slide out into the estuary, Isaac had recovered enough to jump up and down, waving his handkerchief in farewell, but Constance already needed hers to mop away a fresh flood of tears.

'What am I to do without him?'

'Come now.' Sarah gently took her arm and led her towards the waiting carriage. She could so easily have given into grief as well but Constance needed someone to be strong for her and she had given Sir Hugh her word that she would take care of his wife.

She helped the weeping woman up into the carriage.

'Goodbye, Mrs Weston.'

Constance seemed too distressed to reply, and with a gentle smile Sarah turned away to collect Isaac. It was a long walk back to Borthwick and a light rain was blowing in on the wind. Soon it would be heavier. She hoped the soaking wouldn't make the little boy ill.

'Miss Penghalion!' Constance had pulled down the carriage window and was peering out. 'Won't you ride back to Borthwick with me?'

'Thank you.' Sarah felt a surge of relief. 'I will just fetch Isaac.'

'You're very kind,' she said as she climbed up into the relative warmth of the carriage a little later.

'Not at all.' Constance managed to give a feeble smile. 'And if the truth be told, I'm really being selfish. I would much appreciate your company.'

The carriage made slow progress as the crowd on the quayside began to disperse and, glancing out of the window as they passed the row of buildings opposite the harbour, Sarah saw two men leaving the inn. The older of the two looked in her direction and their eyes met briefly before she quickly jerked her head back. It was the disagreeable character who had reprimanded her father for greeting Isaac. Time spent in the inn had clearly done nothing to improve his nature. There was still an unfriendly frown etched on his features and Sarah wondered why his companion, who appeared to be in a jovial mood, wished to spend time with him.

'Do you live in the village itself, Miss Penghalion?'

'Yes.' Sarah was happy to turn her attention back to Constance. 'Please do call me Sarah. I live with my grandmother behind the village shop. I am the postmistress there.'

'Then you have plenty to fill your day.' Constance gave a little sigh. 'I sometimes wish I could seek some kind of employment. You must have such an interesting time.'

'Not entirely.' Sarah laughed. 'On the whole my duties can be monotonous but I do enjoy the company of my customers. They keep me from being lonely and, when the local gossips meet there, it's impossible not to overhear all the village news whether I wish to or not.'

'I know what it is to be lonely,' Constance said quietly and to Sarah's surprise. She knew that Captain Weston employed at least three servants in the house. Surely Mrs Weston had no reason to feel alone there. She was on the verge of saying that she and her grandmother would be happy to welcome a visitor into their home at any time when she recalled who she was addressing and bit back the words. A lady of such high birth who was used to London society wouldn't wish to take tea in the kitchen of their cottage.

'I am sure you will quickly make new friends in the area,' she said instead. 'The weather will improve soon and then you will meet more people.'

'Yes, that's what Hugh said.' Constance gave a wan smile. 'I hope you are both right. I would like to make a friend.'

Sarah smiled back and the two lapsed into silence. As Sarah thought of her father and wondered if the bad weather was making the start of his voyage rough, she guessed that Constance's thoughts were also with her husband.

Exhausted by the day's excitement, Isaac

30

had nestled up against Sarah and fallen asleep with his thumb tucked firmly into the corner of his mouth. Looking down, Sarah gently stroked his hair and prayed it wouldn't be too long until he saw his grandfather again.

By the time the carriage rumbled down the main street of Borthwick, the wind was turning into a gale and heavy rain was lashing against the small windows.

'If not for your kindness we would have been out in this,' Sarah said.

'I hope that no one is without shelter tonight,' Constance replied with a shiver. 'I wouldn't put a dog out in such a storm.'

'This is my home.' Sarah saw a lamp shining in the window where her grandmother must have left it to guide her. She and Lucy would no doubt both be frantic with worry. 'Come, Isaac.' She gently roused the boy as the carriage stopped and he started into a grumpy wakefulness.

'I must thank you and Captain Weston again for your consideration towards us.' In a bold gesture, she held her hand out to Constance who took it.

'I am glad we could help.' Constance suddenly spoke again as Sarah was lifting Isaac out of the carriage. 'Miss Penghalion . . . Sarah, I hope that we may meet again in the near future.'

'I hope so too.'

Sarah kept Isaac in her arms to try and

protect him from the worst of the weather as the carriage pulled away. 'Let's go and see if Grandma has supper ready for us.'

There were no other lights burning in the post office and Sarah guessed her grandmother must have closed up for the night after despatching the evening post.

'We must go in by the back door,' she told Isaac as the wind howled again and made the shop sign creak as it swung about. Although she knew what it was, Sarah couldn't help thinking it was an eerie sound and she was glad they were almost inside. The flickering shadows around them were unnerving. There were so many stories told in these parts about spectres and fairy folk that it was hard not to think of them on such a night.

Another blast of wind hit them and made it almost impossible to walk. As the rain stung at her face, Sarah pressed Isaac closer to her and struggled towards the path that ran round the side of the shop. It was then that she saw something that scared her more than any ghost could. There was a dark figure huddled against the wall near the entrance to the shop. No one from the village would behave in such a way. It had to be a stranger and one who was up to no good. Why else would they be lurking in the darkness? With Papa gone there was no one left to protect the women from an intruder and Sarah shuddered at the thought of her grandmother and sister facing such peril alone.

'Who's there?' She tried to make her voice sound authoritative but her throat had gone dry and her words were almost lost in the wind. 'If you don't leave at once, I'll run for the constable.'

Instead of running, however, the figure turned and moved towards her. Sarah realized with horror that he could be armed and that she and Isaac were in terrible danger.

'I have a child here,' she cried. 'At least let him go unhurt.'

'Please don't get the constable on to me.' A woman's voice came out of the darkness. 'I ain't gonna hurt no one.'

Sarah's fear subsided a little. The speaker sounded more frightened than she was.

'Who are you?' she asked.

'My name's Hepzi.' The stranger moved forward again and was silhouetted in the light of the lamp in the window. 'Are you the postmistress?'

'Yes.' Was this a robbery after all? Who was to say there weren't accomplices waiting in the shadows?

'Then it's you I need.' The woman sounded desperate. 'You must help me. You're the only person who can.'

CHAPTER TWO

The evident despair in the woman's voice pushed all thoughts of robbery from Sarah's mind. If anyone needed help badly enough to come out on such a night then their plight had to be serious.

'Come inside,' she said. 'We need shelter before anything else'

Lucy came hurrying out into the hallway as soon as Sarah opened the cottage door.

'Sarah, thank the Lord. I was out of my mind with worry over you both.' Sarah suspected her sister's greatest concern had been for Isaac but that was only as it should be and she didn't mind.

'Don't worry, Lucy. Mrs Weston was kind enough to bring us home in her carriage so we are not as wet as we would have been.'

'Mrs Weston? How did you come to—?' Lucy's voice tailed away as she caught sight of the figure Sarah was ushering in through the door. 'Who is this?'

'Someone seeking our help. Please bring a lamp.' Sarah put Isaac down and he hurried into his mother's arms before they both disappeared back into the kitchen. A few seconds later the door opened again and Anne came out with a lamp.

'Lucy said we have a guest.'

'Yes.'

As her grandmother brought the lamp closer Sarah was able to see the stranger properly in the flickering light and she was barely able to suppress a shocked gasp. The person standing in front of her was little more than a girl and her clothing was woefully inadequate for the winter weather. Her threadbare dress barely skimmed her ankles and the rough woollen shawl that was pulled up over her head was so wet there was already a small pool of water forming around her bare feet. Sarah guessed she was one of the gypsies who travelled through the area looking for work in the local farms. She'd heard that some had recently set up camp near the village.

'Heaven save us, you're soaked to the skin, child.' Anne was the first to speak. 'Come away inside at once and warm yourself by the fire. You look sorely in need of a hot drink.'

'No, I can't,' the girl gasped. Then she seemed to recollect herself. 'Thanking you for your kindness but I've got to get back. If I'm missed then there'll be trouble.'

'What help do you need?' Sarah asked.

'I've got to send a letter, urgent like, and I've heard it said as how you'll write them for those as can't do it for themselves. I can pay you.' The girl opened her hand and held out two pennies.

'I don't charge for the writing,' Sarah replied, 'and it's only one penny for the stamp but the last post has gone for tonight. It might be better if you returned in the morning.'

'I can't do that.' A stricken look came into the girl's eyes. 'I've got to be in the fields by first light or me Da'll take his strap to me. Please help me, Miss. I wouldn't be asking you if it weren't important.'

Sarah saw a tear slip down onto the girl's cheek and felt a rush of pity for her. She was tired and hungry and there was nothing she wanted more than to join her family by the fire but it was clear that her own sufferings were nothing compared to this stranger's.

'Then we will write it now and it will leave with the first post,' she said. 'Grandma, may we take the lamp through to the shop with us?'

'Of course.' Anne handed the lamp to her granddaughter. 'Wait and I'll fetch the keys for you.'

'I fear it will be cold in here,' Sarah said as she unlocked the door to the shop a few minutes later. 'The stove has been out for some time.'

'I don't mind the cold,' the girl replied. 'I'm used to being out in all weathers.' It sounded almost like a boast but Sarah couldn't help thinking that it was a hard way to live.

'What's your name?' she asked as she fumbled on the large ring of keys for the one that would unlock the post office drawers.

'Hepzi. Hepzi Briar.' The girl watched Sarah take out paper and an ink pot. 'How

36

long will it take to get the letter there?'

'That very much depends on where you are sending it.'

'Combe Langley.'

'Then it will be delivered by tomorrow afternoon.' Combe Langley was a village on the far side of Otterly and no more than half a day's walk from Borthwick. Sarah dipped her pen into the ink and then looked at Hepzi expectantly. 'I am ready to start.'

There was silence. In the flickering lamplight Sarah saw Hepzi look down at the ground before speaking in a subdued tone.

'I ain't never sent no letters before.'

Suddenly Sarah understood. The girl had no idea how to begin. 'Well, it is usual to head the paper with the address you wish any reply to be sent to. Where is that?'

'Can it be here?' Hepzi asked.

'You mean this post office?'

'Yes. I could fetch it from here. There's no place else it can go and that way no one as shouldn't is going to see it.'

Hepzi seemed determined to keep this letter a secret and Sarah wondered what she was trying to hide and from whom.

'That won't be a problem.' Sarah wrote down 'Hepzi Briar, in the care of Borthwick Post Office' and then looked at the girl again. 'Most letters begin with "Dear" followed by the name of the person you are sending it to.'

'Noah,' Hepzi said at once. 'It's "Dear

Noah".' Her voice broke as she said the name for the second time and Sarah pretended not to see her dash a tear away.

'Dear Noah,' she repeated as she wrote the words down. 'Now what do you wish to say to the gentleman.'

'It's not to a gentleman.' Hepzi sounded alarmed. 'It's to my Noah.'

'Of course. How remiss of me.' Sarah had no desire to embarrass Hepzi any further by pointing out her misunderstanding. 'What do you wish to tell Noah?'

'That I'm sorry.' Hepzi's dark eyes clouded. 'I didn't mean to say what I did and I wish I could take it all back. I know he's every right to hate me now but I've got to talk to him. There's something as he has to know and it's a matter of life or death to me. Tell him he's got to come. He's got to come now.'

As she transcribed this into the first person and a coherent message, Sarah wished there was a way she could better convey the anguish in Hepzi's voice through the written words. What if she had failed to communicate the obvious sense of urgency to Noah and he didn't come to see Hepzi? She felt that the consequences of this could somehow be serious and that she would then be partly to blame. She didn't want to let Hepzi down.

'Shall I end with best wishes from you?' she asked.

Hepzi considered this for a moment and

then nodded.

'All my best wishes,' she breathed and in that moment Sarah saw exactly what the situation was. Hepzi was in love with Noah. Clearly there had been a lovers' tiff. That would explain Hepzi's distress. Love made people behave in desperate ways. Sarah smiled to herself as she remembered how Lucy hadn't eaten for two whole days when she and Henry had quarrelled shortly before their wedding. Now she felt happier about the letter she'd written. With luck, it would bring about reconciliation and a happy outcome. She blotted and folded the sheet of paper before reaching for an envelope.

'To what address should I send this?'

'Bishopston Manor. That's where Noah works in the gardens. He's no home of his own but he bides with the cattleman and his wife.'

Sarah had heard of Bishopston. It was a large estate and a great many people worked for the landowner there. She had to make sure the letter reached its intended recipient.

'Does Noah have a surname?' she asked.

'Kettley.'

Sarah put as much information as she could on the envelope and then lit a candle to warm some sealing wax. As she did so the clock above the shop counter chimed the hour and Hepzi started.

'What time is that?'

'Seven o'clock.'

'Oh no!' Hepzi clutched at her shawl. 'I've got to go else Da'll get back before me and know I've been out.' She slammed the coins she'd been holding down on the counter beside Sarah, then turned without another word and ran out through the door they'd entered by.

'Wait.' Sarah tried to call her back. 'At least let me give you a dry shawl before you go.' She hurried after Hepzi but by the time she reached the hallway it was empty. She quickly opened the cottage door and peered out into the stormy darkness hoping to call the girl back. However, there was no sign of life in the rain-beaten street. Hepzi had gone.

*   *   *

The storm took three days to blow itself out. No one ventured far unless they had to and as a result the shop was quieter than usual. Sarah took advantage of the lull to dust down shelves and carry fresh bags of stock up from the cellar. She knew people would be in need of supplies when the weather improved and she was proved right when the skies finally cleared on the morning of the fourth day. The first hints of pale spring sunshine brought customers in from the outlying rural areas. The shop bell rang constantly from the moment the door was unlocked and neither Sarah, who was kept busy in the post office,

40

nor her grandmother in the shop, had a chance to take a break all morning.

The local housewives used the shop as much as a meeting place as a means of making purchases and the air rang with noisy conversation as they queued up to be served.

'Ged Watkins reckons as how he's missing a whole pile of taters out of his barn. It's always the same whenever they come here. I'm half afeared to leave my laundry out on the line in case one of 'em swipes it.'

'No one in their right mind would want your Joe's breeches, Carrie.' This remark was accompanied by a burst of laughter. 'Still, I know what you mean. I'll sleep a lot easier in my bed when they've moved on again.' The speaker reached the front of the Post Office queue. 'Don't you agree, Miss Penghalion?'

'Agree with what, Mrs Harper?'

'That having the gypsies hereabouts is a risk to decent folk like you and I. They're nothing but thieves, the whole lot of them.'

'I really couldn't say.' Sarah found that the generalization upset her far more than it would have done a few days earlier. Hepzi had certainly been no thief. In fact, she had left more money than required to pay for the stamp on her letter.

'Well, you should think on it, especially as your da isn't around to look out for you and your grandma.'

'Is there word from him yet?' the next

41

woman in the queue asked.

'Not yet. He will be at sea for a few days more.'

'Better that than being speared by a Zulu,' Mrs Harper interjected loudly. Sarah quickly glanced over to see if her grandmother had heard and was relieved to see that she appeared not to have done.

'I am sure we are all grateful for your good wishes,' she muttered. 'Now, what can I do for you this morning?'

Sarah was still feeling unsettled by Mrs Harper's thoughtless remarks long after the woman had left and was relieved when she saw her sister enter the shop a little before the midday post was due to arrive. She beckoned her over.

'Lucy, would you have a moment to make a pot of tea? We've had nothing since breakfast and Grandma must be as parched as I am.'

'Of course, but I mustn't stay too long. I only came in for a bag of oatmeal and I've left Isaac in the smithy with Henry.' Lucy hitched baby Georgina up in her arms and went through into the cottage.

A few minutes later she reappeared without Georgina and carrying two earthenware mugs of tea. She put one under the counter where Anne was still busy with customers and then placed the other down next to Sarah just as the carrier from Otterly station came in to drop off and collect the midday post.

'Will I sort it for you?' she asked Sarah who gave her a grateful smile.

'If you could spare the time. It's so busy today and Jake will be in to collect his second delivery soon.'

'I can take a minute. Georgina's asleep in Grandma's linen drawer and I'm sure Isaac will be happy for a while yet. He loves to watch Henry make the horse-shoes.'

Sarah returned to her duties and Lucy began to sort through the bag of letters.

'There's one here for us from John,' she said a few minutes later. 'I recognize his hand. Grandma will be pleased to see it.'

'Indeed. It seems such a long time now since he was home for Christmas.' Their brother was a teacher in Exeter and although he didn't manage to get home very often, his family looked forward to the times when he could.

'And there's another for you here, Sarah.' Lucy held out a pale blue envelope. 'I don't recognize this writing.'

'Nor do I.' Sarah took the envelope and slipped it into her apron pocket. There would be no time to read it until the rush in the shop was over.

'That's the last of them,' Lucy said a few minutes later. 'All sorted and ready for Jake. Now I must get back and take Henry his dinner. He won't be in a pretty mood if he has to go—'

A loud crash from the other end of the shop

interrupted her and both sisters turned to see what had happened. One of the weights from the scales had fallen and dislodged the bag of tea on the other balance. It was scattered across the floor but Sarah was far more alarmed to see that her grandmother was slumped against the counter looking very pale.

'Grandma! What's wrong?' She hurried to her side.

'It's nothing, dear.' Anne's reassurance did nothing to ease Sarah's concern. 'I just went dizzy for a moment and dropped the weight. It's made such a mess. I'm just a silly old woman.'

'Of course you're not. You need to rest.'

'Yes,' Lucy agreed taking hold of her grandmother's arm to support her. 'Come through to the house and sit for a while.'

Henry's dinner would be late today. Sarah was glad that her sister was there to care for Grandma but Anne's failure to protest that she didn't need a rest worried her. As she set about sweeping up the spilt tea and filling another bag for the waiting customer, Sarah was troubled by what had happened. Grandma was old now and, although she would never admit as much, the work in the shop was getting to be too much for her. If only Papa had been able to stay at home and run the shop instead of going to war. Now there was no saying when he would be back. When or if. Sarah's hand shook and she pushed that awful

44

thought from her mind. She had to have faith that he would be safe. In the meantime, however, she had to face up to the fact that she couldn't expect her grandmother to keep working as hard as she was. The problem was that the shop and post office combined were too much work for one person to cope with alone for any length of time. She would need to consider taking on an assistant but first she would have to convince her grandmother to permit someone to take her place and then try to find a suitable applicant. She wasn't sure which would prove to be the harder task.

With queues in both the shop and the post office, Sarah didn't have another chance to ponder these problems until two o'clock came and she was able to close for her half day. At least, she told herself, as she pulled down the blind on the door, it was Wednesday or she would have been rushed off her feet until after six.

As soon as she had locked up the post office drawers, she went through into the cottage and found Lucy making a pot of tea.

'I thought you'd be in need of this.'

'I can't deny that.' Sarah began to cut a slice from the loaf of bread on the table. 'How's Grandma?'

'Sleeping by the fire in the front room. I wonder if we ought to have sent for Doctor Heggerty.'

'And have Grandma tell us off as soon as he

was gone? You know how she hates doctors.' Sarah smiled but could see worry lines etched in her sister's face. 'Don't worry,' she assured her. 'If she's no better when she wakes then I'll fetch him myself.'

The kettle began to sing. Lucy lifted it from the range and poured water into the large and sturdy teapot that had served the family for as long as the sisters could remember.

'I'll have to go and see to Henry. May I take a can of tea from here? He'll be dry as bone by now.'

'Of course, and I hope he's not too ill humoured at you for staying.'

'Oh, even if he is, we'll have kissed and made up by supper time,' Lucy laughed. 'We always do.'

When Lucy had gone, Sarah took her simple meal into the front room and quietly sat down in the armchair opposite her grandmother. The old woman was still softly snoring and so Sarah silently watched the flames in the hearth until she suddenly remembered the letter in her pocket and pulled it out.

'What do you have there?' While she was reading the short note, she hadn't noticed that Anne had opened her eyes.

'How are you feeling now, Grandma?'

'Quite well other than being angry at myself for causing so much trouble in the first place.' The old woman's softly lined cheeks had colour in them again.

'It was no trouble. The shop was very quiet after you left.' One small lie wouldn't hurt on this occasion.

'I don't suppose for a moment that it really was,' Anne replied with a knowing look. Sarah could never fool her.

'I have a letter from Lady Weston.' Sarah held out the note for her Grandmother's scrutiny. 'She asks me to take tea with her this afternoon at four and says she will send the carriage to collect me.'

'I don't doubt she's feeling lonely, the poor thing. She'll be missing her man just as much as we miss your papa.' Anne's sigh was heavy and Sarah wondered if she had overheard the remarks in the shop that morning after all.

'They'll soon be home,' she said instinctively and Anne chuckled. 'Come now lass, I know better than that. They won't even arrive in Africa for days yet. It's Lady Weston who needs to hear pretty words like that, so save them for her.'

'But I can't go,' Sarah protested. 'I'll have to tell the carriage driver that when it comes.'

'And just why not?' Anne asked in a way that made Sarah think she already knew the answer.

'I won't leave you while you're ill.'

'Now just you listen to me, Sarah Penghalion.' Anne's face set into the familiar determined lines that Sarah knew made any

47

argument pointless. 'I'm no more ill than that teacup is. You take yourself out to tea and cheer Lady Weston up. It'll do you good to have some company of your own age as well. We're just going to sit here by the fire and rest a while longer, aren't we Bosun?' She nodded at the hearth rug and Sarah saw that the ginger cat was curled up in a contented ball in front of the flames.

'One day someone is going to realize that our cat doesn't earn his wage.' Every post office in the country received a small annual sum to pay for the upkeep of a cat. They were supposed to control vermin on the premises but it seemed that no one had ever told Bosun this. He much preferred napping to mousing these days.

'Don't change the subject, my girl.' Her grandmother could sound stern when she wanted to. 'Will you be taking tea with Lady Weston?' It was not so much a question as an order and Sarah nodded.

'Yes, Grandma.'

The carriage arrived promptly at quarter to four and Sarah felt like a duchess as the coachman jumped down to open the door for her even though he was Sam Boyer who had been John's boyhood friend and had spent his childhood helping her brother think up ways of teasing her endlessly.

'Afternoon, Sarah.' He made a play of tipping his cap to her.

48

'Hello, Sam.' She was about to step up into the carriage when someone called out.

'Please, Miss.' She turned and found herself facing the girl who had visited her a few days earlier.

'Hepzi?'

'I came to get the letter from Noah. I didn't know you'd be shut at this hour.'

'Only on a Wednesday,' Sarah told her. 'But I'm afraid that no reply has come for you yet.'

'But it must've,' Hepzi insisted. 'You said as how he'd get it the day after and his answer would be back by now, wouldn't it?'

'That would depend on how long it takes for your friend to write a reply.' Or whether he intended to at all. Sarah didn't want to say that aloud but the wretched look that crossed Hepzi's face suggested that the same thought had occurred to her.

'He would've done it by now if he was going to.' She lowered her eyes and Sarah wasn't sure if she was still speaking to her or muttering to herself. 'He's not going to come, is he? He's not going to come and I'll have to face the trouble all alone. What will I do?'

'Hepzi,' Sarah asked, 'do you need some kind of help?'

The sound of Sarah's voice seemed to bring the girl out of her reverie and she shook her head.

'There's nothing no one can do. Nobody but Noah.'

49

'He may reply yet,' Sarah said trying to sound optimistic.

'And he may not.'

Sarah didn't know what else she could say to make the girl feel better. Instead, she opened her reticule and took out a penny which she gave to the girl.

'You gave me too much money when you sent your letter. This belongs to you.'

'Thank you, miss.' The money didn't seem to make Hepzi any happier. When the carriage was pulling away, Sarah looked out of the window and saw the girl standing in the same place with her face in her hands. She wondered what trouble Hepzi had been referring to. Perhaps she had been wrong in seeing the situation as a simple fight between lovers. It seemed it was something far more serious than that and she hoped the letter Hepzi wanted to receive would come very soon.

Farleigh Park was a large house and Sarah was more than a little nervous as she walked up the steps where a footman, who had must have been watching for the carriage, opened the door to her. As she entered the hallway she had to fight down a gasp of surprise. Never in her life had she seen such a large or ornate room. A long marble staircase dominated the space front of her. The stained-glass window above the landing was far more elaborate than anything in Borthwick church and the two willow-patterned urns standing at either side of the bottom step were filled with more flowers than Sarah could have gathered from her entire garden.

'This way.' The butler made no attempt to disguise his disdain of her lowly status as she followed him across the hall and through a door. 'Miss Penghalion,' he announced stiffly.

'Sarah, I'm so glad you could come.' Constance rose to greet her and Sarah was unsure what dazzled her the most—the rich red furnishings and opulent rugs in the room or her hostess, who was wearing a primrose yellow tea gown that matched her fair curls and made her blue eyes shine.

'It was very kind of you to invite me, Lady Weston.'

'I'm afraid it was down to yet more selfishness on my part,' Constance admitted with a smile. 'I was in sore need of companionship but now, as you see, I am quite spoilt. A friend of my husband's has come to call on me as well.'

For the first time, Sarah noticed the figure standing with his back to the fireplace and a teacup in his hand. She drew in a sharp breath. She knew this man. He was the disagreeable civilian who had so rudely chastised her father on the quayside.

'May I introduce you to Mr Ewart Davenport,' Constance said. 'Ewart, this is Miss Sarah Penghalion from Borthwick.'

'Miss Penghalion. I'm proud to say I know your father. He is a fine soldier.' Stepping forward, Ewart extended his hand. He didn't seem to remember their previous encounter but it wasn't so easy for her to forget his unpleasantness.

'How do you do,' she said coolly, withdrawing her own hand almost as soon as he had touched it. She was glad to see that he looked taken aback.

'Come and sit by me, Sarah.' Constance, who was busy with the silver teapot, hadn't noticed the stilted exchange between her guests. 'I was just telling Ewart about the fright I gave myself the other night.' It was clear she was relishing the chance to have someone to talk to and she chattered on quite happily.

'Do help yourself to cake. Cook made it especially for your visit. She has such a light hand for baking. In fact, she made a cherry cake just like this one to raise my spirits on the day my dearest Hugh sailed. Of course, I was in no mood to enjoy it then and I took to my bed quite early that night.

'However, I didn't sleep. The storm was so bad that I couldn't rest for the very idea of Hugh being out at sea in such a tempest. I'm sure you must have been equally concerned about your papa, Sarah. Wasn't it dreadful to watch them sail away from us?'

'Indeed.' Out of the corner of her eye, Sarah saw Ewart start. Had he just recalled their first meeting?

'Anyway, a little after midnight I got up and went to the window. The trees in the avenue were quite bent over in the wind and I feared some of them would come down before morning. That was when I saw the lights. There were three of them bobbing about in the darkness and drawing closer to the house. I was most alarmed.' Constance gave a self deprecating laugh but her light-hearted smile didn't reach her eyes.

'I called for Matthews but by the time he went to investigate they were gone. Mrs Norris says they were likely to have been fairy lights. I thought that such a pretty notion.'

'It doesn't do to listen to the irrational nonsense spouted by your servants,' Ewart interjected sharply. 'Most of the tales of fairy folk told in these parts are the products of little more than some overactive imaginations and too much ale.'

'I think you will find that a great many of them have their roots deep in the past, Mr Davenport.' Sarah, herself, was a sceptic where most of the tales were involved but it irked her to hear this man belittle the culture she'd known since childhood in such an offhand manner.

'Surely, Miss Penghalion, you do not expect Constance to believe that the fairy folk were dancing on her lawn?' Ewart raised a disdainful eyebrow and Sarah felt herself colour.

'Of course not. I merely wished to say that the stories are important to many people in these parts.'

'Ewart, how is Race?' Constance had been raised to be a skilled hostess. She saw that the current topic was raising discord between her guests and quickly moved to change it to a less contentious one. However, judging by the way Ewart frowned as he replied, she wasn't sure her question had been the right one.

'As profligate as he ever was. Since leaving Oxford he has had the idea of assisting the gamekeeper on the estate but is hardly ever there to do so. He spends most of his time in Exeter where, rumour has it, he's taken up with an actress, of all people.' He gave a derisive snort. 'I can only hope Mother doesn't come to hear of it. She has dealt with enough pain this year without the added shame of that.'

'Poor Mrs Davenport', Sarah thought as she stirred her tea with a more vigour than it required. 'One son is dissolute and the other is unbearable. It cannot be easy for her.'

'Sarah,' Constance turned to her 'I see you are wearing your pretty brooch again. Did it you say it belonged to your mother?'

'Yes. It is all I have of hers,' Sarah said quietly and with a pang of regret. Although she couldn't mourn a mother she had never known, she had always felt the sense of something missing her life.

'I'm so sorry.' Constance reached out to touch her hand and Sarah saw genuine tears of sympathy fill her eyes. 'I can't imagine life without my mama. She is travelling in Europe at present and I can't wait for her to return so she can visit me here.'

'I am sure she'll be eager to see you, as well.' As she spoke Sarah happened to glance in Ewart's direction and was disconcerted to find that he was staring at her intently. It made her voice tail away and an awkward silence settled over the room.

'I will take my leave of you.' It was Ewart who broke it. 'It was only my intention to ensure that you needed nothing, Constance.'

'I am indebted to you for thinking of me.' Constance gave him a gracious smile as she laid his tea cup on the tray.

'Good day, Miss Penghalion.' He nodded brusquely at Sarah. She inclined her head slightly in acknowledgement but felt no desire to speak to him any more than she had to. As he walked to the door, she noticed that he was limping and recalled that he'd used a stick in Otterly. It was a pity that some degree of recovery had done nothing to improve his disposition.

'Poor Ewart.' Constance visibly relaxed when she and Sarah were alone. 'It was considerate of him to call but, unlike his brother, he is never fully at ease in the company of our fair sex and that does make him such hard work.' She grimaced. 'No doubt it is cruel of me to say such things when he was good enough to visit, especially as his estate lies a good hour's ride from here.

'He and Hugh met at school, you know, and then spent time together during the summers of their boyhood. Ewart became a soldier as soon as he came of age to acquire a commission and was utterly crushed not to sail to Africa with the regiment. He was injured by a horse a few months ago. Hugh says any other man might have lost the leg altogether but sheer doggedness on Ewart's part has him walking and riding again already.'

'I can see that he might be inclined towards tenacity.' Tenacity, intransigence and down-right rudeness, just to name a few of his better qualities. Now that she knew he had served in the Lancers, Sarah could see why he had spoken to her father as he had, although it didn't make her consider him any more kindly She could think of a great many more things she could say about Ewart Davenport but it would be ill-mannered to criticize another of Constance's guests. She would entertain Anne with her opinion of him that evening.

'What do you think the lights in my garden were?' Constance suddenly asked.

'I can't say,' Sarah replied. 'I don't suppose they were fairies and am quite sure there will be a sound and far less fantastic explanation for them. It could be that they weren't in the garden at all but simply appeared to be. Sometimes I can see the lights from ships even when they are some way out.'

'Perhaps that's the case.' Constance seemed keen to seize at a practical explanation. 'I didn't want to admit to it in front of Ewart but I didn't sleep a wink after seeing them. I felt so uneasy. It isn't at all like London here. I feel so very isolated, and now that Hugh's gone I'm alone.'

'Not completely so,' Sarah pointed out. 'You have your servants.'

'Yes and I am glad of their presence but they cannot make up for the lack of company.' Constance sighed. 'Before I married I often accompanied Mama on her visits and to the meetings of her charity committees. My days here are so empty. I must find some way to occupy them.'

'I'm sure you will,' Sarah said but she was unable to offer any suggestions. She had no idea how the wives of the local gentry filled their time. They certainly never came into the shop.

Constance finished her tea and then stood up.

'It's such a pleasant afternoon. Would you care to take a turn in the garden before you go home?'

—*My dearest Hugh, I wish you were here to*

see the snowdrops dancing in the breeze and the daffodils all ready to burst into bloom. It won't be a proper spring without you. Miss Penghalion is pleasant company and she knows a great deal about the natural world. Today she pointed out a bird perching in one of our rose bushes and told me it was called a chiffchaff. It was such a pretty little thing.

I close this letter with fond kisses and a thousand warm wishes for your well being.

Know that I am always your beloved wife.

Constance laid down her pen and pressed the letter against the blotting pad. Every evening, after dinner, she recorded the day's events in great detail for Hugh. She had no idea when or where her letters might reach him but she dutifully wrote them in the hope that they would bring him a taste of home.

The fresh air and company in the afternoon must have had a beneficial effect on her because, for the first time since her husband's departure, she was aware of becoming drowsy shortly after she'd retired for the night and was soon asleep. However, just as the clock in the hall chimed one, she woke abruptly and for no apparent reason.

She lay still in the darkness, hoping that she'd return to the dream of Hugh she'd been having and was finally drifting back into semi-somnolence when a loud crash made her sit up in fright. It had been the unmistakable sound of breaking glass and it had come from below. There was somebody moving about downstairs.

CHAPTER THREE

The next morning it was barely light when Sarah forced herself to get up. Worries about her grandmother's health and her father's safety had conspired to give her an uneasy night. She wished she could stay snuggled up under her blankets and try to catch up on some of the sleep that had eluded her but that was a luxury she simply didn't have. The first post would soon be on its way from Otterly and the shop would have to be swept out before opening time.

It was bitterly cold in the small bedroom and, after having to break a thin layer of ice that had formed on the water in her washing jug she wasn't surprised, on opening the curtains, to find that a heavy frost had turned the landscape white and formed spirals of ice on her windows. Although it would be March in a few days it seemed that winter was determined to linger this year.

When she had dressed, she went downstairs and was surprised to find a fire already burning in the kitchen grate.

'Grandma, I thought you'd stay in bed today.'

'Now why would I want to be doing a thing like that?' Anne asked as she poured out two cups of strong hot tea. 'I've to get to the bakers and catch the dairy cart for milk before we open up this morning.'

'But surely you don't intend to work in the shop today?' Sarah stared at her in concern. 'You need to rest after yesterday.'

'I need nothing of the sort.' Anne's bright eyes flashed. 'Don't you be in such a hurry to try and turn me into an invalid because I won't have it. Do you hear me, my girl?'

'Yes, Grandma.' As she tried to sound suitably admonished, Sarah tried hard not to let her smile show. Seeing that her grandmother had returned to her full fighting spirit meant that one of her worries was abated at least.

After breakfast Sarah went to attend to her duties in the shop and was about to unlock the door when Anne returned from her errands with a worried frown on her face.

'The baker's boy says there was a robbery at Farleigh Park last night.'

'Oh no!' Sarah's first thought was for Constance. 'Was anyone hurt?'

'He didn't say. I reckon he was just keen to pass a story on but hadn't heard it all himself. Try not to fret about Mrs Weston until you've heard it a'right. You know what a devil that lad is for giving his tales wings and making them fly. If it's true then I've no doubt we'll hear all about it as soon as you open that door.'

Anne was right. News of the robbery had reached the village via the constable's wife and every customer in the shop was eager to voice an opinion on the subject.

'I told you no good would come of having gypsies in the area,' Mrs Harper said smugly as Anne packed her basket. 'Not that they are any more. The constable went a-looking for 'em this morning and it seems they've gone— in a hurry too by all accounts. The ashes were still warm where they'd had a fire.'

Then Hepzi would be gone as well. Now she would never know if Noah replied to her letter. Sarah felt a pang of sadness for the girl. She couldn't believe that she would be caught up in any wrongdoing. Perhaps none of her family had been either. Was it possible that after hearing about the theft they had fled because they knew that suspicion would immediately fall on them whether they were guilty or not?

'Is there any news of Lady Weston?' Anne asked. Sarah was in the middle of totalling a column of numbers but she lost count when she heard Mrs Harper's reply.

'I should say. Poor woman. It seems she was confronted by the villain on her own staircase. I've heard it said he knocked her to the ground

61

and left her for dead before fleeing.'

'Was she injured?' Sarah asked in concern.

'Well, all I know is that Doctor Heggarty rode out that way at first light. I imagine it must have been to attend to her.'

'Poor Constance.' As soon as Mrs Harper left the shop Sarah turned to her grandmother with an anguished expression. 'I hope she hasn't been seriously injured. She was in such high spirits after our walk yesterday. She intended to write to Captain Weston.'

'Maybe you should go and call on her,' Anne suggested but Sarah shook her head.

'It wouldn't be proper for me to call without her asking for it. She's a lady. Her butler seemed unwilling to admit me yesterday and I've no doubt he'll send me packing if I go there uninvited.' She frowned. Observing social protocol wouldn't keep her from worrying.

'Perhaps I could write a note enquiring after her health,' she said at last. 'That wouldn't be as presumptuous, would it?'

'There's nothing presumptuous about showing kindness to anyone, no matter who they are,' Anne said firmly. 'The world would be a better place and your dear father might not be in the peril he is if a few more people were inclined to think the same way now and again. I'm sure she'll be pleased to find that you're asking after her.'

'Then I will write and send it up with Jake

62

when he comes in.' Sarah immediately took a fresh sheet of paper out of her desk drawer and dipped her pen in the ink bottle.

My dear . . . She stopped at once. That was too familiar by far. She took out a fresh page. *Dear* . . . She had been urged to call Constance by her first name but found that she simply could not do it in writing.

Dear Lady Weston,
Alarming reports of a violent incident at your house have reached our ears this morning and my grandmother and I find ourselves greatly concerned for your well-being. I hope that you will overlook my boldness in writing to enquire after your health and to offer any assistance that I can at such a distressing time.
Yours sincerely,
Sarah Penghalion.

It sounded cold and informal when she read it over and she wished she could replace it with a more expressive note. However, Jake would soon be in and there was no time to labour over finding better words. She addressed an envelope and was melting a piece of sealing wax when a small child entered the shop carrying a basket that was almost as big as she was.

'Why, Tilly Luckins, what are you doing coming all this way into town alone?' Anne

63

asked in surprise. Tilly had only recently turned five and she lived in a farm cottage a good way out of the village.

'Please, Missis Penghalion, Mam's poorly and she says can you please give her the things on the list for me to carry back to her. I've got three shillings stitched into my pocket to give you for it.'

'Of course I can. Let me see your list.' Anne took the tattered piece of paper from the child and read it before drawing close to Sarah and speaking in a hushed voice. 'This poor wee lamb will never manage to carry such a heavy basket all the way home. Why, she could barely lift it empty as it was.'

'I'll take it out this afternoon,' Sarah said at once and Anne went back to speak to the little girl.

'Tell your mama that Sarah will carry her shopping out to her later today.' She opened one of the glass jars that stood on the counter. 'And in the meantime here is a barley sugar stick to reward you for coming all this way so cleverly.'

'Thank you, Missis Penghalion.' The little girl grinned at her unexpected good fortune and skipped out of the shop.

'You're a good girl too,' Anne told her granddaughter when they were alone. 'This basket will be heavy for you as well.'

'I'll manage and besides now that the sun is out, it's a pleasant day for a walk.' Sarah finished sealing her letter and hoped that Constance was feeling well enough to appreciate the sunshine too.

*   *   *

From her position on the chaise longue in her drawing room Constance watched as the parlour maid poured coffee for Ewart and Race.

'Thank you, Grace. That will be all.' As she took her own cup from the maid it rattled loudly against its saucer and she realized that her hands were still shaking. She felt as though they would never stop.

'It is very kind of you to ride out to enquire after me especially on such a frosty morning. I apologize that you find me in such a state of déshabillé.' In the aftermath of the robbery and her terrifying experience she had not had her hair curled that morning and there were no tightly laced stays beneath her morning gown and Kashmir shawl.

'My dear Constance, you look as delightfully pretty as ever.' Race gave her one of his charming smiles. 'A great many ladies cannot achieve such elegance even after half a day spent under the care of a coiffeuse and dressmaker.'

'You flatter me,' Constance demurred with lowered eyes. She didn't believe Race's polished compliments for a moment but it was

65

nice to hear them and his light-hearted attitude made her feel a little better after her ordeal.

'Does the constable offer any hope of redeeming your goods?' Ewart lacked his brother's sense of subtlety and his question forced the robbery back into her thoughts again.

'He believes the culprits will already be half way to Exeter where they can sell them. We lost two silver candlesticks and a canteen of cutlery given to us as a wedding gift from Hugh's aunt.' Her unsettled emotions threatened to overwhelm her for what seemed like the hundredth time that morning and she pressed her fingers to her trembling lips. 'Poor Hugh will be so upset. We didn't even have a chance to use it before he was sent off to war.'

'Dear Constance, do not distress yourself.' Race sat forward and laid a comforting hand on her shoulder. 'When Hugh returns it will be to you not his cutlery. I am sure his greatest concern will be for your safety.'

'Indeed.' There was a distinct edge in Ewart's voice. 'Your husband will not care about his silver as long as you are untouched.' She felt Race's hand slip away from her shoulder. 'It is most fortunate that the felon ran when you confronted him.'

'It was scarcely a confrontation.' Constance wished he hadn't raised the subject. She was trying so hard to put the memory of her terror and the thief's fearsome face from her mind. She wished now that she hadn't ventured out onto the landing after hearing the crash. 'I fainted clean away when I saw him.'

'But your scream alerted the servants and was enough to scare him off,' Race said consolingly. 'In my mind, that marks you as a true hero of the hour.'

'I do not feel like a hero,' Constance admitted. 'Indeed, were it not for the draught that Doctor Heggarty administered I should still be in my bed and unable to receive you.'

'Then we must all be indebted to Doctor Heggarty,' Race said with another of his smiles and a slight lift of his eyebrows that made Constance want to giggle. Ewart, however, sounded anything but amused when he spoke.

'You must forgive my brother's indelicacy, Constance. He seems to be adopting the vulgarity of his associates in Exeter.'

'My associates in Exeter do not criticize me on an hourly basis.' A tight smile didn't conceal Race's antagonism. 'I find that most refreshing.'

Constance dreaded Ewart's response and was relieved when there was a tap on the door and her butler entered carrying a small silver tray.

'There is a letter for you, madam.'

'Thank you, Matthews.' Constance wondered if the servant could hear the genuine gratitude in her voice. His appearance had been so timely.

'It is from Miss Penghalion,' she told Ewart as she read the note. 'It is very good of her to take the time to write. I must call on her as soon as I am recovered again.'

Ewart made no comment on this. He was still glaring at his brother. The air of hostility between her guests was so strong that Constance felt as though it was pressing down on her. Her head was beginning to ache and she seized on this as a chance for reprieve.

'I am a little fatigued,' she told them. 'Will you forgive me if I rest now?'

*   *   *

As they left Farleigh Park, Ewart and Race rode in stony silence and for the first mile the only sound in their ears was the hammer of hoofs on the frost-hardened ground.

'I think it would be best,' Ewart said eventually, 'if you did not visit Constance again while Hugh is absent.'

'I shall visit whomsoever I choose to,' Race said in a sullen voice. 'I do not require your permission to do anything.'

'It isn't appropriate,' Ewart snapped back. 'She is the wife of a family friend and you were openly playing the libertine with her.'

'I meant nothing by it.' Race shrugged. 'I was merely trying to raise her spirits a little. Is it a crime to tell a pretty woman that she is?'

'In these circumstances it is irresponsible. You are playing fast and loose with the reputation of a lady, not one of your music hall girls.' Ewart scowled at him. 'I do not know why I continue to lecture you on responsibility when it is clear that you lack any. When you were sent down from Oxford I was under the impression you intended to turn what little knowledge you did attain to assisting me on the estate. Instead you spend your days finding ways to entertain yourself and all the estate sees of you are the bills that arrive in your name. Only this morning I find that you have spent a hundred guineas on tailoring.'

'Surely you wouldn't see me going about in rags?' Race asked with a laugh. 'I thought that a modest price to pay for such workmanship. The waistcoat I have on today is worth that much alone.'

'I beg to disagree,' Ewart said. 'Don't you understand that as landowners we have a God-given duty to exercise restraint and set a worthy example to those less privileged than us? Wanton profligacy is no less a crime whatever your annual income.'

'Even the most poorly paid labourer in your fields knows how to enjoy himself once in a while, Ewart,' Race pointed out. 'You might do well to benefit from his example before your heart turns completely to stone.'

'Better that than losing my soul in a life of dissolution,' Ewart snapped but then his harsh

69

tone softened slightly. 'I have no desire to see you come to harm, Race.'

'And you won't. I have fate on my side.' Race laughed and spurred his horse up into a canter. 'If you don't believe me then watch this.'

As Race kicked his horse up to a gallop, Ewart realized that he intended to jump the wall that bounded the woods at the start of their estate. It was a dangerous thing to do at any time but the ice and the hard ground made his behaviour utterly reckless.

'Race, no!' Ewart's warning was lost in the sound of Race's laughter. He felt his hands tense involuntarily around his reins as his brother's horse left the ground and leapt over the wall. Its back hoofs grazed against the top stones. A stone dislodged and, for one dreadful moment, it looked as though both horse and rider would come to grief as they landed. However, Race managed to steady the animal and Ewart watched as he continued to gallop up the hill and into the trees. It seemed that fate had saved his brother once more.

'I pray that your luck never deserts you, Race,' he muttered as he urged on his own horse and continued along the safer road back to the house.

*   *   *

It was early afternoon when Sarah started out

70

in the direction of the Luckins's house with their basket of groceries. Her grandmother had packed it and Sarah suspected she had slipped in one or two little luxuries that were not on Mrs Luckins's list but which would provide a treat for the invalid. Papa joked that his mother's soft heart meant the shop would never turn a good profit but Anne was adamant that she would continue to help others where and when she could.

Although the sun was out, it was still cold. Sarah watched her breath form soft curls in front of her and her boots crunched on the frost-whitened grass when she crossed the verge outside the post office and took the road out of the village.

'That looks like a heavy load, Sarah. Can I relieve of you of it?' Albert Eden, who worked as a groom at the rectory had crossed the road to speak to her.

'I won't refuse an offer like that,' Sarah said handing him the basket. 'It is a heavy one today. I'm going out to the Luckins's. Is that anywhere along the road you intend to follow?'

'You know I'd happily walk along any road with you, Sarah.' Albert winked and Sarah blushed.

'Really, Albert, if you insist on saying such things every time we meet then I may begin to believe them one day.'

'Who's to say that I don't mean every

word?' he asked. 'I should be sore affronted if I was to ask you to come to the Shrovetide dance with me and you thought I was speaking in jest.'

'Then perhaps it's as well that you haven't asked me.' Sarah said with a toss of her head that Lucy would have called coquettish. She was sure Albert meant nothing by his flattering speeches and that made her bolder than she might have been with anyone else. Sometimes she wondered how she would react if he were to seriously pay court to her. With his honey-gold hair, blue eyes and open features he was widely regarded as one of the handsomest bachelors in the village. It might not be that unpleasant a prospect. It was certainly enjoyable to have his company this afternoon.

'Does life at the rectory still suit you as well as it did?' she asked.

'It's agreeable enough,' Albert said with a dismissive shrug. 'Reverend and Mrs Yates are good to me and I take pride in seeing the carriage going out with a shine on its wheels and a gleam on the horses' manes but I do sometimes think I could make more of myself. What was the good of going to school for five years if I'm never to make use of my writing and arithmetic? One day I intend to leave service and be my own man.'

Albert had been saying this for as long as Sarah could remember but he had never made any effort to fulfil his dream and she wondered

72

if it would ever be more than that.

'Shall we take the path through the churchyard?' she asked. 'It will make our journey a little shorter.'

'Why would I wish to take any course that will mean less time in such charming company?' Albert pulled a mournful face but he opened the lychgate and stood back to let Sarah pass through first.

No matter how busy the village streets were there was always an air of tranquillity in the churchyard where generations of Borthwick's inhabitants had been laid to rest over hundreds of years. There were rabbits grazing on the grass beside the church and a blackbird, perched in the top branches of the yew tree by the gate, was singing in clear, piping notes.

'I'm glad that spring is almost upon us at last.' Sarah took a deep breath and could almost smell the new life in the buds and grass around her.

'You wouldn't have called it springlike if you'd been breaking ice in the troughs this morning,' Albert said. 'My fingers were numb with the cold for a good part of an hour after it.'

'Before we know where the time has gone it will be summer and you'll be longing for respite from the heat. You always say it makes the horses fractious.'

'It's the flies as do that,' Albert muttered.

'They make us all fractious.' Sarah

remembered how last summer her father had spent most of his leave working in the vegetable garden with a neckerchief tied over his mouth to give him some relief from them. She wondered how he would fare with the insects in Africa. He'd explained to his family that the seasons were reversed there and that winter would be approaching on the African continent by the time he landed there. It was hard to imagine such a thing.

'Sarah?' Albert's voice disturbed her thoughts. 'About the dance. Do you think you might— What's that?' His tone changed abruptly and he pointed to a grave stone a short distance in front of them where a dark shape was huddled close to the ground.

'It looks like a person.' Sarah hurried forward.

'Be careful.' Albert advised as he tried to catch up with her. 'It could be one of those that robbed Farleigh Park. They might be set on violence.'

Whoever it was didn't seem capable of any aggression. As she drew closer, Sarah could hear muffled sobs and see that the person was shivering so hard it was a wonder they didn't shake themselves apart.

'Are you all right?'

The figure stirred a little at the sound of her voice and drew back the shawl covering its face. Sarah gave a shocked cry.

'Hepzi!' She knelt down on the damp grass

beside the girl. 'What are you doing here?'

Hepzi tried to reply but her trembling lips were unable to articulate any coherent words. Sarah took hold of one of her ice-cold hands. 'Have you been here all night?'

This time the girl managed to nod weakly.

'It's a wonder she survived.' Albert was staring down at the girl with an expression that seemed to be a mixture of pity and distaste.

'I think she barely has.' Sarah put a hand to Hepzi's forehead and felt the alarming warmth of a fever in her skin. 'Albert, I must take care of her. Will you deliver the basket for me?'

'Yes, but what do you intend to do with her?'

'I'm taking her home with me.' Sarah hadn't hesitated to come to that decision. 'Grandma will know what to do for the best.'

The short journey back to the shop felt like one of the longest of Sarah's life. Hepzi was so weak she could scarcely stand. Sarah did her best to support her but every step seemed like an ordeal for the girl and Sarah was afraid she would collapse completely before they had reached their destination.

She was relieved to see that the shop was empty when they finally struggled through the door.

'Grandma, it's Hepzi. She's very sick.'

'Oh my Lord.' Anne hurried out from behind the counter and helped to hold up Hepzi's limp body. 'Bring her through to the

75

kitchen. The fire will still be burning and there's hot water. The first thing we must do is get her out of these wet clothes.'

'She's been out in the elements all night,' Sarah said and Anne clucked sympathetically.

'Poor soul. It's no wonder she's half frozen.'

As soon as Hepzi was settled by the fire Anne sent Sarah to fetch some dry clothes. She selected one of her warmest woollen nightgowns and a shawl that Anne had knitted for her, then hurried back down to the kitchen.

Hepzi was still collapsed in a chair by the fire. Her wet clothes had been removed and she was wrapped in a blanket while Anne was gently bathing her hands and face with warm water.

'There now, we'll soon have you warmed up again,' she said in the same tender tone that Sarah could recall her using whenever she, John or Lucy had been ill as children. Hepzi murmured something but Sarah couldn't make out what she'd said.

'Don't you fret yourself about that.' Anne squeezed the girl's hand and then looked up at Sarah. 'Good lass. Help me get her dressed and then make up the fire in your father's room. She needs a warm bed and some tender care.' As she stood up and eased the blanket off Hepzi's shoulders, she said nothing but drew Sarah's attention to the girl's back with her eyes.

'Oh!' Sarah couldn't bite back her horrified

gasp. Hepzi's thin shoulders were marked with long red weals that criss-crossed over her pale skin. There was only one explanation for such appalling injuries. Someone had beaten her.

'We'll look after her now.' Sarah heard the resolve in her grandmother's voice. 'It won't happen again.'

There was so little colour in Hepzi's cheeks that only her flame-coloured hair showed up on the white pillows when she was settled into bed.

'She looks so—' Sarah whispered to her grandmother. 'I think I should get the doctor.'

'No.' Anne shook her head. 'If you're going to fetch anyone then make it Maggie Price.'

'Maggie?' Sarah looked at her grandmother first in bewilderment and then, as realization slowly set in, with a more questioning look. That's right,' Anne said briskly. 'Unless I'm mistaken, and I don't for one minute think I am, it's not a doctor this poor child needs, it's a midwife. She's going to have a child of her own before the summer's out.'

'A baby?' Sarah asked in surprise.

'I doubt it will be a kitten,' Anne gently teased. 'Now go and fetch Maggie but tell her it's a matter of some delicacy and discretion. We don't need the whole village knowing our business at the moment and the last thing we want is the person who beat Hepzi hearing where she is and coming a-looking for her.'

After examining Hepzi, Maggie quickly confirmed Anne's suspicions. 'I reckon this little one will come around harvest time,' she said as she drew the blankets back up over Hepzi.

'Then it's true,' Hepzi said bleakly. 'I thought it but I was feared to ask me Ma if there was a baby coming. It's what I had to tell Noah but he don't care about me no more. He's not coming and I don't know what I'm going to do now.' Her voice broke on the final words and she began to sob.

'There now,' Maggie said consolingly. 'You're not the first lass to find herself in this pickle and I doubt you'll be the last. You'll get by and find that things aren't as bad as you think.'

'They'll be worse,' Hepzi gulped between sobs. 'I can't go back to my folks now. Me da'll kill me for sure.'

'I'm sure he won't.' The placating words came easily to Maggie but she hadn't seen the marks on Hepzi's back. If her father had been responsible for those then Sarah wasn't convinced that Hepzi was exaggerating.

'He will and I know it!' Hepzi was inconsolable. She buried her face in the blankets and cried out loud with no signs of stopping.

'This amount of upset is doing no good to

either her or the baby,' Maggie told Anne and Sarah. 'You need to try and keep her calm if you can.'

Sarah didn't know how she could begin to make Hepzi feel any better but her grandmother didn't hesitate. She went and sat down on the bed next to Hepzi and spoke in a kindly but firm voice.

'Come along, my dear, taking on like this isn't going to help you or your baby. You're safe here now and I give you my word that no one will hurt you again while I'm looking out for you.' Hepzi's sobs abated slightly and now that she knew the girl was listening, Anne continued. 'This young man of yours may not have answered your letter but he still has responsibilities to face up to. You need to go and put him right on the matter. It's a wedding ring you need from him now, not a letter.'

'Do you know where the young man in question is to be found?' Maggie asked Sarah.

'Over at Combe Langley. I believe he works at Bishopston Manor.'

'Then there's no question of her going to look for him.' Maggie frowned. 'She's too weak to walk to this door and back. She's had a rough time of it and if she doesn't take care to rest now then there might not be a baby for her to worry about.'

'Then I'll go for her.' Sarah moved closer to the bed and addressed the shape under the blankets. 'Hepzi, I'm going to Bishopston to

79

fetch Noah. I'll ride with the post wagon and bring him back with me.'

The blankets stirred and Hepzi's red-rimmed eyes came back into view.

'Would you really do such a thing for me, Miss?'

'Yes, and I'll bring Noah back with me, I promise you.'

'You're so kind.' Hepzi's eyes filled with tears again. 'No one's never been so good to me as you afore.'

'I'm happy to help you.' Sarah quickly turned away so that Hepzi couldn't see the tears of compassion forming in her own eyes. She couldn't bear to think of the suffering Hepzi had already endured in her short life. At least now she could do something to ease some of it. She would find this Noah Kettley and leave him in no doubt of her opinion of him. What made him think he had the right to treat a girl in such a way and then abandon her, refusing to even acknowledge the letter asking him for help? Well, he would have a different view of things by the time she'd put him right. Sarah was determined to make sure that he came to Borthwick and did the right thing by Hepzi no matter what she had to do to ensure it.

*   *   *

'I'll have to drop you here.' Dart Gregory, the

wagon driver brought his horse to a halt at a fork in the road and pointed to the left. 'Bishopston Manor's up that road there. About half a mile on from here you'll come to a stile. Go over that and take the path through the woods to the farm. That'll cut a good bit off your journey.'

'Thank you, Dan.' Sarah carefully climbed down from her place beside him on the plank seat and picked up her basket. 'I'm most grateful to you for bringing me this far.'

'It was good to have a bit of company.' The old man tapped his pipe on the board in front of him and began to fill it with fresh tobacco. 'Now, just you take care to stick to the path in those woods. We don't want you getting lost in there.'

Sarah set out along the road to Bishopston with a determined stride and began to rehearse exactly what she would say to Noah when she found him. She would be indignant but not judgemental and firm but not too harsh. At least Hepzi had been looking better by the time she set out. Anne had made her eat a bowl of hot chicken broth and she had settled down to sleep.

Lucy had been called in to serve in the shop for the remainder of the afternoon. Isaac had found this very exciting and was eager to help open the door for customers. Sarah knew everyone would want to know where she had gone and there would no doubt be endless questions when she got back but by then Noah would be reunited with Hepzi and there would be nothing more to worry about.

She saw the stile Dan had told her about. There was no one in the road to witness her trying to negotiate it but she had no desire to be inelegant. She gathered her skirts carefully about her ankles, climbed over it with as much grace as she could and then took the path that led into the woods.

The sun was already low in the sky and long shadows fell on the ground around the trees where tightly curled up liquorice wheel-like ferns were poised ready to unfurl in the spring. The previous autumn's leaf fall was like a thick, damp carpet and beech nut cases crunched underneath Sarah's feet as she walked. There seemed to be no one else around but the path she was following was well trodden and Sarah wasn't worried until she came to the place where the track divided in two. She came to an abrupt halt. Dan hadn't mentioned this to her. Each branch of the path led in opposite directions and there was nothing to indicate which one went to Bishopston. It would soon be dark and Sarah recalled Dan's warnings about getting lost. She had to make a decision and hope that it was the right one.

The left-hand path looked as though it had seen more use. This seemed as good a guide as any other she could think of. She took that one and walked along briskly. There was no telling where she would end up but she consoled herself with the thought that it was a well-defined path and that if so many people used it, it had to lead somewhere eventually. Her only hope was that it would be somewhere inhabited and not a glade that people liked to visit in the summer. Her grandmother had sent her off with enough sandwiches to feed at least three people but this wasn't the best of days for a picnic, no matter how pretty the spot.

A sharp crack echoed around the trees and Sarah felt a stab of anxiety. It had sounded very much like gunfire and she had no desire to be mistaken for game. There was another shot and this time she laughed at her own fears. It was too muted to be that close to her. The odds were that the gunman wasn't even in the woods.

Something else was though. She heard a sudden scuffling on the path behind her and then a pounding so loud it seemed as though a herd of horses was galloping towards her. She turned round. It wasn't horses. Granted the three dogs that were running at her were almost big enough to be mistaken for ponies but ponies didn't have teeth that big and they didn't growl with such menace. Sarah dropped her basket and started to run. She knew it was the worst thing to do and that she had no hope of getting away from the dogs but she'd had no desire to stand still and let them maul her. She could hear their rasping breath closing in behind her and was sure she was going to be caught when she saw a tree a few feet ahead. Unlike the others around her, it had some low branches that looked sturdy enough to take her weight. Sarah had no thought for grace or dignity now as she hitched up her skirt and scrabbled her way into the branches. A dog jumped beneath her. She felt a sudden tugging on the back of her dress and heard the fabric rip as the dog landed again. She had to get higher yet. She tore her stocking and skinned her knee on a piece of sharp bark but didn't stop climbing until she was sure she was out of the dogs' reach.

Eventually she was safe from their snarls and snapping jowls. Safe but a prisoner. The dogs circled the tree and showed no signs of leaving their quarry. Sarah clung to the tree trunk for support and wondered how she was going to get down or if she was going to be forced to spend the night huddled in the branches.

CHAPTER FOUR

Several slow minutes passed. The dogs showed no sign of moving and Sarah was beginning to resign herself to the unpleasant prospect of a night in the tree when she heard first a whistle and then a shout.

'Nero, Julius? Where are you? Cassius, come here.'

There was someone coming. Sarah tried to call for help but the dogs had started barking in response to the calls and her voice was drowned out. A few minutes later, the undergrowth rustled and a young man came into view, carrying her basket in one hand and a shotgun in the other.

'What have you got there, boys? Sit down.' The dogs obeyed and Sarah called out again.

'Please help me.'

'What do we have here then?' The man came to stand under the tree where he peered up at her. 'My, my, the poachers are growing prettier these days.'

'I'm not a poacher.' Sarah's predicament had done nothing for her sense of humour. 'Do I look like a poacher? I'm Sarah Penghalion, the postmistress at Borthwick.'

'Really.' The man grinned. 'In that case, the postmistresses are getting prettier as well.'

Sarah scowled at him. She couldn't help thinking there was something vaguely familiar about his appearance but she was in no mood for his teasing.

'Do you intend to spout inanities all day or will you call off these brutes which I assume are yours?'

'They wouldn't have harmed you. They probably wanted to play.'

85

'Play?' Sarah held out the tattered hem of her skirt. 'You have a strange sense of play, sir. Now please call them off and then have the decency to turn your back so I can get down and complete my journey. I have urgent business at Bishopston.'

'They won't bother you while I'm here.' Her rescuer put down the items he was carrying and held out his arms. 'And if you will forgive such forwardness, I'll help you down.'

It was either that or risk another skinned knee as she tried to shinny down the bark. Sarah permitted him to place his hands on her waist and lift her down.

'Thank you.' She was aware of a hint of bad grace in her voice. If it hadn't been for his dogs she wouldn't have needed rescuing in the first place.

'You're welcome.' He smiled at her. 'Now tell me what the postmistress of Borthwick is doing wandering about in these woods so late in the day.'

'As I have explained, I am travelling to Bishopston.'

'Then you're taking the wrong path.' He bestowed another smile on her. 'But fortunately for you I am heading back there myself and so will guide you.'

'I would be much obliged.' Sarah eyed the dogs a little warily as they stood up but they trotted off ahead of their master and paid no further attention to her.

'Is it far to Bishopston?' she asked when they had been walking for a few minutes.

'No, it's only a short distance away,' her companion replied. 'I suspect you took the wrong turn at the fork in the path or you would have arrived there a long time since. This is Bishopston Estate land.'

'Then you work for the landlord?' Sarah guessed he must be the gamekeeper. It explained the presence of the dogs and the gun he was carrying.

'In a manner of speaking.' Her question seemed to have amused him.

'Then you'll know everyone on the estate. Where will I find Noah Kettley?'

'Ah, I should have known a gentleman would be involved in your quest.' To Sarah's indignation he winked at her. 'It's obvious that a pretty girl like you would have a sweetheart.'

'I am carrying an urgent message to Mr Kettley,' Sarah said stiffly. 'And I would thank you to refrain from making such personal remarks.'

'I'm sorry.' The gamekeeper looked genuinely abashed and even a little surprised at her outburst. 'It wasn't my intention to cause offence.'

After that they walked in silence until they reached a small cluster of cottages.

'These are estate houses,' the man told her. 'But there are others at the far side of the farm and I don't know where you'll find Noah. I'll take you up to the main house. Mr Davenport will be best able to help you.'

'Davenport?' Sarah felt a rush of dismay. 'Do you mean Mr Ewart Davenport?' There was no one she wanted to discuss her errand with less.

'Yes.' He chuckled in a way that seemed entirely inappropriate for an employee. 'And by the expression of utter dread on your face, I suspect you've encountered him before but don't worry. I'll see to it he doesn't frighten you.'

'I'm sure there's no need for you to do so.' She wondered if Ewart knew how an employee was speaking about him. 'After all, he cannot be as alarming as your dogs.'

To her amazement the man threw back his head and laughed so loudly that people in the cottage gardens looked across to see what was happening.

'Oh Miss Penghalion, I assure you he can.'

Bishopston House wasn't the grand building Sarah had been expecting. She'd imagined it to be like Farleigh Park with colonnades and turrets but although the building her guide led her to was large, it was a plain, stone-built farmhouse set behind a small formal garden.

'Come this way.' Closely followed by his dogs, the man bounded up the steps to the house and swung the front door open. Sarah followed him but paused in the doorway waiting to be formally invited to enter by the owner. She was just wondering why someone like Ewart would permit his gamekeeper to behave in such a familiar fashion when a door inside the house opened and the man himself came out into the hall.

'Race, where the devil have you been? Mother insisted on delaying tea until you returned and we've been waiting for an hour now.'

As she heard this exchange, Sarah wished she could turn and run away. She would rather be anywhere other than on those steps in the circumstances she was in. What a fool she'd been. The man she'd taken for a gamekeeper and spoken to so haughtily was evidently a member of the family. He must have been laughing at her ignorance. No doubt, he and Ewart would share the joke later.

'Ewart, we have a guest.' Race turned to beckon Sarah in. 'I found her in Temple Woods. The dogs had been a little too playful and she'd been obliged to seek shelter up a tree.'

Ewart glanced towards her and she saw the look of surprise on his face.

'Miss Penghalion?'

'She has urgent business here,' Race interjected before she could speak. 'I thought it best she speak to you.'

'Edwin, is that you at last?' A woman came out of the same door that Ewart had and stopped when she saw Sarah. 'I didn't know we

89

had company.'

'Mother, this is Miss Penghalion.' Ewart stepped forward, took Sarah's arm and gently led her over the threshold. 'She has had the misfortune to encounter Race and his pack of hounds in the woods and I believe she must be in need of a quiet place to rest.'

'Oh my dear.' Mrs Davenport looked at her in concern. 'You must have had quite an ordeal. Come and have a cup of tea. You look sorely in need of it.'

'You're very kind.' Sarah finally found her voice and overcame her sense of mortification to help Hepzi. 'However, I must find the person I came to see. It's a matter of great importance and I believe you can help me, Mr Davenport.'

'I will do whatever I can, Miss Penghalion, but my mother is right. You should take time to recover from your fright. We will discuss your business over tea.' It was the first time Sarah had heard Ewart sound so cordial and she was beginning to wonder if she'd misjudged him when he turned to Race and his voice hardened again. 'I assume you have apologized to Miss Penghalion for the distress you've caused her.'

Sarah saw the younger man colour and decided she'd been wrong to think he'd ever be able to share a joke with Ewart.

'Yes he has, thank you.' The ease with which she told an untruth shocked her but she justified it to herself by thinking that she had spared Race from any more of Ewart's unpleasantness. Race stared at her in surprise but she didn't have the nerve to meet his questioning glance as she allowed Mrs Davenport to lead her into the parlour and settle her into an armchair.

'You said you had a matter to discuss with me.' When Sarah had been served with a cup of tea and the plate of food that Mrs Davenport insisted on preparing for her, Ewart came and stood beside her.

'Yes, I'm looking for someone called Noah Kettley. I'm told he works on your estate.'

'He did.' Ewart nodded to himself as he spoke. 'He was a good, hardworking lad, too. Then at the end of the year he took into his head that he wanted to improve his prospects and asked if I would permit him to give notice so he could take the Queen's shilling. I was happy to do so and to recommend him to Major Kilwinning. He'll be a fine asset to the Lancers.'

'The Lancers?' Sarah repeated in dismay. 'Has he left to join them already?'

'Some time ago,' Ewart confirmed. 'Indeed, he sailed to Africa on the same day as your father.'

'Oh no!' Sarah slumped back into her chair and pressed her hand against her mouth. She'd promised Hepzi she would bring Noah back and now she'd have to tell her he'd left the country and was sailing to war. The girl was already so frail looking. She dreaded to think how such bad news would affect her.

'Is something wrong, Miss Penghalion?' Mrs Davenport asked. She was a kindly looking woman who, despite her widow's dress and cap, had a slight upward curl on her lips which suggested that she smiled a lot. Sarah thought she would be able to understand Hepzi's plight and she might have told her if Ewart hadn't been in the room. She doubted he would understand even if she could bring herself to mention such a delicate matter in front of him. From the little she had seen of Ewart Davenport she already knew he lacked any kind of compassion or understanding. She wouldn't expose Hepzi to his condemnation.

'No,' she was aware she was lying for the second time that day. 'It is just so difficult to think of Papa at such a worrying time.' At least that was the truth.

'Oh my dear, I know how you're suffering.' The gentle smile Sarah had known she would have softened Mrs Davenport's cheeks. 'I spent so many years worrying; first about my dear husband and then over Ewart when he followed his father into the Lancers. It isn't easy for us to watch them go. Take comfort from the fact that the Lord will be watching over him.'

Sarah nodded but at that moment it was hard for her to feel any comfort knowing she had to give Hepzi such bad news.

* * *

'You're looking a good deal less peaky than you were earlier.' Anne smiled when she carried a tray into the room where Hepzi was resting and found the girl sitting up in bed.

'I'm feeling better now,' Hepzi said with a faint smile. 'I can be up and out of your way right away if you're wanting it.'

'You'll do nothing of the sort,' Anne retorted as she set the tray down on a small table by the bed. 'What are we supposed to say to Mr Kettley when Sarah brings him and he learns you've left? Besides, where exactly do you intend to go? Sarah said you slept in the churchyard last night.'

'I was there but there weren't much sleeping to be had.' Hepzi's smile faded. 'My folks have moved on. I was supposed to be going with them but I was wanting to see if the letter came. Da said I shouldn't be expecting any thing else from him if I weren't going to come and work for the good of the family.'

Anne thought of the bruises on Hepzi's back and hoped her father would be true to his word not to give her anything else if he'd been responsible for them.

'Was he very angry at you?' she asked. Hepzi nodded and the way that the memory made the colour drain from her cheeks confirmed Anne's suspicions. Her lips tightened as she held back the stream of angry words that welled up inside her. Whatever he had done, the man was still Hepzi's father and it wasn't her place to vilify him in front of the girl.

'I've brought you cocoa,' she said, handing Hepzi a mug. 'Then you should try and rest again. We want you looking your best when Sarah comes with Noah.'

'Do you think he'll really come?' Hepzi asked quietly.

'He will if my Sarah has anything to do with it.' Anne smiled. 'Once she's set her mind on something it's a brave man who tries to oppose her.'

'She's been so kind,' Hepzi said. 'You both have. I don't know how I can ever be repaying you.'

'We'll be repaid enough when your Noah comes and we see you setting off to church as a bride.' Anne looked at the girl and finally voiced the idea she'd been mulling ever since Sarah had set out for Bishopston. 'Given as how your folks are away and we've got the space. I reckon you should stay here until that day. You and your little one need a safe, warm place to sleep.'

When Anne had finished speaking Hepzi stared at her for a moment and then burst into tears.

'Heaven help us, whatever's wrong?' Anne

asked.

'No one's never done such good things for me,' Hepzi sniffed. 'And I've never been in such a nice place as this. I didn't know a bed could be so soft. I'm crying 'cos I'm so happy.'

'Oh there now,' Anne's cheeks flushed and she looked a little tearful herself. 'There's no need to take on so. A bride is supposed to smile, not cry.' She took a handkerchief out of her apron pocket and used it to dab at Hepzi's eyes. 'There now, no more tears Make sure Noah sees the pretty girl he fell in love with when he arrives.'

*　　　*　　　*

Sarah was finding tea at Bishopton a trying event. Mrs Davenport seemed glad to have company and kept up a steady stream of conversation. Sarah liked her very much and, under different circumstances, she would have more readily joined in the conversation but her thoughts were on Hepzi and what the future would bring to the girl now. Ewart's presence was another distraction. Even though she was careful not to look in his direction she was sure she could feel his eyes on her whenever she replied to one of Mrs Davenport's remarks.

'Did Sarah tell you she is a postmistress, Mama?' Race was sitting on a chair across from hers and had taken an active part in the

95

conversation.

'No.' Mrs Davenport smiled at her. 'You must be very clever to deal with all that arithmetic. It takes me all my time to add up the weekly accounts when cook brings them to me. I'm sure I couldn't cope with a business of my own.'

'It's my grandmother's business. I merely help her.' Sarah saw a means of making her escape without causing offence. 'Speaking of Grandma, I really ought to set out for home. She will be wondering where I am.'

'Of course.' Mrs Davenport laid down her tea cup and addressed her younger son. 'Edwin, you'll drive Miss Penghalion home, won't you?'

'It would be my pleasure.' Sarah noticed he had inherited his ready smile from his mother.

'I think not,' Ewart said. Sarah supposed he took after his father. There was certainly no smile on his face. 'I will take her.'

Sarah saw Race roll his eyes and had to smother down a laugh. The idea of a carriage drive with Ewart had the same effect on her but she wouldn't have dared to show it.

'Ewart, you can't,' Mrs Davenport said. 'You're expected to dine at Reverend Healy's tonight and you wouldn't get back in time if you went to Borthwick now.'

'That settles it, then.' Race leapt to his feet and grinned at his brother. 'I'll go and ask for the gig now.'

Sarah was lost in her own thoughts about Hepzi as the gig left Bishopston behind and pulled out onto the main road but good manners told her she ought at least to apologize for her earlier error.

'I'm sorry for thinking you were the gamekeeper, Mr Davenport.'

'I took no offence.' Race laughed. 'And please call me Race. Everyone but Mama does. She still insists on Edwin.'

'Is that your given name?'

'Yes, but they called me Race at school because I have no love of being kept still for too long. I decided it suited me better.'

'I think it does too.'

Race stole a look at the girl at his side. It was clear she had a quick wit and lively mind and she was so pretty when she smiled in the way she just had. She seemed troubled, however, and his natural inclination was to offer his help. Unfortunately, Ewart had made it very clear that he was to forgo any natural inclinations concerning Miss Penghalion when he'd followed him out to the stable earlier.

'Sergeant Penghalion is a good man, Race. Treat his daughter with the respect she deserves.'

'I don't know what you mean, brother.' Race had tried to look indifferent but Ewart hadn't been fooled by it.

'I saw the way you looked at her in the parlour and I've seen such a look on your face before. Don't dally with her affections. She merits better than that.'

Race had busied himself with the harness then and hoped Ewart wouldn't see the colour creep up his cheeks. The truth was that from the minute he'd seen her up the tree, he'd found Miss Penghalion to be utterly captivating and he'd very much hoped to better his acquaintance with her as he drove her home.

Now he watched her twist her fingers anxiously in her lap and decided he had no more desire to pay heed to any of Ewart's lectures than he had in the past.

'You seem anxious,' he remarked. 'I trust it's not my driving that makes you look so worried.'

'No, not all.' He was rewarded with another sweet but fleeting smile. 'The message I had for Mr Kettley was important to someone and I am perturbed not to have delivered it.'

'You did your best,' he told her. 'And all is not as gloomy as it might have been. You might have had to ride with Ewart instead of me.'

'I am glad it was you.' Another girl might have batted her eyes or given him a coy smile as she said it but Miss Penghalion kept her eyes fixed firmly in front of her and didn't smile. However, her words had a ring of sincerity about them and that made Race's heart pound more than any flirtation might have done.

As soon as the words left her mouth, Sarah was aware they could have been misconstrued and she coloured. She'd meant to say she was relieved not to have to converse with Ewart but she'd been thinking about Hepzi and her reply had come out all wrong.

'Do you not have a dinner invitation this evening also?' she asked in a bid to change the subject.

'No, Reverend Healy doesn't view me as a prospective son-in-law so my invitations are few and far between. A fact for which I never cease to give thanks.' Race laughed. 'Reverend Healy and Ewart are well matched when it comes to dull conversation and Miss Healy lacks any sense of humour.'

'Will your brother marry her?'

'Probably.' Race shook his head. 'If they contrive not to bore each other to death in the meantime.'

Sarah found herself feeling sorry for Miss Healy. Ewart would be a difficult man to be married to even if his wife was of a humorous disposition.

'Running a business must be time consuming,' Race said a little later. 'Do you ever manage to escape from the post office?'

'Not very often,' Sarah admitted. 'Today is most unusual. Normally I have only Wednesday and Saturday afternoons to myself and Sunday after church, of course.'

'Of course.' Race nodded sombrely in agreement.

Sarah didn't feel her usual sense of happiness to be home when they arrived in Borthwick. Most of the way home she'd been trying to think of a gentle way to break her news to Hepzi and had concluded that there was none.

'That's such a heavy sigh.' She didn't realize she'd let her worries slip again until Race spoke. 'Are you sure I can do nothing to assist you, Miss Penghalion?'

'Nothing, but it is kind of you to enquire.' He had been such agreeable company throughout their journey and Sarah wondered how two brothers could be so dissimilar in their natures.

'There, I have brought you safely home.' Race brought the gig to a halt outside the post office and then leapt down in order to assist Sarah. She took the hand he offered her and was a little surprised when he didn't release it as soon as she was standing beside him.

'I'm sorry the dogs made our first meeting such a frightening one for you but I am truly delighted to have made your acquaintance nonetheless, Miss Penghalion.' He smiled at her as he finally let go of her hand. 'That's such a mouthful. May I call you Sarah in future?'

'If you wish it.' Sarah was wondering if Hepzi would be awake when she went in and it was only after she'd entered the cottage that she wondered when Race intended to ever see her again.

*   *   *

'Not there?' Hepzi stared at Sarah in horror. 'How can he not be there? Where has he gone?'

The moment Sarah had been dreading had come. She sat down on the edge of Hepzi's bed and reached for the girl's rough-skinned hand. Hepzi's wide, dark eyes made her face seem so pale. Sarah prayed she wouldn't faint when she heard the news.

'He joined the army just after Christmas. That's why he didn't reply to your letter, not through disinterest but because he didn't receive it.' It was the best comfort she could offer Hepzi and she knew it would do little to assuage the girl's distress.

'A soldier?' Hepzi looked stunned. 'My Noah's too soft natured for being a soldier. Is he barracked near here?'

'Not at the moment,' Sarah said as gently as she could. 'He has sailed to Africa.' She expected this news to break Hepzi completely but the girl only stared at her in confusion.

'Why would he be doing a thing like that?'

She didn't know about the war. Sarah was surprised at first but then understood. Hepzi couldn't read and even if she could, she had no access to newspapers. The way her family kept to themselves also meant they wouldn't hear news from other people. Hepzi simply knew nothing of the battle of Isandlwana and its dreadful aftermath. Sarah considered keeping the truth from her but decided she had no right to do so.

'He has gone to fight there, Hepzi. It's where my father is too. They've both gone to fight in a war.'

'But Noah don't know how to fight.' Hepzi gave Sarah a stricken look and then began to sob. 'He'll be killed for sure, I just knows it.'

Her last words were almost lost as she started to cry hysterically. Sarah couldn't bear to watch the sobs racking the girl's thin body and she put her arms round her.

'Don't cry, Hepzi. It will be all right. The Lancers are well trained and they look out for each other. They'll be safe, I know it.'

But the one thousand, three hundred men who'd died at Isandlwana hadn't been all right and they had been trained too. Sarah tried not to think about her papa in such a place but it was hard not to and soon the tears coursing down her cheeks as the two women clung to each other were as much for him as they were for Hepzi.

*   *   *

'I hope Reverend Yates doesn't plan to give

too long a sermon this morning,' Lucy said as she, Henry and Isaac met Anne and Sarah on the way to church the following Sunday. 'It's the best day of the year so far and it'd be too bad to spend most of it cooped up inside.'

'Lucy Bell!' Anne was indignant. 'What a way to talk about the Lord's Day. I'm sure I didn't raise you to think in such a way.'

'Sorry, Grandma.' Lucy lowered her eyes penitently over baby Georgina in her arms but as soon as Anne wasn't looking she looked up again and winked at Sarah who shook her head. Her headstrong older sister would never change.

'Good morning, Mrs Bell, Mr Bell.' One of the fishermen's wives passed them and Lucy frowned.

'There, I knew it wasn't my imagination as you said, Henry. She did it too.' She turned to her grandmother and sister. 'Everyone is smiling at me very strangely this morning. It's as if they all have a secret and I'm the only one not to know it. What do you suppose it means?'

'Possibly that they are admiring the soot on your nose.' Sarah giggled as Lucy immediately shrieked and started to rub at the nonexistent smut on her nose and Anne tutted.

'I thought you two would tease each other less when you were grown. If anything, you get worse.'

'Papa,' Isaac said excitedly. 'Look at the

carriage. It's very shiny.'

'It certainly is,' Henry agreed. The landau sitting outside the church gate had been well polished and was pulled by a pair of striking grey horses that one of the village boys was holding. He grinned as Sarah and her family approached.

'A gentleman is going to give me a shilling for watching the horses while he's at the service.'

'I wonder who the gentleman is,' Lucy said, and Henry shook his head.

'Not a local man, anyway. I'd remember such handsome horses had been to me for shoeing.'

'Perhaps it's a visitor,' Sarah said. She wondered if Constance had guests and whether she had come to church with them that morning. So much had happened since she'd heard of the robbery at Farleigh Park she'd almost forgotten that she hadn't seen Constance since.

They made their way into the church and Sarah glanced at the people already in the pews to see if Constance was there. She wasn't, but another familiar figure raised his hand in silent greeting as Sarah passed and she stared at him in surprise. It was Race Davenport. What was he doing here?

She learned the answer to that question when the service was over and the congregation were gathering to pass the time of day in the spring sunshine.

'Sarah.' Race seemed to have been looking for her and came directly across with a cheery smile. 'What a charming hat you're wearing. It suits your colouring so well.'

'Thank you.' Sarah flushed. She wasn't used to receiving compliments. 'Are you visiting someone here?'

'No.' He smiled again. 'It's such a glorious day, I came in the hope that I could persuade a pretty postmistress to come for a drive.'

'Then it's your carriage outside?'

'Yes and there's a picnic packed inside it. All I need now is a delightful companion to share it with me. What do you say?'

Sarah suddenly realized that his invitation was a genuine one and she was too astonished to reply. To her relief, she saw her grandmother approaching them.

'Grandma, this is Mr Race Davenport from Bishopston. He brought me home last week.'

'Mr Davenport.' Anne spoke deferentially but Sarah knew her well enough to see reservation in her eyes.

'Mrs Penghalion.' Race bowed as though he was greeting a duchess.

'I was just asking Sarah to accompany me on a drive this afternoon. I trust that would meet with your approval.'

Anne's brow creased and Sarah was sure she was about to withhold her permission when Lucy came hurrying up with Henry and

Isaac following close behind.

'You will not believe what I've just heard,' she said indignantly. 'It seems the entire village is smiling at me because they believe I am to be a mother again. The midwife was seen entering your cottage and because she was carrying her bag, everyone has assumed she was there in a professional capacity and that I was the patient.' She hitched Georgina up in her arms. 'Well, I have ensured that rumour is halted before it travels any further.'

Sarah and Anne exchanged a troubled look. Hepzi was still staying with them in the cottage. She had nowhere else to go and they had decided it was best for her to do so until the men came back from the war. They had believed her secret to be safe for the moment but if people were already speculating about the presence of the midwife it wouldn't be easy to keep it for much longer.

Sarah frowned and then recalled that Race was still standing with them.

'This is my sister, Lucy, and her husband, Henry Bell.'

'I am delighted to meet you.' Race seemed to have an easy grace with whoever he met and even Isaac, who was sometimes intimidated by strangers, felt bold enough to address him.

'Is that your carriage?'

'Yes. I've come to take your Aunt Sarah for a drive.'

'I want to come too!' Isaac tugged at Sarah's

hand. 'Can I come too, Aunt Sarah?'

'I have no objections.' Lucy looked both impressed and surprised that her sister should have received such an invitation.

'In that case, you're very welcome to come,' Race told him and Sarah realized she was going on the drive without having had the opportunity to decide whether she wanted to or not.

She was aware of a great many pairs of eyes watching as Race helped her into the carriage and she wished their departure could have been less public. No doubt this would keep the village talking for days. Isaac was delighted to have an audience, however, and waved excitedly to everyone he passed, including Albert who was bringing the gig down to collect Reverend Yates. Sarah saw a stunned look start to form on his face but they had passed before she had time to wave to him.

Race had chosen a pleasant spot for a picnic. It was sheltered from the still-cool spring breeze and there was a stream running past that kept Isaac happily occupied sailing twig boats and looking for fish.

'Don't fall in,' Sarah called to him as he leant over a little too far for her liking. 'Your mama won't thank me for bringing you home wet.'

'He's a splendid little chap,' Race said helping himself to a slice of the pie he'd unpacked from the basket. 'Is Lucy your only sister?'

'Yes, but we have a brother, John, as well. He's a teacher in Exeter and sadly doesn't get home as much as we would like. We haven't seen him since last summer.'

'That's a pity.' Race held a plate of thinly sliced cucumber sandwiches out to her and she took one. 'And with your father away fighting for his country you must live with your mother and grandmother.'

'With Grandma, yes.' Sarah stared at the sandwich in her hand. 'Mama died when I was born.'

'Then you never knew her?'

'No. I wish I had.' She gave a gentle sigh.

'I'm sorry. I didn't mean to upset you, Sarah. I wouldn't want to do that. Truly I wouldn't.' The humour had left Race's voice. Sarah looked up again and found he was looking at her in such open regard that it made her warm with discomfiture. 'I admire you too highly to wish to do that.'

'I should tend to Isaac.' Sarah scrambled to her feet and hurried down the bank to the stream. Race was a witty and lively companion. She had been enjoying herself this afternoon but his sudden declaration had caught her unawares and she didn't know if her increased pulse and sudden sense of confusion meant that she welcomed it or not.

*   *   *

108

'I had no idea you were so well connected, Miss Penghalion. Is the gentleman with the carriage a friend of your family?'

'No. I met him only recently.' Sarah was beginning to wish she could close the shop rather than endure any more of the same questions. She'd known her departure in Race's carriage would spark curiosity in the village and she'd been right. When the shop had opened the following morning it seemed that everyone had found some pretext to come in and ask her about it. Her ambiguous feelings about Race didn't make it any easier to field the questions about him. Was he an acquaintance or should she view him as a friend or more?

After the incident by the stream he had reverted to his friendly style of conversation and she had enjoyed the remainder of the afternoon a great deal. If she was honest, she suspected that had a great deal to do with having been with Race but she didn't know if her feelings extended to any more than friendship and even that was more than she should seek with a man of his station. She wished she could discuss the matter with Grandma but she seemed to have taken an instant dislike to Race, and Sarah had yet to raise the matter of the offer he'd made as he'd driven her home. There was no telling how Grandma would react to that.

'He was certainly a handsome gent,' her customer pressed.

'I can't say I'd noticed.' Sarah slapped the packet of tea she'd been wrapping down on the counter. 'Will there be anything else today?' The bell above the door jangled and she sighed. No doubt she would be exposed to the same questions all over again.

'Sarah!' The last person Sarah expected to see was an agitated-looking Constance. 'Have you seen the paper?'

Constance hurried up to Sarah and laid a copy of the *Times* down on the counter with shaking hands.

'I didn't know where else to come when I saw it,' she babbled. 'I'm so scared. Do you think the Lancers were there?'

Sarah stared at the words in front of her and felt a cold lump settle in her stomach.

'British Army confronted by Zulu forces at Devils Pass. Reports of one hundred British casualties.'

She knew Constance was looking for words of comfort but she had none to give. The thought that their loved ones might have been in that battle was too awful to contemplate.

'I don't know,' she whispered. 'We can only pray they weren't.'

CHAPTER FIVE

Althought the spring days were gradually growing warmer, the nights still brought a chill with them and Sarah was glad of the hearty blaze in the stove when she, Constance and Hepzi gathered in the kitchen of her cottage one evening after the post office had closed. As she carried Anne's best china to the table she wondered how three women of such different backgrounds had come to be sitting together like this. The answer was the common bond that they shared. Each woman had a loved one in Africa and was desperate to hear news of them.

Sarah laid the cups and saucers down on the white embroidered cloth Anne had made as a bride and which only saw service on birthdays and at Christmas. When her grandmother heard Lady Weston was coming to call she'd started to clean and bake as though it was the Queen herself who was expected and, despite Sarah's reassurances that Constance would be unlikely to check the top of the dresser for dust, she hadn't been happy until the small room was immaculate and the copper kettle on the stove top was shining as brightly as it had on the day it was made.

'What a delightful room,' Constance said looking round her in delight. 'It's so much cosier and prettier than the one I sit in at home. I'd feel much more comfortable in a room like this.'

'Thank you.' Sarah looked forward to telling her grandmother that all her efforts hadn't been in vain and that Lady Weston was enchanted. How much things had changed. Only a few weeks ago she'd told herself that a lady like Constance would never accept an invitation to the cottage and yet now she was sitting in its kitchen looking quite at home. The catalyst for this change was sitting at the other side of the table with Bosun curled up on her lap. Hepzi looked completely in awe of Constance and as she stroked the cat her fingers curled deep into its thick fur as though she was finding some comfort in its softness.

'Have you had news of Captain Weston yet?' Sarah asked and Constance shook her head.

'No. I had hoped for a letter by now but I suppose they do not have the leisure we do in which to write. At least there has been news of a victory at last.'

'At Eshowe.' Sarah nodded. 'I saw it in the newspaper. After three months under siege Colonel Pearson and his men must have feared they would never be relieved. Thank the Lord they have been.'

'I wonder if the Lancers were there,' Constance said, quietly voicing the question that was uppermost in all their minds. Sarah felt her stomach start to tense and jump in the way it always did when she thought of her father being caught up in fighting. When she was busy with the hustle of the daily routine she could sometimes forget how much danger he was in, but talk of battles brought it forcefully back to her and disturbed her sleep at night.

'Do you intend to send another letter to Captain Weston soon?' She wasn't the only person longing for news of someone and she had asked Constance here in order to help Hepzi.

'Of course. I write every day although I can't tell if he receives them and can only hope he does.'

'I wonder if you would be good enough to ask him to seek out a private who has recently joined the Lancers.' Sarah sat down and moved to draw the gypsy girl into the conversation. 'Hepzi is seeking word of Noah Kettley. We know he joined up after Christmas and has sailed to Africa.' She glanced quickly at Hepzi. 'It's important to get a message to him.'

'Of course I'll be happy to help.' Constance smiled across the table at Hepzi. 'But wouldn't you rather write to Noah yourself? I'm sure a letter from you would make him much happier than a message from Hugh.'

'I can't.' Hepzi's face turned scarlet and she bent low over Bosun's head, letting her cheek rest against his velvet-soft ears. Sarah was uncomfortable on her behalf and tried to ease the situation for her.

'Hepzi's family travels a great deal and she hasn't been able to attend school as much as she would have liked.' Constance didn't have to know that the girl had never set foot inside a classroom.

'You mean you don't know how to write?' Constance made a poor job of hiding her surprise.

'No,' Hepzi admitted. 'Nor read neither.'

'The message is one of some delicacy.' Sarah tried to spare Hepzi any further embarrassment but knew it would be hard to divulge the nature of her message without shaming her any further. 'That is why I thought it would be better coming from Captain Weston than from my papa. The fact is that Hepzi has learned something that directly affects Noah.' Would Constance be scandalized? Sarah took a deep breath. 'She is going to have a child in the summer.'

'Oh.' Constance didn't reply at first and Sarah was afraid she had taken offence. However, Constance smiled then and a soft glow shone in her cheeks as she reached out to Hepzi in a gesture of understanding. 'Of course I'll ask Hugh to tell Noah. I'm sure he'll be only too happy to, as in the same letter he will learn that he is to be a father as well.' Her blush deepened. 'I saw the doctor this afternoon. My baby will be born in the autumn.'

'I'm sorry for making you travel out on such a cold night,' Sarah said later as she helped Constance into her coat. 'If I had known you were indisposed I wouldn't have asked you to come.'

'Nonsense. I feel perfectly well and I'm happy to help Hepzi.' Constance paused for a moment. 'Is it true that she really can't read or write?'

'Yes.' Now that they were alone Sarah was able to be more candid. 'It is not uncommon amongst the children of farm workers. The nearest school here is at Otterly and a great many children don't make the journey. They are of greater use to their families in the fields than in the schoolhouse.'

'But still they should have some education.' Constance frowned. 'It's not right to deny them that and surely the law insists that they should.'

'It's not always such an easy matter,' Sarah said. Constance, with her privileged background, could have no idea how hard life was for most of the people in the countryside. No one checked that children under twelve were in school when they were supposed to be. Unscrupulous landowners often employed children rather than their parents in the fields, as the lower wages they could pay them increased their profits. Faced with such a choice, was it any wonder the parents preferred to see food on the table than a book in their child's hands?

'There must be something that can be done.' Constance's thin eyebrows gathered into a tight frown as she went out the door to her waiting carriage. 'Something really should be done.'

Hepzi was still in her place at the table when Sarah returned to the kitchen.

'There, I told you it would be all right,' Sarah said as she began to gather the tea things. 'Noah will have your message before you know it. Lady Weston intends to write to her husband as soon as she returns to Farleigh Park.'

'Farleigh Park?' Hepzi's head jerked up. 'That's the house as was robbed isn't it? Does she live there?'

'Yes.'

'I should be getting to me bed now.' Hepzi jumped up so abruptly that Bosun almost fell off her lap and registered his disapproval with a hiss as he landed on the hearth rug.

'Am you feeling all right?' Sarah asked.

'Yes, I'm fine.' Hepzi was already at the door. 'Leave the dishes. I can wash 'em first thing.'

Sarah watched as the door closed behind Hepzi. The mention of Farleigh Park seemed to have upset her and Sarah wondered if the gossips had been right after all. Perhaps Hepzi

116

knew more about the break-in and the identity of the thieves than she was prepared to say.

*   *   *

Before going to her own room Sarah tapped lightly on her grandmother's door. Anne, who had decided to stay in her room rather than make the small kitchen seem overcrowded, was sitting in the chair next to her bed, knitting, and she looked up as Sarah entered.

'Is it all settled?'

'Yes.' Lady Weston will ask her husband to pass word to Noah.' Sarah sat down on the patchwork counterpane that covered Anne's bed. 'And all your fussing was for nothing. She called the house charming.'

'That's nice.' Anne gave her granddaughter a wry smile. 'But of course there's no saying she would have done if I hadn't cleaned it as I did.'

'Oh Grandma, I will never have the last word, will I?' As she and her grandmother laughed, Sarah decided this was the moment to discuss the offer Race had made on the day he took for her a drive. She had planned to do so many times over the past few days but somehow the time had never quite seemed right, especially as she wasn't sure that Anne approved of Race or would agree. However, if she didn't speak soon it would be too late and a precious opportunity would be lost.

117

'Grandma,' she began tentatively. 'Race Davenport has offered to drive us to Exeter at Easter so we might see John. He knows of a respectable hotel close to John's lodgings where we can stay. It's been so long since he was home. I thought it would be wonderful for us to see him again.'

'It has been a long while, right enough.' Anne seemed to be considering the suggestion and Sarah was daring to hope they might go, when the older woman finally shook her head. 'No. It's a nice idea but I'm too old to travel so far and besides we can't just take off and leave the shop. You know that.'

'Yes, Grandma.' Sarah tried to hide her disappointment but it was hard. She'd been so excited at the idea of spending time with John and the notion of being in Race's company for three days had not been an unpleasant one either.

'Of course there's no saying that you shouldn't go,' Anne added at last. 'Provided you're properly chaperoned, and I don't think Isaac will suffice on this occasion.' She frowned. 'Lucy would be the most obvious choice but you know how she is about Henry. You'd never persuade her to go so far from him and besides, if you're away she can help in the shop.' Her fingers raced at her knitting for a few moments longer as she contemplated the situation. 'What about Hepzi?' She said eventually. 'She's well enough to travel now. A

118

trip would take her mind off Noah and get her away from the village for a few days.' She looked up sharply. 'We can't keep her hidden away for ever and I don't know if you've noticed it but that baby's not going to be hidden for much longer either. I've had to let out two of her skirts already.'

'I'll ask her.' Sarah felt her hopes start to soar again. 'I'm sure she'd love to come.'

'I dare say.' Anne fixed her granddaughter with a meaningful look. 'And it would make things a lot easier on her if she was to come home with a ring on her finger. You'll be able to buy a penny one at the market and no one here will be any the wiser, if you take my meaning.'

'I do. Goodnight, Grandma.' Sarah kissed Anne's cheek and then went to her room to light the lamp. Before she went to sleep she had to write to John and Race.

*　　*　　*

'I'm glad it's Saturday and we can close early,' Sarah said as she bagged up the last of the post. 'I'm in sore need of a rest today.'

'You wouldn't be if you hadn't stayed up half the night writing letters,' Anne observed from her place behind the shop counter.

'I know, but once I had completed notes for John and Race it seemed natural to write a letter to Papa and I didn't realize how late it had got.' She wrapped a length of string tightly round the top of the bag and tied it in the firm knot her grandfather had taught her to use when she'd been a child. 'I'm glad Hepzi has agreed to come with me. It will be such fun to take a trip.'

'Especially in the company of Mr Davenport, I dare say.' Anne fixed her with a piercing look and she felt her cheeks start to burn. Grandma always seemed to know exactly what was in her mind.

'It's almost time to lock the door,' she said, trying to sound less disconcerted than she felt. 'Why don't you go through and have a cup of tea? I'm sure Hepzi will have a pot ready for us.'

'Aye, she's proving to be a real help about the place, there's no doubt about that. Will I ask her to bring you a cup while you're finishing off in here?'

'Yes, thank you. I need to count the stamps, so may be a while yet.'

When the post had been collected, Sarah took the heavy key out of a drawer in her desk and went to lock the front door. However, before she could do so, a tall figure blocked the light coming through the small pane of glass in the door. A last-minute customer wanted something. Sarah sighed but didn't have the heart to turn them away. Hopefully their errand would be a quick one. She stepped away from the door as it opened and, to her utter astonishment, Ewart Davenport walked in.

'Miss Penghalion.' He tipped his felt hat before removing it. 'Forgive me for disturbing you so late in the day but I have received word of the Lancers and wished to bring it to you as quickly as possible.'

'Oh no!' Sarah clasped a hand to her mouth. Something terrible had happened to Papa and Ewart had been despatched to break the bad news. She knew she would have to be strong for Grandma's sake but her knees went weak and she would have fallen if Ewart hadn't reached out to catch hold of her elbow and steady her.

'Has he been injured?' She could barely force the words out. It seemed dreadful to hope that her father was hurt but that was infinitely preferable to the other news Ewart might have to impart.

'No, Miss Penghalion . . . Sarah, please do not distress yourself.' She felt his grasp on her arm tighten. 'I came to reassure you that he is well.'

'He is?' The room slowly came back into focus but her heart was still pounding so hard she was sure its palpitations must be visible through her blouse.

'Yes.' He drew a roll of paper out of his coat pocket. 'I have received a report from Colonel Mortimer, my former commanding officer. The Lancers have sustained no serious casualties. Your father and Captain Weston are both in good health.'

'Is there word of Noah Kettley?' Sarah wanted to have good news for Hepzi as well.

'No, but in view of the general report we must conclude that he is also uninjured.'

'But you're not sure of it.' Neither of them had noticed Hepzi come out into the shop and they turned to find her staring at them with wide, anxious eyes and the fingers of both hands tightly gripping the mug she was carrying. Ewart scrutinized the girl for a moment, then nodded almost imperceptibly and spoke.

'It's Hepzi Briar, isn't it? You worked for me a few months ago.'

'Yes, sir.' Hepzi dropped an awkward half curtsy as she replied. 'And I presume you are the reason Miss Penghalion has been seeking word of Noah?'

'Yes, sir.' Hepzi went as red as the uniform worn by the Lancers and a hint of a smile crossed Ewart's lips.

'As I was telling Miss Penghalion, I am sure he is well but I will endeavour to obtain more information for you as quickly as I can.'

'Thank you, sir.' Hepzi put the mug down on the counter, cast one more awed glance at Ewart and then fled back into the cottage.

'Am I to assume that Noah and Miss Briar formed a romantic attachment while she was working for me?' Ewart asked as he watched the door close behind the girl.

'Yes.' Sarah was surprised Ewart had remembered Hepzi's name when so many itinerant workers must spend time on his estate.

'Strange then that Noah should choose to enlist,' he mused. 'She clearly still holds him in her affections.'

'I believe there was a quarrel.'

'And now you seek to see it resolved.' He turned to look at Sarah. 'Are you always so concerned for the welfare of others, Miss Penghalion?'

'I do my best.' The unexpected question caught Sarah off guard. 'Grandma says the world would be a better place if we all looked out for others more.'

'She sounds like a very prudent woman.' Ewart nodded. 'And she is right. There would be far less discord if we all did our Christian duty.'

Sarah was sure Grandma had never once viewed her kindness to others as a duty. She was a naturally compassionate woman, but that seemed to be a trait Ewart lacked. She recalled the way he had chastised her father for speaking to Isaac on the day the Lancers had sailed. Duty had certainly won out over compassion then and she wondered if he would have offered the same ready assistance to Hepzi if he'd known that she had failed to live up to the high moral standards he seemed to live by. She would have been happy to see him leave but hospitality was another virtue that Grandma set great store by.

'It is a long ride to here from Bishopston. Will you take some refreshment before you leave?'

'Thank you, but I must decline your offer.' Sarah hoped her relief didn't show too clearly in her features when he spoke. 'I have a dinner invitation this evening and am obliged to return for that.'

No doubt it was with Miss Healy again. Sarah still couldn't help but pity the young woman.

'Race told me that congratulations are in order,' she said.

'Congratulations?' Ewart frowned at her in obvious bewilderment, and she wished she hadn't spoken.

'He said you were to be married,' she stammered. 'That you are about to announce your engagement to Miss Healy.'

'Race said.' Ewart's sigh was audible and his eyes, that were the same deep shade of brown as his brother's, met Sarah's before he spoke again. 'You would be wise not to believe everything Race tells you, Miss Penghalion. Please remember that.'

'Surely you are not implying he is dishonest?' Sarah was filled with indignation on Race's behalf.

'No.' Ewart sounded weary. 'At least he

124

never intends to be, I am sure of it. However, he can sometimes let his imagination run away with him. I wouldn't care to see you suffer in any way because of it.'

'I thank you for your dutiful concern, Mr Davenport.' Sarah was fighting to keep her temper. How dare he speak in such a way about his brother when he wasn't here to defend himself? As if Race, who had been so kind already, would do anything to hurt her. 'However, I assure I am very well able to take care of myself.'

'I'm sure you are.' Ewart's voice was tight. 'And I will not take up any more of your time. Good day, Miss Penghalion.'

'And to you, Mr Davenport.' Sarah knew she ought to thank him for bringing news of her father but she wasn't inclined to be polite at that moment.

He put on his hat and she was about to open the door for him when the door to the cottage burst open and Hepzi hurried in again.

'Miss Sarah!' she cried. 'You'd best come quick. Your granny's sick. She's fallen and I can't wake her.'

*　　*　　*

Anne had regained consciousness by the time Sarah raced to her side but she was still on the floor and there was a greyish tinge to her skin.

'Grandma?' Sarah dropped to her knees

125

and took Anne's hand into hers. It felt icy cold.

'Someone must go for a doctor at once.' Ewart came to Anne's other side and bent over her.

'No.' Anne's voice was little more than a whisper but her stubbornness hadn't diminished. 'I don't want the doctor.'

'Whether you want him or not, he must be sent for.' Ewart looked up at Hepzi. 'Do you know where he is to be found?'

'Yes.'

'Then run and fetch him. Tell him to come at once.'

Hepzi obeyed the instruction without question and Ewart turned his attention back to Anne. 'Now, Mrs Penghalion, let's endeavour to make you more comfortable. A stone floor is no place to be any longer than you have to.'

Sarah gave as much help as she could as Ewart lifted her grandmother into a chair. Once she saw him wince and remembered the injury that had forced him to use a stick only a few weeks earlier. Anne seemed almost incapacitated and Sarah wondered what she would have done if Ewart hadn't been there to calmly take charge of the situation as he had.

'Try not to worry.' She looked up and realized he was speaking to her. 'The doctor will be here soon. I'm sure he will set your mind at rest.'

Between them, the doctor and Ewart
126

managed to carry Anne up to her bed and, after a lengthy examination, the doctor drew Sarah out of the older woman's room with him.

'It's her heart,' he said solemnly. 'I told her some time back that she needed to slow down but she refused to listen. Now she will have to.'

'I didn't know she'd been to see you.' Sarah was shocked.

'I'm sure I don't need to tell you how strong willed your grandmother is.' The doctor frowned. 'She'd been feeling unwell for some months before she consulted me. I told her then she would have to rest but she said it wasn't an option open to her until your father returned.'

'Can you treat her?' Sarah asked.

'There's little I can do.' The doctor shook his head. 'She's growing old and works too hard. Please try and keep her in bed for at least a few days and then make her rest completely for some weeks.'

'I'll do my best,' Sarah promised, 'but it won't be easy. I know she'll be trying to get back into the shop as soon as she can.'

'That would be most unwise.' The doctor looked at her gravely. 'In my opinion, she should not return to the shop at all.'

When she had shown the doctor out, Sarah went into the kitchen and was surprised to see that Ewart was still there. He and Hepzi were seated at the table with a pot of tea between them. Hepzi had used the everyday mugs and it occurred to Sarah that her grandmother would be mortified to see a guest of Ewart's social standing using those instead of the best china. Only her grandmother wasn't well enough to see what was happening and might not be again if she didn't take care of herself. Tears welled into her eyes.

'Oh Miss Sarah.' She heard Hepzi's worried cry but it was Ewart who leapt to his feet and guided her to a chair with unexpected gentleness. 'Come now. It will not do to make yourself ill as well.'

'I fear we have made you late for your dinner engagement, Mr Davenport.' She tried to regain a sense of normality but the tears wouldn't stop and she was grateful when Ewart thrust a silk handkerchief into her shaking hand.

'I am not concerned about dinner. How is your grandmother?'

'The doctor says she has been unwell for some time and that she must have complete rest now. She has been damaging her health and I had no idea. What kind of a person am I not to have noticed?'

'You must not blame yourself,' Ewart told her, but his words had no effect. Sarah was wracked with guilt.

'I should have insisted that she stop working when she had the dizzy turn.' She looked up at Hepzi. 'I'm afraid we must cancel our trip to

Exeter. John will understand.'

'I'm sorry for that, Miss Sarah.' Although the cancelled trip must have been a disappointment to Hepzi as well, the sorrow in her eyes seemed to be solely for Sarah.

Anne still looked ashen when Sarah took a tray of supper up to her later that evening.

'There will be no argument this time,' she told her grandmother. 'You will do as the doctor has instructed.'

'Yes.' Anne's uncharacteristic acquiescence worried Sarah more than her pale cheeks did.

'Has Mr Davenport gone now?' Anne asked.

'Yes, some time back.'

'I must take time to write a note of thanks when I feel a little stronger. He was very kind.'

'He was no doubt doing what he considered his duty,' Sarah said sharply and her grandmother frowned at her.

'I don't see why you're so taken against him. He seemed very pleasant to me and he has a more responsible air than his brother.'

'You don't know him as I do, Grandma. He has no heart.'

'Is that so?' Anne let her head drop back against the pillows. Mr Davenport had been kindness itself as he had helped her up the stairs, and coming all the way to Borthwick with word of George didn't seem like a heartless act to her. If she didn't know better she would have called it the behaviour of a man who not only had a heart but one which was being swayed by feelings that went beyond duty or even mere friendship. She had seen Ewart's face when Sarah's name was mentioned and, to her, he had seemed very much like a man who was falling in love.

*   *   *

It was, Sarah thought grimly, a fact of village life that any hint of gossip brought more people into the shop than usual. It could be said to be good for business but, when the subject of the latest rumour was the shop itself and there was only one person left to serve all the extra customers as well as answer all their questions about Anne, it also meant a lot of exhausting work. For the first few nights after locking the door, she'd flopped into an armchair, too tired to think of much else, but on the fifth day she hurried into the kitchen with renewed vigour and waving an envelope.

'There's a letter from Papa at last.'

'Thank the Lord.' Anne was out of bed for the first time and was resting in a chair by the fireside. 'What does he say?'

'I've had no chance to open it yet, we were so busy and it only came in the last post.' Sarah opened the letter. It seemed so flimsy and yet it had come so far to them. She had known her father's neat handwriting at once and had been longing for the chance to read the letter ever since.

'I'll go to my room.' Hepzi stood up. 'You'll not be wanting strangers to hear your private news.'

'No, stay, Hepzi.' Sarah almost thought of the girl as part of the family by now. 'It may give you some idea of how life is for Noah too.' She opened the letter and began to read aloud

> *My dearest family,*
> *We have made camp for a few days and so I take this opportunity to write and assure you all that I am in good health and spirits. I hope this letter will find you the same way.*

Sarah's voice trembled slightly as she read this sentence and she glanced at her grandmother. She prayed the frail woman would be on the road to recovery by the time the Lancers returned and didn't want to think of any other possible outcome.

'Well what else does he say?' Anne asked briskly. If she sensed her granddaughter's worries, she clearly wasn't going to let her dwell on them.

'Let me see.' Sarah found her place on the page and began to read again.

> *I know it will soon be spring in Borthwick and yet here in Africa we feel the approach of winter more each day. I will*

*miss the sight of snowdrops and new buds
on the trees. The landscape here is mostly
barren. The earth is burnt orange by the sun
and the only greenery we see are the clusters
of thorn bushes that we are obliged to cut
our way through when creating a track
through the terrain.*

*When we arrived here, the veterans of the
war showed us how to soak our helmets in
strong tea. This has turned them the colour
of the earth and rendered us less obvious to
the eyes of the enemy but I fear we will
never pass an inspection with them in such
a condition.*

'What a sight that must be,' Anne muttered.
'They'll look very strange when they come
marching home again.'

*The climate is harsher than we are
accustomed to. By day we bake beneath the
sun and long for it to set while at night,
bone-chilling frosts make us complain
about the cold and wish the sun would rise
again. In addition to this we are often
soaked by sudden torrents of rain that soak
us through to our skins and makes the
progress of our ox-drawn wagons slower
than it already it is.*

*I wish now that I had filled my pack with
your baking, Ma. Our meals are substantial
but consist of little more than bully beef*

and biscuits washed down with tea. Even one stale fairing would be a luxury. Be sure to have one of your delicious seed cakes baked for me upon my return. I will fall on it with relish.

'I will.' Anne was smiling now and Sarah was glad to see the letter having such a positive effect on her.

We have seen very little of the enemy as yet. I am told that Amazulu means the People of the Heavens and can only think that they have a poor impression of paradise if they consider this place to represent it. If they had once seen the countryside around Borthwick on a bright spring day they would know what Heaven truly looks like.

Rest assured that you are all always uppermost in my thoughts. I often think of the day when I will lay down my gun for the last time and became a simple, contented shopkeeper. I send a kiss for Isaac and Georgina and remain your devoted son and father,

George.

'I wish he could come home now.' Sarah folded the letter and put it carefully back into the envelope before laying it down on the table.

'So do I, lass,' Anne said quietly. 'But at least we know he's safe and our moping won't make the time pass any faster.'

'You're so clever.' Hepzi had picked up the envelope. 'You can look at all those squiggles and learn so much from them. I wish I'd had some schooling.'

She sounded so forlorn that Sarah wished there was some way she could help her. If the shop didn't take up so much of her time she would offer to help her but she didn't think she would make a good teacher but perhaps there was someone else.

A sudden knock at the cottage door interrupted her train of thought.

'Who could that be?' She went out into the hallway and opened the door to Ewart and another man.

'Miss Penghalion, I hope it is not too late to call on you.' Ewart raised his hat. 'How is your grandmother?'

'Recovering well, thank you.'

'May we come in? I have a proposition to put to you.'

'Of course.' Sarah had no idea what Ewart could possibly wish to discuss with her but she showed them into the kitchen and saw how warmly her grandmother smiled when Ewart greeted her before turning back to Sarah.

'Last week Miss Briar explained to me that you hoped to visit your brother and that it had been some considerable time since you had seen him. Then you said you would be unable to go and I have been giving the matter some thought since.' He turned to introduce his companion. 'This is William Hogg. He works on my estate but was previously employed by a grocer so he has knowledge of commercial matters. I have discussed the matter with him and he is happy to work in your shop for a few days so you can make your trip as planned. I understand from Miss Briar that your sister was to have run the post office.'

He finished speaking and Sarah realized he was waiting for a reply but didn't know what to say. Was this another act of duty? Her first reaction was that it was arrogant presumption on Ewart's part. Did he really think she would leave Grandma now?

'I have served with your father for many years and have great respect for him.' Had he seen her annoyance? 'I do not wish to offend you, simply to assist his family in a time of need exacerbated by his absence.'

'I think it's a grand idea,' Anne said, but Sarah shook her head.

'No, who will care for you, Grandma?'

'Why, Lucy, of course. She loves to play at nurse and I'll endure her ministrations for a few days so you can take a break.' Her eyes met her granddaughter's gravely. 'Have a rest while you've got the chance, lass I'm afraid it may be some time before I'm fit to get back to work and the burden will fall heaviest on you.'

'Very well.' Those words made Sarah even more unwilling to go but she seemed to have little choice. 'I will not stay for as long as I had planned, however.'

'I'm glad you will have some time with your brother.' She had seen Ewart smile so rarely that when he did it came as a surprise. His entire demeanour seemed lighter somehow. She was equally astonished that he was encouraging the trip. He was usually so set against anything Race did. Suddenly she understood. Ewart had no idea she was going with Race. He hadn't mentioned him once. She considered telling him and then thought better of it. There would only be strife and what she and Race did was really of no concern to him.

*   *   *

Exeter was a much more exciting place than Sarah had imagined. She had gazed up in awe at the immense vaulted roof of the cathedral and seen shops that Borthwick post office would fit into five times over. Now, at an hour when most people there would be taking to their beds, she was doing the most daring thing she had ever done in her life. She was at the music hall.

At first she had demurred when Race suggested the outing. She'd heard they were far from salubrious places and wasn't sure her grandmother would approve. Race had been persuasive, however, and now she was glad she'd changed her mind. It was magical. The enormous chandelier above them shone and twinkled in the glare of the lights that burned across the centre of the stage below. It was decorated with a brightly painted backdrop representing a garden and Sarah had watched in awe as the artistes had performed here. Dressed in exotic and dazzling costumes they had sung, danced and told jokes. One woman had even swung high above the stage on a trapeze.

'Wasn't it wonderful?' When the show was over she turned to John who was sitting beside her. 'If I lived here I would come all the time. Do you?'

'No.' Her brother shook his head. 'I must take to my bed early at nights or I wouldn't be fit to take charge of my pupils. However, this has been a most enjoyable evening, especially as it has been in your company. I'm very grateful to you for bringing Sarah to visit me, Mr Davenport.'

'Call me Race. There should be no formality between friends.' Their companion grinned. 'Was I right to prevail on you to come here, Sarah?'

'Oh yes. It's such a shame that Hepzi was too tired to accompany us, though. I'm sure she would have found it great fun as well.' She glanced back at the stage, now covered by a

137

heavy red velvet curtain. 'The artistes are so talented. I'm sure performing so well can't be as easy as they make it look. Do you think they feel nervous before stepping onto the stage? I'm sure I would.'

'Well now you'll have the opportunity to ask them.' Race had risen from his seat and was offering her his arm. 'Lydia Prescott and Daisy Banks are good friends of mine and would be delighted to meet you, I'm sure.'

When they left the theatre instead of catching a cab back to the hotel, John and Sarah followed Race down a narrow, dimly lit alleyway that ran down the side of the building. A rickety wooden stairway led up to a shabby-looking entrance which had the words 'stage door' painted across it in uneven red letters.

'In here.' Race opened the door and flicked a shilling in the direction of the old man who sat on a chair just inside. 'Evening, Dawkins. The ladies are expecting me.'

'Good evening to you, Mr Davenport.' The man caught the coin and doffed his cap as the three of them passed.

The corridors Race now led them down were full of people and noise. The confusion reigning here bore little resemblance to the polished performance they had just witnessed. A man in evening dress was trying to manoeuvre a double bass through a door and a woman in little more than her corsets and petticoats suddenly burst out of a room and almost collided with them, causing Sarah to gasp and John to hurriedly avert his eyes.

Race, however, seemed unaffected by the mayhem. He paused in front of one green door and, after knocking loudly, walked in before receiving an invitation to do so.

'I hope you're decent, ladies, I've brought company.'

'Race, darling! I thought you were never going to come back and see me.' A pretty blonde-haired girl in an evening gown gave a shriek and flung her arms round his neck in an exuberant embrace.

'As if I would miss a chance to see you, my dear Daisy.' Race seemed to be in no hurry to extricate himself from the girl's clutches. They clearly knew each other very well and Sarah found that the scene took the edge off her good mood.

'And Lydia.' Race finally disengaged Daisy's arms and turned to an older woman who was standing by a mirror, pinning up her long black hair. 'You're as beautiful as ever and you sang like an angel tonight. May I introduce two friends of mine, Sarah and her brother John? We're hoping you ladies will be kind enough to join us for a late supper.'

Sarah had to try and conceal her surprise on hearing this. Race had made no mention of supper before and his plans made her feel a little uneasy. It had been one thing to attend the music hall but she was sure Anne wouldn't be happy to think of her grandchildren consorting with actresses. Everyone knew of their reputation. Besides, if she was honest, she knew she would feel dowdy sitting at the same table as them. Her Sunday coat and hat were drab and plain compared to the richly coloured silk gowns they were wearing.

Lydia had turned from the mirror when Race made the introductions and Sarah watched as Race bent to kiss her hand. On the day of the picnic he'd kissed hers in such a way and she'd believed it to be a gesture of genuine affection on his part. Now she was unsure. If it was in his nature to be so charming to all women, then did he care for her or not?

'Why can't we go alone?' Daisy asked in a resentful voice. 'It's been so long since I've seen you.' She shot Sarah an openly hostile glance and yet again Sarah wondered just what Race's relationship with the young actress was.

'We will the next time I'm in town. I give you my word.' Race seemed unaware of Daisy's obvious antagonism and patted her arm as though she was merely a sulky child. 'Will you come, Lydia?'

'Of course.' The older woman didn't sound any happier about the arrangement than Daisy and the smile she gave them was a tight, forced one which made Sarah feel that she resented her presence. She glanced at Lydia, wondering what she also could have done to upset her, and then realized that the actress was staring at the brooch on her lapel. Her obvious interest in it perturbed Sarah and she wished she hadn't worn it that evening.

'What a pretty brooch and such an unusual design.' When she realized that Sarah had noticed her preoccupation, Lydia spoke. 'Have you had it for a long time?'

'Since I was a little girl. It was my mother's before that.'

'Sarah is very fond of it,' John added. 'It has our father's initials worked into the back of it.'

'Indeed.' Lydia seemed unable to take her eyes off it. 'I am quite taken with it. Might I examine it more closely?'

'If you wish.' Sarah carefully unpinned the small cameo and handed it to Lydia, who looked at it for a moment and then quickly returned it.

'It's most attractive.' She sunk into a chair by the mirror and rubbed a hand over her forehead. 'Race, I'm more tired than I thought tonight. I don't think I'll come to supper after all.'

'Oh Lydia, it will be no fun without you,' Race protested but she dismissed him with a wave of her hand.

'I'm sure the company will be gay enough without me. Now please go and let me rest.'

'Very well.' Race pouted, but in the next second his disappointment seemed forgotten. 'Let's go or we may not get a table.'

He left the room with Daisy clinging tightly to his arm. Sarah and John followed but as she left the room, Sarah couldn't help looking back at Lydia. She had risen from the chair and was advancing to close the door behind them but she had turned so white Sarah was sure she must be ill.

'Are you all right?' she asked in concern.

'Yes.' Lydia's voice sounded strained. 'I simply wish to be alone.'

'Are you sure?' Lydia looked as though she was on the verge of fainting and Sarah was unwilling to leave her. 'If you wish I can—'

'Please just go.' Lydia frowned and, with one last shake of her head, slammed the door abruptly in Sarah's face.

CHAPTER SIX

Rain beat steadily on the window of Lydia Prescott's attic room and the dark clouds were so low they seemed to be resting oppressively on the roof of the lodging house. She shivered, wrapped her peignoir more tightly around her and edged her chair closer to the stove that gave out more smoke than heat. The weather suited her mood that morning. She felt as black and cheerless as the sky outside.

Paper, a pen and an open bottle of ink lay on the table in front of her. The top sheet of paper was blotted and covered in crossed-out words where she had begun to write and then changed her mind many times. She stared at it for a moment and then strengthened her resolve. Screwing the page into a ball, she picked up the pen and began to write on a fresh sheet with a hurried and uneven hand.

My dear Miss Penghalion,

I begin this letter formally as I cannot bring myself to call you Sarah. It is not the name you were given at birth although I understand why your family saw fit to change it. Last night at the theatre, Race introduced me as Lydia Prescott. That is no more my given name than Sarah is yours. I am Betsy Penghalion, wife of George and your mother. I admit I have no claim to that title since I abandoned you when you were but a few weeks old but now that I have seen you I must confess and make some attempt to explain my actions.

When I met your papa I was seventeen years old and struggling to earn a living in the theatre. I'd lost a glove in the park and, seeing my distress, George offered to help me find it. He looked splendid in his uniform and he was so kind that I fell in love with him at once. His first wife, Sarah, had died three months previously leaving him with two small children to care for. My heart went out to them and when, a few weeks later, George asked me to marry him, I readily agreed.

Perhaps I should not have been so hasty. Marriage was not at all as I had imagined it would be. Otterly was dull in comparison to city life. Your papa was often away with the regiment and I found it hard to care for Lucy and John alone. His parents disapproved both of me and my former profession so I dared not admit my difficulties to them. When I learned I was to have a child of my own it seemed more than I could bear.

There were complications at the time of your birth. I was weak and confined to bed for several days afterwards but holding you in my arms for the first time brought me greater joy than I have ever known. You were my own sweet child and I understood at that moment how a mother could give her life for her infant. I named you Elizabeth after me and hoped that the five of us could now be a happy family together.

It was not to be. George was sent to Sebastopol with his regiment and I was alone again. I did my best to be a good mother but failed miserably at every turn. You took colic and after pacing the floor with you each night I had no energy to tend to John and Lucy's needs by day. They grew fractious and I could scarcely muster the strength to feed them let alone tend to household tasks. We rarely left the house and no one ever came to see us. Eventually I became so filled with despair that I stopped bothering to dress and spent a great deal of the day weeping in my bed. I realized then that my marriage had been a terrible mistake. I was in love with George but now I had cause to doubt his love for me. It seemed he had been in search of a nursemaid rather than a wife.

My dearest daughter, I wanted so much to see you grow healthy and happy and my inability to be a good mother to you broke my heart. After yet another night when I was powerless to soothe your cries I made the hardest decision of my life. I took you, John and Lucy to your grandparents in Borthwick and asked them to care for you while I carried out an urgent errand. Then I left the village with no intention of returning. I knew they would care for you better than I was able to.

You must believe me when I tell you I have thought of you every day since that terrible one. I have longed to see you just once but never found the courage to go back where I knew I would not be welcome. Yet now you have come to me. The brooch you wear was indeed mine. George carved his initials in it and gave it to me on our wedding day. When I left our home I took nothing but the clothes I was wearing and I am glad to know you have something of mine—perhaps you will not want it now that you know the truth.

You are truly a beautiful young woman and I'm gratified to see how John cares for you. He was always a good boy. I wish I could know more of your life but understand that I have forfeited that right. Nor do I ask your forgiveness. How can I ask that when I cannot forgive myself? I only ask that . . .

'Lydia!' Daisy's voice accompanied an insistent rap on the door. 'Are you there? I must speak with you.'

'I'm just coming.' Lydia rubbed the tears from her cheeks and went to open the door. 'It's a little early to head to rehearsals yet.'

'I don't want to go to rehearsals,' Daisy burst into the room and Lydia could see she was highly agitated. 'What's the point of rehearsals? What's the point of anything?' She threw herself down on the top of an ottoman and started to cry.

'What's wrong?' Lydia guessed what the answer would be before Daisy replied.

'Race,' she sobbed. 'He treats me so cruelly. Last time he was here he told me I was his sweetheart. Then he went away for weeks without so much as a word and returned with that floozy in tow.'

Lydia drew in a sharp breath.

'She looked most respectable to me,' she said quietly.

'Respectable!' Daisy gave an indignant sniff. 'She was dull and dowdy, yet Race flirted wildly with her all through supper without a thought for my feelings. Why does he treat me so, Lydia?'

Lydia sighed. She'd tried to warn Daisy about Race but the silly girl hadn't listened and now she imagined herself in love with him.

'I told you he would not be constant.' She bit down on her lower lip. Daisy wasn't the only girl whose heart now stood to be broken by him. 'Are you sure he was paying court to the other lady?' she asked.

'He was charm itself.'

'And do you think she welcomed his advances?'

'How would I know?' The question had irritated Daisy. 'It was bad enough to watch him make them.' She jumped to her feet. 'I cannot bear to think about it for another moment. Let's go to the market. I need some new ribbons and shopping will help to occupy my mind.'

'Very well.' Lydia wished she could cast her cares off with the same ease. 'I'll have to dress first.'

When she was ready, Lydia followed Daisy to the door and, as she turned to close it behind her, her glance fell on the letter, still lying on the table. She had hoped to post it today. Now it seemed it would have to wait a little longer.

*   *   *

The rain had done little to dampen the spirits of Sarah and Hepzi as Race drove them back to Borthwick. He had pulled the sturdy black hood over the gig and, although he was slightly exposed to the elements behind the horses, they were both snug and dry inside.

Sarah had spent the journey teaching Hepzi some of the songs she'd heard at the theatre and now as the gig reached the top of the hill overlooking Borthwick all three of them were singing with gusto.

' 'Twas on a Monday morning when I beheld my darling. She looked so sweet and charming in every high degree . . .'

They reached the last verse as they came to a halt outside the post office and Sarah and Hepzi ended up giggling as much as singing as they raced to finish the song before Race opened the door of the gig for them.

'What beautiful voices,' he said with a wink as he helped them down. 'I'm sure I've heard nothing better in the theatre.'

'I think you exaggerate, sir,' Sarah said with a laugh. 'My voice is nowhere near as sweet as Lydia Prescott's was.'

'But your face is prettier and that counts for a lot on the stage.'

148

Sarah felt her cheeks colour. It was undeniably pleasant to be on the receiving end of compliments from Race, even if it was nothing but flattery.

'It must have been cold sitting out in the wind,' she said. 'Would you like to come in for some tea so you can warm up? I'm sure Grandma would be happy to see you again.'

'Perhaps some other time.' Race gave a charm-filled but regretful smile. 'I should get back and take tea with Mama.'

'Of course.'

Sarah couldn't help a small sigh escaping as the gig drove away.

'It's a shame he couldn't stay a little longer. He makes everything such fun, but it's kind of him to be concerned for his mama.'

Hepzi chose not to comment on this. In all the time she'd worked at Bishopston she couldn't recall Mr Race showing that much devotion to his mother. She thought it far more likely that he was trying to avoid Anne.

'Thank goodness you're back.' When Sarah entered the shop a dishevelled looking Lucy came out from behind the counter and caught her up into a welcoming hug. 'I don't know how you do this every day. You've no idea what a trial I've had this afternoon. This is the first time there's been no queue of customers getting impatient and I've had to clear up flour twice when Isaac spilled it.'

'I've been helping,' Isaac announced in

149

blissful innocence of his mother's frustration. 'I like working in the shop.'

'I'm glad to hear it.' Sarah stooped to brush flour out of her nephew's hair. 'When you're a little older you can come and help more often.'

'You'll live to regret that offer,' Lucy muttered and Sarah smiled. 'But why are you alone? Where's Mr Hogg?'

'He had to go back this morning,' Lucy explained. 'I thought you might be back a little earlier than this.'

'I'm sorry.' Sarah had a pang of remorse. They would have been if Race hadn't persuaded her to stop for luncheon at an inn on the way. 'Can you bear to stay for just five more minutes while I go and see Grandma? I promise I'll come straight back.'

When Sarah found Anne in her seat by the fire she was pleased to see that her knitting was in her hands and that she looked a lot better than she had a few days ago.

'Hello, Grandma.' She bent down to kiss her soft cheek. 'How are you feeling?'

'Quite well and idle,' Anne replied. 'It's about time I was getting back to work.'

'Not yet,' Sarah said firmly. 'You know what Doctor Heggarty said.'

'Doctors!' Anne tutted. 'It's all very well for him to say that but you can't cope alone in that shop for ever.'

'I won't have to. Papa's sure to be home soon.'

'And if he isn't for a while yet?' Anne asked doubtfully.

'Then I'll have to think of taking on an assistant.' Sarah tried to sound unconcerned but her grandmother was shaking her head.

'And how will we pay them?' she enquired. 'You know we couldn't cover the rent here and a salary for someone outside the family.'

'Well, Isaac's offered to help and he'd be content to take his pay in sugar canes,' Sarah joked. She was unwilling to let her worries overcome the holiday mood she was in. 'John is well and sends his love,' she said changing the subject.

'And did you enjoy yourself?'

'Oh yes.' Sarah smiled as memories came rushing back. 'The city's such an exciting place. You wouldn't believe how many people live there. We went to the cathedral, an art gallery and—' She stopped abruptly. She'd been about to tell her about the trip to the theatre but wasn't sure her grandmother would approve, especially if she found out that she and John had dined with an actress after the show. She had never held the profession in very high regard.

'And?' Anne prompted.

'And I bought Hepzi a ring,' Sarah finished lamely. It wasn't really a lie, she told herself, just an omission. There was no need to upset Grandma with the truth and she hadn't really done anything wrong, after all. So why, she wondered, did she feel so guilty.

*　　　*　　　*

'Good day, Mr Davenport.' When Constance's butler opened the door to him, Ewart was surprised to see that the man's livery was dusty and there was a cobweb dangling from his shoulder.

'Are you spring cleaning, Matthews?'

'Not exactly, sir.' The butler's eyebrows rose and the scepticism in his voice was evident. 'Lady Weston's taken it into her head to clear out the old schoolroom. I believe she has plans to set herself up as a school mistress.'

'Indeed?' This came as some surprise to Ewart. 'Whom does she intend to teach?'

'That's the problem, sir.' Matthews seemed glad to have someone to confide in. 'She's talking about local urchins coming into the house. It's hardly appropriate. We've already had one robbery and I've enough to do without cleaning up behind ragamuffins. I'm sure Sir Hugh won't be happy to come back and find the house full of them.'

'Probably not.' Ewart handed his hat to the butler. 'Is her ladyship still in the schoolroom?'

'Yes, sir. Would you like me to show you up?'

'No, that's all right, Matthews.' A faint smile crossed Ewart's face. 'I spent a lot of time there as a boy. I'm sure I can still find my way.'

When Ewart tapped on the open schoolroom door, he saw Constance balanced on a low stool dusting down a bookshelf. She had a large white apron on over her dress and, with the feather duster in her hand, looked more like a maid than the mistress.

'Oh Ewart, you've come to visit me again.' She turned at the sound of the knock. 'I'm sorry for not receiving you downstairs but I'm a little occupied this morning.'

'So I see.' He felt a rush of nostalgia as he entered the room. How many times had he, Hugh and Race fought battles on this floor with their tin soldiers? 'Matthews seems a little out of humour today.'

'Oh dear, is he still complaining?' Constance came down from the stool with a sigh.

'He seems to think you're turning the house into a school.'

'And is prone to exaggeration,' Constance said with a smile. 'One pupil hardly constitutes a school. I want to teach Hepzi to read and write. The poor girl is quite illiterate.'

'Many in her position are.' Ewart picked up a pile of old books and blew a layer of dust off them before reaching up to put them back on the shelf for Constance. 'There was a time when Hugh wished he was. I recall him threatening to burn these when he had to read one of them on a summer's day instead of going fishing. Do you intend to give Hepzi lessons here?'

'Yes. Learning her letters and perhaps some numbers can only be of benefit to her and it will give me a way to fill my days until Mama arrives.' Constance smiled. 'I've had a letter from her and she intends to visit as soon as she returns from Europe.'

'That will be most pleasant for you. Does she intend to stay long?'

'I hope she'll remain for some months.' A faint and very becoming flush glowed in Constance's cheeks.

'Then you must both come and dine at Bishopston when she arrives. My mother would be delighted to make her acquaintance.'

'We will.' Constance picked up a slate that was lying on top of another heap of books. 'Ah, this is the very thing I need. I wonder if there is still any chalk.'

'It used to be kept in here.' Ewart opened a drawer in the side of the large oak table where Hugh's tutor had sat and searched through it for some minutes. 'I'm afraid there doesn't appear to be any,' he said at last.

'Well, it's not a disaster,' Constance was polishing the slate with a wet rag. 'I'm sure Sarah stocks all the chalk I could possibly need in her shop.'

'How is Miss Penghalion?' Ewart asked, picking up a picture book and flicking through its faded pictures of knights and dragons.

'Quite well but very busy now that she's

154

alone in the shop. I've only managed to speak to her once since she returned from Exeter. She really enjoyed her time there and said that Race was a most entertaining companion.'

'Race?' Ewart let the book drop back onto the table, his interest in it now completely gone.

'Yes. It was very good of him to take her there, wasn't it?'

'I was unaware that he had,' Ewart said stiffly.

'Why, the whole trip was his idea.' Constance seemed blithely unaware of her guest's mounting displeasure. 'She was so happy to see her brother again and Race took time to show her all the sights. It was so kind of him.'

'I doubt altruism played a great part in it,' Ewart muttered under his breath.

'Oh, I've had quite enough dust for today.' Constance put the cloth down. 'Shall we go to the drawing room and take some refreshment?'

'I'm afraid I must decline.' Ewart was struggling to maintain his composure. 'There is a matter I must attend to.'

He barely heard Constance's goodbyes as he turned and strode from the room. Race had obviously ignored his last warning about dallying with Sarah. This time he would have to make the point a little more forcefully.

'One for you today, Miss Sarah.' Jake fished an envelope out of his sack and handed it to her. 'Looks like it's come from Exeter.'

'It must be from John.' Sarah took the letter eagerly. Her recent visit had made her more acutely aware of how much she missed her elder brother. She was looking forward to reading his impressions of their few days together.

The shop was empty for the moment and so she slit the envelope open noting that the letter inside was much longer than his usual one-page notes.

Dearest Sarah,
How good it was to see you last week. I am now all the more eager to come home during the summer and spend time with Grandma and Lucy too. Did you like the city?

The next few paragraphs were full of the things they had done together and Sarah enjoyed reliving her experiences through them. Then John wrote about their trip to the theatre and a surprised smile broke across her face. She had never before thought of her brother as a romantic.

I am so glad we had the opportunity to

meet Miss Banks. She is quite the prettiest girl I have ever laid eyes on and I found her utterly charming at supper.

Sarah frowned. Had they met the same person? She thought Daisy had been sullen and peevish for most of the evening but then she hadn't been viewing her through John's eyes, and it was clear from his letter that he had been smitten.

I have been back to the theatre twice since that night and waited at the stage door for her to emerge. Once I took her flowers and she seemed pleased with them but has declined my invitations to dinner. At first I was disappointed by this but now I realize that, being the sweet natured, and modest girl that she is, she must feel the need of a chaperone before accepting. I had hoped Miss Prescott would oblige us in this matter but she seems to dislike me for some reason. Whenever I endeavour to speak to her, she makes an excuse to hurry away. Once I saw her in the street and greeted her but she hurried into a shop as though she hadn't seen me although I'm sure she did. I can't think how I may have offended her. If only she would give me a chance to speak I could assure her that my intentions towards Daisy are highly honourable.

Intentions? John sounded serious. Whatever would Grandma say if an actress joined the family? Sarah stifled a giggle as she imagined the ensuing uproar. However, her laughter quickly faded as she read the next few lines.

While I am on the subject of honour I must speak of Mr Davenport. He seems to be an affable enough character but there were times when I felt his behaviour towards you was a little more familiar than it ought to be. I trust you are wise enough to insist on a chaperone whenever you are with him. While Papa is away, the burden of protecting you from harm falls to me.

'Oh really!' Without finishing what her brother had to say, Sarah folded the letter and stuffed it into her apron pocket with a disbelieving shake of her head. She wouldn't have imagined John could sound so pompous. She was hardly a child and perfectly able to protect herself from harm. Besides, Race was scarcely a threat. He had been kind, that was all. If she had once imagined that he might have had feelings for her, the notion had been quashed by seeing how attentive he was to all of her sex. What harm could there be in enjoying his company from time to time?

'I've brought you a cup of tea, Sarah.' Hepzi came through from the cottage and handed her a mug.

'Thank you.' Sarah sipped at the warm liquid and felt her irritation with John turn to amused exasperation. Brothers would be brothers and she supposed his concern only showed how much he cared for her. She must be sure to tease him about Daisy when she next wrote to him.

'Is there anything I can be doing to help you?' Hepzi had lingered in the shop. 'I've dusted through the cottage and your grandma's sleeping so she won't be needing me for a while.'

'Are you sure you wouldn't like to rest as well?' Sarah asked. She seemed to recall that Lucy had never missed an opportunity to do so during her pregnancies.

'No.' Hepzi shook her head. 'I'm used to working. Too much sitting about makes me feel twitchy.'

'Well, if you're sure, you could tidy up the shelves a little.'

'And sweep the floor, too, if you'd like.' Hepzi seemed pleased to be helpful. She set to rearranging the packets on the lower shelf at once and Sarah began weighing out bags of sugar to fill the spaces.

'Good day, Sarah.' A few minutes later the shop door opened and Mrs Thomas bustled in dragging her youngest child along by the hand. 'Gracious me, what a chill's in that breeze today. You'd hardly believe we were so far into spring. Now just give me a moment and I'll find my list.'

She was still rummaging in her coat pocket when Mrs Harper came through the door. She wasn't as distracted as Mrs Thomas and noticed Hepzi at once.

'Is this you getting some help while your Grandma's poorly?' She asked subjecting Hepzi to an intense scrutiny. 'You don't come from these parts do you, my dear?'

'No.' Colour flooded into Hepzi's cheeks and she looked like a startled rabbit on the point of running.

'Hepzi is staying with us for a while,' Sarah said coming to her aid. 'Her . . . husband is in the same regiment as Papa.'

'I see.' She saw Mrs Harper glance at the thin golden band on Hepzi's finger and knew the woman had already taken in her thickening waistline.

'Hepzi,' she said wishing to spare the girl any further embarrassment. 'Why don't you go and see whether Grandma needs anything.'

'Yes, Miss Sarah.' Hepzi shot her a grateful look and hurried back into the cottage.

'Why, Sarah.' Now Mrs Thomas joined the conversation. 'You've been keeping secrets from us. I didn't know there was anyone staying with you. I certainly haven't seen her out and about—not even at church, which is most unusual.'

'She hasn't been well. That's why we've been caring for her until the Lancers return.'

'And you say that her husband serves with them. Is he a local boy?'

'He comes from Bishopston.' Sarah wished she could think of a way of stopping the questions but it seemed that each careful statement she made only sparked the women's interest more.

'That's the Davenport estate, isn't it?' Mrs Harper interjected. 'I wondered why young Mr Davenport had been seen in these parts so often lately.' She gave Sarah a knowing smile. 'Or is there perhaps some other reason for his presence?'

'Was your brother well when you visited?' Mrs Thomas added and, from the juxtaposition of the two questions, Sarah realized that the entire village knew she'd travelled to Exeter with Race.

'Yes,' she stammered as she struggled to maintain her composure. 'He was very well, thank you.'

'And I dare say you enjoyed yourself. It's certainly very kind for a high-born gentleman like that to take an interest in a village girl like yourself, isn't it?' There was a distinct edge in her voice and Sarah felt ill as she comprehended the meaning implicit in her words. Was this what the village thought of her? Suddenly her simple and innocent friendship with Race had been reduced to a tawdry piece of village gossip.

'He has been a true gentleman and very

kind to both me and Miss Briar,' she said
quietly.

'Miss Briar?' Mrs Thomas noticed her
mistake at once. 'I thought you said she was
married.'

'Of course.' Sarah was mortified by her own
stupidity. 'I still think of her as Miss Briar,
that's all.'

'Really?' Mrs Thomas didn't look convinced
but Mrs Harper had a more thoughtful
expression on her face.

'Briar?' she repeated. 'Wasn't that the name
of that band of thieves that came here at the
start of the year? Those ones as took off in
such a rush when Farleigh Park was robbed.'

'She's one of those gypsies?' Mrs Thomas
looked horrified. 'Sarah, how could you keep
such a person under your roof? You're lucky
you and Anne haven't been murdered in your
beds or robbed blind.'

'Hepzi's not a thief,' Sarah protested. It hurt
her to hear someone she now regarded as one
of her family slandered in such a malicious
way.

'Well, don't say we didn't warn you.' Mrs
Thomas finally located her list and handed it
over. 'I wouldn't trust her to be out of my
sight, if I was you.'

That evening, as soon as the last post was
gone, Sarah locked the shop door early and
slipped out into the late spring sunshine. Her
encounter with the women that afternoon had

left her feeling agitated and unhappy for the rest of the day and now a headache had built up behind her temples. She needed some air and some time to think.

Mrs Thomas had been right about the cool wind and she wrapped her shawl tightly across her chest as she began to walk down the lane that led past the side of the church and down to the stream.

The things that had been said about Hepzi had upset her but she knew they weren't true and was therefore able to dismiss them, although she was glad the girl hadn't heard them. The sly insinuations about her friendship with Race weren't so easy to ignore and she'd been reflecting about them all afternoon. Eventually she had decided that, up to a point, the women had been right. A member of the gentry like Race didn't cultivate friendships with lower class girls like her for no reason and she'd been flattered enough by his intentions to forget her station in life. She hoped his kindness had been nothing more dubious than charity towards her. No doubt it had made him feel benevolent but it had been disastrous for her reputation in a small village where everyone would always be ready to believe the worst. In future she would remember her place and avoid Race. Perhaps she shouldn't call on Constance again either. After all, she was Lady Weston, and assuming they could be friends too was presumptuousness on her part. It wouldn't be easy to carry out her resolve. She liked them both and would miss them but she didn't belong in their social circle and had no right to behave as though she did.

'I didn't expect to see you here, Sarah.'

She turned at the sound of the voice to see Albert coming towards her with a bunch of bluebells in his hand At least she could still speak to him. She waited for him to catch up and when he did, he thrust the flowers at her.

'These are for you. I was going to bring them to the shop but then I saw you walking down here.'

'Thank you, Albert. They're lovely.' She buried her nose in the deep lavender blue petals and absorbed the sweet spring scent that clung to them.

'You've closed the shop early.' Albert glanced up at the clock on the church tower.

'Just a little. I had a headache and thought a walk would cure it. I'm going down to the stream.'

'Then I'll come with you if you'd like.'

'All right.' It would be nice to talk to someone and take her mind off her troubled thoughts for a while.

'You never did come to the Shrove Dance with me,' Albert said as they continued along their way.

'No, and I'm sorry for it, but events ran away with me.' Sarah had been referring to

Hepzi and her grandmother's illness but the comment made Albert frown.

'I suppose you mean the gentleman in the fine carriage,' he said sullenly. 'I've heard it said you went to Exeter with him.'

'Yes.' She'd been mistaken to think she could forget about Race so easily. However, Albert's next question caught her completely off guard.

'Are you his paramour?'

'No.' She recoiled in horror and knew Albert was only expressing what the rest of the village suspected. 'Race—' She recalled her new resolution to be less familiar with the gentry. 'Mr Davenport has been very kind at a difficult time. That is all.'

'Sorry, Sarah.' Albert didn't look as apologetic as he sounded. In fact, she thought she saw a smile cross his lips. 'I suppose this has been a very trying time for you. How is your grandma now?'

'A little better but I don't believe she will ever regain her former health. I'm still very concerned about her.'

'And struggling alone in the shop. That must be hard for you as well.'

'Yes.' Albert's understanding tone was touching and she found she could unburden her worries onto him in a way she hadn't been able to with anyone else. 'It is exhausting but Papa will come home eventually and then we'll work together.'

165

'Can't you find someone to help you in the meantime?' Albert asked gently. 'Such a strain will take its toll on your health eventually.'

'It's not as easy as that. We have to pay rent on the shop and cottage and we don't make enough to cover another wage. Lucy used to help out when she could but she's busy with her own family now and it's not fair to ask her to do more.'

'It's not an easy situation,' Albert agreed. 'There is a solution though, I think.'

'Really? What is it?' Sarah was eager to hear any idea that might resolve her difficulties but she didn't expect to hear what Albert said next.

'I could help you. In fact, we could run the business together as partners.'

'I don't understand.' She frowned. 'You have your own work and how could we be partners?'

'By extending the union to more than just the shop.' With a sudden smile, Albert reached out and caught hold of her hand. 'Oh dearest Sarah, don't you see how easy it could be? Marry me and your problems will be over.'

CHAPTER SEVEN

'Look at me, Aunt Sarah. I'm weighing things.'
'Oh Isaac, please be careful. You might fall.'

Sarah turned to discover that her nephew had climbed up onto her high stool and was balanced precariously over the counter as he stretched to drop a weight heavily on the scales. The loud clang resounded around the shop and woke Georgina who immediately reverted to the ear-splitting crying she'd been indulging in for ten minutes before Sarah had managed to rock her to sleep.

'There, there.' Sarah held the baby against her shoulder with one arm while she used the other to make sure Isaac didn't come to grief as he clambered down from the stool.

'Can I play in the flour again?'

'No!' She was beginning to think that even the busiest morning in the shop was easier than caring for children. 'Why don't you come and see if you can make Georgina happy again?'

'Don't want to.' Isaac pouted. 'I want to help in the shop. You said I could.'

'I know I did.' Sarah sighed. How Lucy would laugh if she was here to see this. When she'd asked Sarah to watch the children, she'd promised it would be for no more than five minutes while she ran down to the bakers. That had been quarter of an hour ago and there was still no sign of her.

Georgina drew breath for a fresh outburst of screaming and Sarah was relieved to finally hear the bell above the door jangle as someone entered the shop. Was Lucy back at last?

'Hello, Albert.' Isaac grinned up at the newcomer and Sarah tried not to let dismay show on her face. Albert had become a frequent customer over the past few weeks and every visit ended with him asking her the same question.

'Dear me, Georgina isn't in good humour today.' Albert bent over to smile at the baby but this did nothing to alleviate her yells.

'No.' Sarah renewed her efforts to lull her niece back to sleep. 'I don't suppose you chanced upon Lucy in the street?'

'She's talking to Maud Cooper outside the bakers. I'm sure she'll be along in a moment.'

'Thank goodness for that. Now what can I get for you today?'

'Nothing. I'm simply here to see if you've got an answer for me yet.'

Sarah sighed. Albert was impatient for her response to his proposal and yet she was no closer to making a decision than she'd been when he first asked her to marry him. She knew he was a decent man who'd worked hard to make something of himself and would always provide well for a family. He was kind, too, and she enjoyed his company but was that enough? No doubt some folk would call her foolish but she'd always believed she would be hopelessly in love with the man she married. She was fond of Albert but that was all. The sight of him had never made her heart race

168

and he certainly didn't haunt her thoughts when they were apart. She didn't know if it was fair to either of them to settle for less than her dreams.

'I'm sorry, Albert. I need a little longer.'

'But it's been weeks already!' Albert heaved a frustrated sigh. 'Surely you've had time to make a hundred decisions by now.'

'Albert, I barely have time to catch my breath at the moment.' His impatience and Georgina's continuing cries combined to drive her to exasperation. 'You know how busy I am through the day and even when the doors are closed I have to work on to ensure the post office records are kept up to date. I need to consider your kind offer most carefully and I've had little chance to do so.'

'I'm sure you could find some time if you wanted to,' Albert protested.

'I wish it was that easy.' She pulled an envelope out of her pocket. 'This letter arrived this morning and I haven't even had an opportunity to open it, far less read it. Please give me a little longer.'

'It seems I have little other choice.' Albert looked distinctly unhappy but Lucy's arrival put an end to any further discussion on the subject and he left with nothing more than a wounded glance in Sarah's direction.

'I'm sorry I was delayed, Sarah.' Lucy took Georgina back into her arms and the baby quietened almost at once. 'I met Maud. Her husband's just brought news of Africa back from Otterly. Prince Louis Napoleon has been killed.'

'Oh no!' Sarah gasped. Only a few weeks earlier the newspapers had told the story of the young exiled French prince. He wanted to join the British Army but when his nationality had barred him doing so he'd volunteered to serve as Lord Chelmsford's aide-de-camp. His death was a demoralizing blow to the British and an unspoken question hung in the air between Sarah and her sister. If someone of his birth wasn't safe then who was?

'Why don't you take the children through to the house?' Sarah didn't want Isaac to sense their anxiety. 'I've a letter from Papa in my pocket. I'll come through as soon as I've locked up and we can all read it together. I'm sure that will cheer us up.'

*   *   *

By the time Sarah was able to join her family in the kitchen there was a pot of tea on the table and Isaac was chewing contentedly on a slice of bread and jam.

Hepzi was also in the room. She had a slate resting on the table in front of her and was carefully etching out the letters Constance had taught her. Sarah noticed she was squinting over her work and put a candlestick down in front of her.

170

'Use this. It's getting dark now that the clouds are coming in off the sea.'

'Thank you.' Hepzi frowned at her work. 'I'm not sure light will be making these look any better though. It's fair difficult to get the lines straight.'

'I think you're doing very well,' Sarah told her. 'You'll be reading the newspaper to us before you know it.'

'Talking of reading, let's hear what Papa has to say.' Lucy was sitting in the armchair by the fire, nursing Georgina.

'Of course.' Sarah retrieved the letter from her pocket and opened it.

My dearest family, I trust these few lines will find you all well. There has been a good deal sickness among the garrison here within the past few weeks but I have been fortunate enough not to succumb to the fevers and agues that have afflicted so many. The rains have descended upon us in earnest and continual sogginess makes us all miserable. The wagons can barely make progress through the mud and our uniforms are permanently heavy with damp.

'It seems to be raining everywhere,' Lucy said. 'We haven't had a dry day this week either.'

'At least we can put on dry clothes when we need to.' Sarah hoped their father had

171

continued to avoid illness whilst living in such appalling conditions.

The cook has been unable to keep a fire alight long enough to produce hot vitals and although we have plenty to eat we long to taste warm . . .

There was a sudden crash and Hepzi cried out. While she was reaching for a fresh piece of chalk she had knocked against the candlestick and it had fallen over. The flame had gone out as it tumbled but she and Lucy were both staring at it with horrified expressions on their faces.

'A fallen candle is a sure sign of coming disaster,' Lucy murmured. 'Something terrible's going to happen.'

'That's just superstition,' Sarah said quickly. 'It means nothing.'

'Then why does everyone say it?' Hepzi whispered.

'For the same reason they talk of fairies.' Sarah was trying to sound unconcerned but she too had heard the superstition many times and it was hard not to let it affect her, especially when her father's letter was still in her hand.

'Mama, I'm scared.' Isaac had noticed their anxiety and was beginning to look tearful. 'What bad thing will happen?'

'Nothing will happen,' Sarah assured him

172

but he looked no more convinced of this than Lucy and Hepzi. The tense atmosphere in the room wasn't good for any of them and Sarah decided that she had to lighten it.

'Who wants to see a dance?' She snatched Isaac's hat up off the table and balanced it on top of her head. She knew it must look preposterous and was pleased to see that Isaac was already smiling. 'One of the singers at the theatre wore a hat like this and he did a funny dance as well.' Sarah tried to imitate the jerky movements she'd seen the performer make and started to sing the song he'd entertained the audience with.

'When I was a bachelor, I lived all alone. I worked at the weaver's trade. And the only, only thing I ever did wrong was to woo a fair young maid.'

'Oh Sarah, that's so funny.' Lucy was smiling now and she and Hepzi began to clap their hands in time to the song. Encouraged by their response, Sarah began to make her dance more energetic, kicking her legs and twirling her skirts.

'And the only, only thing that I ever did was wrong was to keep her from the foggy, foggy dew.'

'Sarah! Stop that at once!' Anne's angry voice brought the performance to an abrupt end. The old woman was standing in the doorway with a look of utter fury on her face. 'What do you think you're doing?'

'Trying to cheer everyone up.' Sarah suddenly remembered about the hat and took it off.

'With that coarse behaviour?' Anne's voice was still scathing. 'Where did you learn such a crude song?'

'At the music hall.' Sarah lowered her head as her cheeks reddened. 'Race took us there when we in Exeter.'

'How could you? You know those places are nothing more than dens of iniquity.' Anne glared at her. 'You want to be careful, my girl, or you'll end up being no better than your mother.'

'What do you mean by that?' Lucy demanded indignantly. 'What was wrong with Mama?'

Lucy's question brought Anne's tirade to an abrupt halt and the woman suddenly looked flustered. 'Nothing,' she stammered. 'Of course there was nothing wrong with her. That wasn't what I meant. I shouldn't have—' She went pale and Sarah guided her to her chair before she could fall.

'Are you all right?' Grandma was ghostly white and it was all her fault. She wouldn't forgive herself if she was responsible for making her ill again.

'I was wrong to speak of it.' Anne was still muttering to herself as she took the cup of tea Hepzi brought her.

'I think I should take the children home.'

Lucy still sounded affronted and she turned on Sarah as soon as they were both out of the kitchen.

'What do you think she meant by such a thing?' she hissed. 'It sounded as though she thought Mama was wicked.'

'I'm sure she didn't.' Sarah was also confused by their grandmother's words but she was more upset at having been the cause of the disturbance. 'She was angry and muddled that's all.'

'If you say so.' Lucy didn't sound convinced. 'I'm sure Grandma meant something and I intend to find out what it was.'

*　　*　　*

Bury Meadow on a sunny Sunday afternoon was a popular place to be. As Lydia walked beneath the row of oak trees that lined the path near the entrance, she could hear children's laughter and see many other people out taking advantage of the summer weather. It really was a lovely day and she might have been able to enjoy it more if she wasn't feeling so apprehensive about the situation she was in.

When John had first taken to waiting by the stage door she'd been sure he would eventually tire of Daisy's disinterest in him but the young man had been persistent and had won his reward. Daisy had agreed to take a walk in the park. John had insisted that they must have a chaperone and Daisy, who had never shown such scruples when she walked out with Race, had begged Lydia to fulfil this role.

'We intend to walk down to the rose garden, Miss Prescott.' John turned to look back at her. 'Will that be agreeable to you?'

'Of course.' Lydia didn't know whether to be distant or not. She was torn between the fear that John would suddenly recognize her and an almost overwhelming longing to question him about Sarah and George.

'It is such a lovely day and there's no need for us to hurry back, is there Lydia?' Daisy, who had once sworn she wanted nothing to do with the young teacher, now seemed unwilling to leave his company and blushed like a schoolgirl when he offered her his arm.

'Have you always lived in Exeter, Mr Penghalion?' There had been no hint of recognition in his eyes and that gave Lydia courage.

'No. I come from a small village called Borthwick.' John smiled. 'I don't suppose you've even heard of it.'

'The name isn't familiar.' She hoped that the faint tremor in her voice wouldn't reveal her lie. 'Do your parents still live there?'

'My father does or at least he will when he returns from Africa. He's in the army and often has to go away. My grandparents mainly raised us as our mother died when my

176

youngest sister, Sarah, was born.'

'Oh.' Lydia couldn't suppress the faint sound of dismay and John looked at her in concern.

'Are you all right? Is it perhaps too warm for you?'

'It's nothing.' She opened her fan and hid her pained expression behind it. So she had been completely written out of the family's history. Her daughter didn't know she had ever existed.

'Of course, you met Sarah a few weeks ago.'

'Indeed, and I thought her quite charming. Does she spend a great deal of time with Race?' Lydia ignored Daisy's scowl as she said this.

'I don't know.' John's brow contracted into a frown and she wondered if he was simply unwilling to discuss his rival or was as concerned about his sister as she was. 'I doubt if she has much time to lately. Our grandmother has been taken ill and Sarah is running the shop alone.'

'Doesn't Lucy help?' As soon as she asked the question she knew she'd made a terrible mistake.

'No, she's busy with her own family.' John looked perplexed. 'How did you know I have a sister called Lucy?'

'You must have mentioned her in a previous conversation.' Lydia hid her confusion behind a laugh that must have sounded as false as it felt. 'I have no talent as a fortune teller so how else could I have known?'

John frowned again but he didn't argue and Lydia was relieved when Daisy demanded his attention.

'I thought you wanted to talk to me,' she said a little petulantly. 'Tell me about the scrapes your pupils get into.'

As the young couple walked on again, Lydia pressed her hand to her mouth. That slip had almost revealed her secret. If she wasn't careful, John would discover who she was before she had decided whether or not she had the courage to post her letter to Sarah. Many times she had taken it out of her trunk and prepared to send it before losing her nerve and concealing it again. If her daughter was to learn the truth, she wanted to be the one to tell it to her. Being around John was dangerous and she would have to tell Daisy to find another chaperone for their meetings.

John, however, had other ideas on the matter. When the trio had walked an entire circuit of the park and Daisy was occupied watching the antics of a hurdy-gurdy man's monkey, he approached Lydia who was resting on a bench.

'May I speak with you?'

'Of course.' Was he going to question her about Lucy again? Her act of composure was more demanding than any performance she'd ever given on the stage.

'I know you haven't encouraged my courtship of Daisy.' John spoke rapidly as though it was a well rehearsed speech. 'If it is because you fear I am dallying with her affections then let me assure you that is not the case. My heart is entirely hers and I can only hope that she might soon return my devotion. To that end I would very much like to take her to meet my family. I'm sure they'll love her as much as I do.'

'I think perhaps you ought to be telling Daisy this.' Lydia was feeling increasingly uncomfortable. 'My feelings in the matter are unimportant compared to hers.'

'I intend to,' John said earnestly. 'But I still have a request to make of you. Daisy must be chaperoned for the journey to Borthwick. You would do me a great service if you would agree to accompany us.'

He looked at her eagerly and Lydia realized he was waiting for her response.

'I cannot answer at once,' she stammered. 'It may not be possible to leave the theatre.' The blood was rushing in her ears so loudly that she was sure John must be able to hear it. If she went to Borthwick she would see her daughter again and there was nothing that would make her happier. However, she would also have to face her former mother-in-law. John might not recall her but there was no doubt that Anne would, and she didn't think her welcome would be a warm one.

*   *   *

Ewart felt the smooth wooden handle of the mallet slip against his palms as he raised it above his head and then smashed it down on the piece of limestone at his feet. The rock split cleanly down the middle and he watched it fall apart with satisfaction. His mother had been surprised when he'd told her that he would build the rock garden she wanted behind the house. She didn't understand how much he missed his physically active life in the army. No one did.

'I'm sure you could find someone to do that for you.' He heard Race speak but chose not to acknowledge him. 'This kind of toil is considered to be a punishment in the prisons.'

'On the contrary, there is deep gratification to be found in good honest labour.' Ewart spoke tersely. 'But, of course, I wouldn't expect you to know about such things.'

He swung the mallet again. Relations between the brothers had been strained ever since he'd heard about Race's trip to Exeter. They'd argued bitterly about it and even their mother's pleas for a truce had done little to resolve matters.

'I am as capable of work as you.' Race removed his jacket and waistcoat and tossed them down on the grass. 'In fact, I can probably do more. I have no injury to hamper me.'

Ewart frowned. His leg was almost fully healed but he still felt a twinge of pain from time to time.

'Assist me, if you wish,' he muttered. 'It will be a more profitable use of your time than visiting the inn or pestering Miss Penghalion.'

'Why is everyone so intent on warning me off Sarah?' Race picked up a lump of broken stone and threw it onto the pile of others. 'The last time I went to Exeter, Lydia spent the better part of an evening telling me that Sarah didn't seem an appropriate companion.' He snorted. 'Of course, she would. She's always telling me I should treat Daisy more kindly. But tell me, Ewart, why are you so concerned about her?'

'Her father was one of my men. I have a duty of care towards all their families in their absence.' Ewart picked up a shovel and began to dig along the lines of the new garden. 'Help me here, if you've a will to.'

'You don't go to visit Reverend Healy as much as you once did.' Race picked up another spade and cast his brother a shrewd look. 'Might there be a reason why Miss Healy's charms have faded for you?'

'Miss Healy is staying with her sister in Plymouth. I believe she intends to marry a doctor there.'

'And aren't you even a little heart broken? Perhaps some other girl has taken your fancy.'

Race laughed and Ewart scowled.

'Perhaps I'm simply too busy with other matters to think of such things.'

'No man should be that busy.'

Ewart didn't reply and the brothers worked in silence for several minutes.

'I intend to go to London for a few days,' Race said when he stopped for a rest.

'Not with Miss Penghalion, I hope,' Ewart muttered and Race glowered at him.

'Alone. I've a mind to seek employment and perhaps a home there.' Ewart stopped digging and turned to look at his brother.

'You would leave Bishopston?' he asked in surprise.

'I have no real role here.' Race gave an awkward shrug. 'I don't share your love of farming and you manage things perfectly well without me. Besides, I imagine you will marry one day and your bride may not wish to share a home with me.'

Ewart stared at him for a moment. It had never occurred to him that Race's seemingly irresponsible attitude might have been caused by a sense of not belonging.

'There will always be a home here for you, no matter what,' he said gruffly.

'Why Brother!' The vulnerable side Race had briefly exposed was gone again and he gave Ewart one of his wicked grins. 'Be careful what you say or people may suspect you have a heart after all.'

'And if you speak of finding employment, they'll be likely to believe in miracles.'

Ewart easily dodged the clod of turf his brother playfully lobbed at him and when their mother came into the garden with a jug of cider for her sons, she was relieved to see that they were laughing together and their quarrel seemed resolved.

*　　*　　*

'Now that you've mastered the alphabet we can begin to create words.' Constance was enjoying her role as Hepzi's teacher and the willingness of her pupil meant the lessons were progressing much faster than she'd expected. 'Copy these three letters and see if you can read the word they make.'

'Yes, miss.' Hepzi set about the task just as Matthews knocked on the schoolroom door.

'Reverend Yates is here to see you, Madam.'

'Oh.' Constance rose from her seat and saw that the butler had brought the vicar up with him. 'How very nice to see you, Reverend.'

'Lady Weston.' The vicar shook her hand and then glanced at Hepzi. 'Have I called at an inappropriate time?'

'Not at all. This is Miss Briar. I have been teaching her to write.'

'Indeed.' This brought a smile to Reverend Yates's face. 'How very propitious that I should find you engaged in the very activity I wished to discuss with you.'

'Really, and what is that?'

'Education, Lady Weston.' Reverend Yates began to explain. 'As you know, the nearest local school is located at Otterly and children have a long walk each day in all kinds of weather. Now we hope to establish a board to oversee the building of a school here in the village. I came to enquire whether we might depend on Sir Hugh's support.'

'Of course you can.' Constance didn't hesitate. 'And on mine as well.'

'Thank you, Lady Weston. The board meets tomorrow and I'm sure they'll be delighted when I tell them of your patronage.'

'Tell them?' Constance shook her head. 'That will be quite unnecessary, Reverend. I will attend the meeting.'

'You, Lady Weston?' The vicar sounded shocked but Constance didn't flinch.

'Of course,' she said resolutely. 'I have a great interest in education. I represent my husband in his absence and will be happy to do so on this occasion.'

As the vicar acknowledged this, she had a momentary fear that Hugh wouldn't entirely approve of her direct involvement but she quickly dismissed it. After all, he was hundreds of miles away and unlikely to hear of her exploits anyway. She was, for the moment, free to act as she wished.

*　　*　　*

'Are you sure I can't get you anything else, Grandma? You need to eat and keep your strength up.'

'No, lass, this tea is all I need. I've no appetite for anything else and besides, you should be down in the shop not fussing about me.'

'I've left Albert in charge for a few minutes.' Sarah smiled. 'He's in there so often these days that he may as well be useful during his visits.'

'After an answer again?' Anne asked and Sarah sighed.

'I expect so. I'm still no closer to a decision though.'

'I think you are.' Anne reached out to touch Sarah's hand. 'You'll find your heart has been sure since he asked you. Listen to what it tells you and you won't go wrong.'

Talking seemed to tire Anne. Her head dropped back against the pillows and Sarah looked on in concern. Over the past few days her grandmother seemed to be growing weaker again. She was barely eating and had been forced to take to her bed once more

'Oh Grandma, I wish I could do something to make you feel better.'

'You do plenty.' Anne smiled at her. 'You're a good girl.'

'I wasn't the other day.' Sarah looked rueful

185

and then curious as she recalled Anne's reaction to the song. 'Grandma, what did you mean when you said I would be no better than Mama?'

'I shouldn't have said that.' Anne shook her head. 'I shouldn't have been as hard on her as I was, either. She was barely more than a girl and the three of you were too much. I should have offered support and instead I did nothing but criticize. It's small wonder she left you as she did.'

'She died, Grandma,' Sarah said softly. 'It was no one's fault.'

'You don't understand.' Anne's rheumy eyes filled with tears and Sarah felt bad for pressing her on the matter.

'Don't cry. You've always done your best for us and we all love you for it.'

'If George ever learned the truth he would hate me.' Anne lapsed into a weary silence and Sarah frowned. Grandma seemed to be growing confused about the past.

'Papa loves you too. I'm sure he'll be home very soon and then everything will be all right again, you'll see.'

Anne didn't reply and Sarah realized she had drifted into sleep. She drew the coverlet gently up over her hands and then crept from the room with a heavy heart.

*   *   *

Sarah heard Albert's voice as she returned to the shop and thought at first that he must be serving a customer. Then she realized that he sounded belligerent and hurried to see what the problem was.

'I've already told you, she's not here.' Albert was standing behind the counter with his arms folded in a determined gesture and Ewart was on the other side with an equally stubborn look on his face.

'What's wrong?' When she spoke both men turned to look at her, Ewart with a complacent smile and Albert with a distinctly annoyed scowl.

'Miss Penghalion.' Ewart spoke first. 'I asked to see you but this gentleman said you were unavailable.' The pointed look he gave Albert and the emphasis he placed on 'gentleman' made it obvious that it wasn't his first choice of word.

'I told him you were with your grandma,' Albert countered.

'How is Mrs Penghalion?'

Ewart ignored Albert's protest.

'Not very well, I'm afraid. She needs a lot of rest.'

'I'm sorry to hear it. Be sure to tell me if there is anything I can do to help.'

'I'll help Sarah if she needs it,' Albert muttered but once again Ewart took no notice of him.

'I've called today because I have received

word from Mr Kettley.'

'Noah?' Sarah smiled. 'Oh, Hepzi will be pleased.'

'As it is a matter of some delicacy might we perhaps discuss it in private?' Ewart glanced at Albert again and this time the young man lost his temper.

'You can talk in front of me. Sarah and I are as good as betrothed. We have no secrets and I know all about Hepzi. I helped save her life.'

'Oh?' For the first time during the exchange Ewart's composure seemed to falter. 'I didn't fully comprehend the situation.'

'Well now you do.' Albert puffed his chest out while Sarah stared at him in irritation. He had no right to say such things and she felt particularly aggrieved that Ewart of all people should be the one to be misinformed.

'Sir Hugh has written on behalf of Noah.' Ewart addressed them both but his eyes were on Sarah as he spoke. 'He is now aware of the situation and has made arrangements for Miss Briar to receive a proportion of his pay until he returns. She can collect it from the clerk's office at the barracks in Otterly.'

'Thank you.' Sarah was sure the money would make a great deal of difference to Hepzi. 'I'll tell her.'

'And if she has any difficulty making the journey I will be happy to provide transport for her.'

'You're very kind.' Sarah bit back a smile as

she realized that was a description she'd once thought would never apply to Ewart Davenport. Perhaps she'd judged him too harshly in the past.

'If Hepzi needs a ride into Otterly then I'll be the one to take her.' Another outburst from Albert brought her amusement to an abrupt end. 'We don't need charity from the gentry.'

'As you wish.' Ewart turned to give him a frosty look. 'I didn't realize you had the means of transportation.'

'We have all we need, don't we, Sarah?' Albert turned to include her in his curt retort and she lost her patience. Albert knew she was worried about Grandma, yet instead of supporting her he was behaving like an ill bred child and provoking Ewart in a shameful way.

'I know I have a great deal of work to do,' she said sharply. 'Thank you for minding the shop for me, Albert.' She gave him a look that left him no doubt that he was dismissed and he coloured as he reached for his hat.

'I will not detain you, either.' Ewart also headed for the door and Sarah raised her eyes in exasperation as there was a short, silent tussle between the two men over who would show the courtesy of allowing the other to exit first. In the end, Albert conceded defeat and Ewart was left alone in the shop for a few seconds.

'Good day, Miss Penghalion.' He raised his hat and his deep brown eyes met hers, holding them in an intense questioning gaze that made her feel both self-conscious and exposed yet strangely unwilling to look away.

'Mr Davenport.' She eventually managed to stammer out a response and the momentary connection between them was broken. Ewart blinked, gave her a stiff bow and then left.

From her vantage point inside, Sarah watched him untie his horse and swing up into the saddle. He glanced back at the shop once more and then rode away while she sighed and sank down onto her stool. She could have done without all that antagonism between Ewart and Albert. The entire incident had left her feeling strangely discomfited and for some reason her heart was pounding as heavily as the hammer in Henry's forge.

CHAPTER EIGHT

'Come on, Sarah!' Dan, the wagon driver hammered on the shop door. 'It's not like ye to linger in your bed. I need to collect the post or I won't make it to the train back at Otterly.' He rattled the door again in case it was just stiff but there was no doubt about it. It was locked. 'Come on, I've got news for you as well. Good news.'

He saw a figure appear behind the blind in the doorway. A key jangled in the lock and

190

eventually the door opened.

'About time too, lass. Now come on, we'll have to look lively if I'm to get to the station in time.'

Sarah's only response was a tearful sniff. Dan looked at her properly for the first time and suddenly realized that something was very wrong. She was in her working clothes but her dark hair still hung loose about her shoulders. He might still have thought she had simply overslept but for the pallor of her cheeks and the tears that were falling from her red rimmed eyes.

'Whatever's wrong with ye?'

'It's Grandma.' Sarah held a handkerchief up to her eyes. 'I went to take her cup of tea as usual and . . . and—' Her voice broke. 'Oh Dan, she's dead.'

'There now, lass.' The old man took the sobbing girl into his arms. 'Let all the grief come out. It's a tragedy and there's no doubt about it.'

'I don't know what I'm going to do.' Sarah's sobs continued. 'I can't imagine life without her.'

'You've had a bad shock and the first thing you should do is take some time to recover. I'll sort the letters as best I can today.'

'The post!' Sarah ran a hand over her eyes. By law she had to ensure that nothing impeded the speedy delivery of the post. Not even this great loss was allowed to affect her duty to Her

Majesty's Mail Service. 'I'll sort it.'

She hurried to carry out the task and Dan watched her in concern. 'You don't want to be all alone in here today.'

'I'm not. Hepzi's here but she's still sleeping. I'll have to go for Lucy and send a telegram to John.' Sarah handed the mail bag over to Jake. 'Please tell anyone you see that the shop will be closed today.'

'I'll do that. Can I be doing anything else for you?'

'No, thank you. You've been very kind.' Sarah looked up at him. 'What news were you going to tell me?'

'News?' Dan looked blank for a moment and then blinked. 'Oh yes. Seeing ye taken so bad clean put it out of my head. In Otterly at first light they were saying how that war in Africa is over. Our boys have won a great victory and they'll be coming home.'

When Sarah had locked the door behind Dan, she sank down onto the floor and buried her face in her hands. She'd waited so long to hear that her father was heading for home but she'd never once imagined she'd feel so utterly heartbroken when she heard it. Now his homecoming would be overshadowed by loss and their little family would never be quite the same again. Tears overwhelmed her and she didn't stir until she heard a faint sound behind her. Hepzi was standing in the shop with a shawl wrapped over her nightgown.

'I heard you crying.' There was fear in her voice. 'What's wrong?'

Sarah took a deep breath. She couldn't indulge her own grief any longer. She would have to be strong for Hepzi and Lucy. One of the hardest days of her life was about to begin.

'Come here.' She held a hand out to Hepzi. 'There's something I must tell you.'

*   *   *

Constance was in high spirits when she returned to Farleigh Park that morning. Not only had she read the newspaper report of the British victory at Ulundi but she had just attended a very productive meeting of the new school board. Everything was progressing most satisfactorily. The site of the new school had been approved and Reverend Yates had offered the use of a large room in the rectory that could be used as a classroom until the new building was completed. Constance had committed money for the purchase of essential equipment and soon they would advertise for a teacher. Other members of the board seemed to think that would be the hardest task and warned that it might not be easy to find qualified staff who would be prepared to live in such a small village. Constance refused to worry about this, however. She was sure the right person would be found and that the children of Borthwick would soon have a school to be proud of.

Matthews was waiting on the steps when the carriage drew up and he approached as the footman helped Constance to descend.

'Lady Hawley is here, Madam.'

'Mama?' Constance looked startled. 'I didn't expect her until later this afternoon.'

'She arrived almost an hour ago,' Matthews replied. 'I have taken the liberty of showing her and her maid to their rooms and of serving coffee in the drawing room.'

'Thank you, and please tell cook to lay out a cold luncheon in the dining room. I'm sure there'll be enough for two if she slices last night's brisket thinly.' She untied the strings of her bonnet, handed it and her shawl to Matthews and then headed towards the drawing room.

'Mama, how lovely to see you again.' She smiled as she hurried across to the settle where her mother was sitting sipping from her coffee cup.

'My dear.' Lady Hawley seemed to bridle as her daughter approached with every intention of hugging her. Constance sensed her stiffness and settled instead for placing a kiss on the cheek that her mother presented.

'You look well, Mama. Did you enjoy Europe?'

'It was most a most enjoyable tour although the travelling was more than a little tiresome at times and one does find that foreign accommodation is rarely to the standard one takes for granted in this country. Some hotels I visited had most unusual ideas about sanitation.'

'I trust you've found your rooms here to your satisfaction.' Constance had spent most of the previous afternoon overseeing the preparation of her mother's suite. She had personally checked every aspect of the furnishing and ensured that books, fresh flowers and a collection of pretty ornaments were displayed throughout.

'They are quite adequate although I would have preferred south-facing windows.' Lady Hawley put down her cup and subjected Constance to a disapproving look. 'I would also have liked my daughter to be here to greet me on my arrival.'

'I'm sorry, Mama. I didn't expect you until much later and I had business to attend to this morning.'

'Business?' Lady Hawley stared at her. 'What kind of business?'

'We're building a school in the village and I am a member of the board overseeing the task.'

'Constance!' Her mother's eyebrows gathered slightly. 'If this is your idea of a joke I must say that I do not find it amusing. If you are serious then I am even more displeased.'

'But why? There is no one else to represent Hugh in his absence and you have always encouraged me to show an interest in charitable works.'

'There is a considerable difference between sewing items to sell at bazaars in order to help the needy and conducting yourself in such an inappropriate way. Whatever would Hugh say?'

'I'm sure he wouldn't mind.' A slight flush rose in Constance's cheeks. The truth was that she hadn't yet mentioned her new interest in her letters to Hugh.

'Well, that's beside the point.' Lady Hawley sniffed. 'You'll have to resign from the board anyway.'

'Why?' Constance asked and her mother shook her head as though unable to believe what she was hearing.

'Correct me if I am wrong but did you not write to inform me of the imminent arrival of a new addition to your family?'

'Yes.' Constance couldn't help smiling.

'Then surely you must understand the implications of your delicate condition. It is absolutely essential that you rest completely.' Her mother frowned. 'It's well known that too much activity and indulging in wholly unwomanly behaviour, as you have been, is detrimental to the welfare of the child and is more likely to result in the mother's death after the birth.'

'I feel perfectly well,' Constance protested. However, Lady Hawley barely seemed to hear her as she continued with her lecture.

'In addition to that it is unacceptable for you to show yourself in public when your condition is obvious.' She took out a pince-nez and squinted at her daughter through the lenses. 'Unless I am very much mistaken you have already loosened your corsets. It would be utterly scandalous for you to continue to go out in mixed company. I think it's just as well I've arrived when I have. Now I can make sure you behave in an appropriate and seemly way. Have you made arrangements to employ the new staff you will require?'

'No, Mama.'

'Well, that is the sort of activity you would be better to occupy yourself with instead of running about the countryside attending meetings. You need a monthly nurse who should be in position as soon as possible to care for you, and of course a nurse maid. I will ask my associates if they can recommend anyone. You can't be too careful in these circumstances.'

Constance felt the last traces of her good mood dissipate. Her baby wasn't due for more than three months yet and if her mother had her way she would spend every day of them shut in the house with only the preparation of a layette to occupy her. She had come to value the freedom Hugh's absence had afforded her and she was unwilling to have it taken from her so abruptly.

'We've been invited to dinner at Bishopston Manor,' she said in an effort to change the subject. 'Mrs Davenport and her son are looking forward to meeting you.'

'Constance, have you heard one word I've been saying?' Lady Hawley asked. 'You can no longer go out, especially not in society. If Mrs Davenport wishes to make my acquaintance then she will have to come here—without her son.'

So every small pleasure was going to be denied her. Constance was beginning to wonder if she would ever have any fun again, when Matthews entered the room.

'A message has arrived for you, Madam.'

'Thank you.' Constance took the note from the silver tray he held out to her and opened it with a faint smile as she recognized Sarah's handwriting. However, her expression quickly changed as she read the few lines on the page.

'Oh no! How terrible.' She rose to her feet. 'Matthews, I'll need the carriage again. I must go into Borthwick at once.'

'What's wrong?' Her mother asked.

'Miss Penghalion writes that Hepzi will not be able to attend her lesson today as Miss Penghalion's grandmother passed away in the night. They were very close and Sarah will be distraught. I must go and see if I can help.'

'I think you had better explain yourself first.' Lady Hawley seemed unmoved by her daughter's apparent distress. 'Who is Miss

198

Penghalion and what lesson does the person called Hepzi attend?'

'Sarah runs the village shop and post office,' Constance explained. 'Her father and Hugh serve in the same regiment where Sergeant Penghalion is held in very high regard by both Hugh and Mr Davenport. Hepzi is a girl who lives with her. She has never learned to read or write and so I've been teaching her.'

'What manner of girl?' Lady Hawley's eyebrows rose. 'Why hasn't she been taught in school as the law requires?'

'Because she has never been able to attend a classroom. Her family are itinerant farm workers and they never stay in one place for very long.'

'Itinerant?' Her mother repeated. 'Do you mean to say she's a gypsy?'

'Yes.' There was little point in trying to conceal the truth now.

'Oh my!' Lady Hawley fell back against the sofa and made a show of fanning herself. 'I feel faint. Whatever has possessed you to forget your position? You simply can't associate with shop girls, and as for the gypsy—' She fanned herself again. 'Is it any wonder you were robbed when you bring such people into the house?'

'Hepzi isn't a thief and Sarah is very respectable.'

'But still not of our class,' Lady Hawley said sharply. 'And I must be firm in this. I forbid

199

you to visit or entertain these people again. If you must express your condolences then a short note of sympathy will suffice.'

For a moment Constance stared at her mother in disbelief then she slowly shook her head.

'No,' she said eventually. 'That would not suffice at all. These people are my friends. I will go and you cannot stop me. I am mistress of my own home now.'

'How dare you speak to me in such a fashion,' Lady Hawley shrieked but Constance didn't remain in the room to hear the rest of her mother's protests. She hurried out into the hall and then stopped to catch her breath. Her heart was racing and she was shocked by her own audacity. The tearful girl who had waved Hugh off to war would never have dared to defy her mother like that. She had changed so much in the intervening months that she sometimes hardly recognized herself and she wondered if Hugh would when he returned.

*   *   *

Lydia couldn't help noticing the smile on Daisy's face as the two women walked along the street where John lodged. She smiled a lot more these days and she was a wearing a new bonnet purchased especially for this occasion.

'It was very nice of John to invite us to tea, wasn't it?' Daisy said and Lydia nodded.

'Indeed, and I thought it particularly thoughtful of him to arrange it for an afternoon when we have no matinee performance to delay us.'

'John is always thoughtful.' A blush crept up Daisy's cheeks.

'And he treats you very kindly.' Lydia glanced at the younger woman. 'Have you had any word from Race of late?'

'No.' Daisy scarcely seemed perturbed by his absence this time. 'I believe he is still in London.'

'I see.' Lydia was glad to hear that. She had feared that his failure to visit Daisy in recent weeks meant he was spending more time with Sarah. She wondered how her daughter was. Perhaps if she was careful she could glean a little more information about her over tea. However, care would have to be her watchword. She had almost given herself away in John's presence before and it wouldn't do to make such foolish errors again. As it was, John was likely to ask if she'd come to a decision about accompanying him and Daisy to Borthwick during the Harvest Holiday period. She frowned. If only he knew how impossible it was for her to go there or how very much she wanted to.

'This is the place.' Daisy stopped in front of a terraced house which had lace curtains hanging in the windows. 'John said his landlady has given permission for us to take tea in the

201

parlour.'

Daisy rapped smartly on the door and Lydia prepared herself to face John again. However, when the door opened it was an old woman wearing black and an old-fashioned mob cap who appeared.

'Are you the ladies who were to visit Mr Penghalion?' she asked in a hushed voice.

'Yes.' A slight furrow appeared between Daisy's eyebrows. 'Isn't he here?'

'He is.' The woman shook her head. 'But I'm afraid he's received very bad news today.'

'Oh.' Lydia felt an icy chill pass over her. Not George. Please let nothing have happened to George.

'You'd best come in and see him.'

They followed the woman along a narrow hallway and into what was obviously the parlour. The table had been laid for tea but John looked in no fit state to receive company. He was slumped in a chair and Lydia trembled when she saw the black-edged telegram that was crumpled in his hand.

'Oh dearest John.' Daisy hurried to his side. 'What's happened?'

'Daisy.' He raised his head and, although he managed to raise a flicker of a smile when he saw her, it was evident he had been crying. 'Please forgive me for not receiving you properly. I regret I am not fully myself this afternoon.' He held out the telegram. 'My grandmother has died.'

Neither of them noticed Lydia gasp and briefly close her eyes. George was safe. How strange that this could matter so much to her after so many years.

'Grandma raised us when our mother died,' John was telling Lucy. 'She was always kind and even when we'd been naughty and angered her, we never went to bed without a goodnight kiss. I was so looking forward to seeing her in August. I just can't believe she won't be there to greet me.'

Tears began to flow down his cheeks again and Lydia recalled what a sensitive little boy he'd been. She'd once seen him broken-hearted over a dead bird in the garden. The loss of his grandmother must be a dreadful blow to him. Filled with sympathy, she went to stand beside Daisy where she reached out to put a comforting hand on his shoulder.

'I'm so sorry, Mommet.'

John didn't respond at first but when he eventually recovered himself, he turned to look at her.

'Someone else use to call me that when I was very young. I can remember hearing it.' He dashed a hand across the tears on his cheeks. 'I suppose it must have been my grandfather. I was always getting grubby as a boy, so it's no wonder he'd call me a scarecrow.'

Lydia didn't trust herself to speak. She'd been the one who called John a scraggy mommet one day after he'd been playing in the haystacks and had come home with straw sticking out all over him. George had roared with laughter and the affectionate little nickname had stuck.

'Will you have to go away?' Daisy asked, and John nodded.

'Yes, I must go back to Borthwick at once. With Papa away I'm the head of the family. I have to organize matters and take care of Lucy and Sarah.'

'But the school holidays aren't for a few more weeks,' Lydia said. 'Will you be granted a leave of absence?'

'No, I will have to leave my post.' He sighed. 'I would have preferred not to but there's no way round it.'

'But you will come back?' There was a tremor in Daisy's voice. 'Won't you?'

'I don't know.' John shook his head. 'Sarah may need me to stay on and help her for a while and then it will all depend on whether I can find another position here.' He turned to look at Daisy and Lydia saw the unmistakable glow of love in his eyes. 'Of course, I very much hope I will be able to. If things were different. If I was able to support you now—' His voice tailed off and Lydia heard Daisy try to stifle a sob of her own.

'Perhaps we could soon come to visit you in Borthwick,' Lydia said and John gave her a grateful smile.

'Thank you for agreeing, Lydia.' He reached out to take Daisy's hand. 'I would like that. I would like it very much.'

'So would I,' Daisy blushed shyly.

'Then it is settled.' Lydia said. It was evident that these two young people were meant to be together and now there was no reason why she couldn't go to Borthwick with them. At last she would be able to see her daughter again.

*　　*　　*

'It's all after being my fault,' Hepzi said tearfully. 'If I hadn't have knocked over that candle when I did it wouldn't have happened.'

'Oh Hepzi, that's not true.' Sarah squeezed the girl's hand. 'Grandma was very old and ill. You mustn't blame yourself.'

'I wish I hadn't been so short with her the last time I was here.' At the far side of the table, Lucy dabbed at her eyes with a handkerchief.

'She knew you meant nothing by it.' Sarah tried to comfort her sister. 'In fact, she probably didn't even notice that you were.'

'But I know I was.' Lucy burst into tears for the third time that morning. Sarah rose and was about to hug her when a knock at the door distracted her.

'I expect that's Reverend Yates. I'll go and let him in.'

When Sarah opened the door, however, she

found Constance and Ewart standing there. Constance looked strangely flushed and it was Ewart who spoke first.

'Please forgive our intrusion, Miss Penghalion. I encountered Lady Weston on the road into the village and she told me of your sad news. We've come to offer our sincerest sympathies.'

'Thank you. You're very kind.' Although Sarah had been trying to put up a brave front for Lucy and Hepzi, her own grief was still raw and she struggled to keep her tears in check. 'Please won't you come in?'

The arrival of the visitors brought some semblance of normality to the house. Hepzi quickly put the kettle on the stove to boil and Lucy, who seemed glad to have some task to do, brought the best china out of the cupboard.

'I am afraid I may have to stop our lessons for a few weeks,' Constance told Hepzi. 'My Mama has come for a visit and is of the opinion I should rest more.' She sighed. 'If she has her way I will never again do anything more strenuous than embroider tray clothes or very occasionally take jars of calves foot jelly to the deserving poor.'

'Is that such a hardship?' Ewart asked. 'I understood you took a great interest in charitable works.'

'I do, but I intend to be far more active than that.' Constance gave a rueful smile.

'However, until Mama leaves I will have to moderate my efforts. I have already caused her to take to her bed with the vapours today. It won't do to upset her any more.'

'Miss Penghalion, I wonder if I might speak with you in private for a moment.' As Lucy began to pour the tea, Ewart turned to Sarah.

'Of course.' She stood up. 'We can go through to the shop. It will be quiet in there.'

The shop felt strangely cold and empty as they entered it. Usually at this time of day it would be filled with the noise and bustle of customers. Today it was silent. Their footsteps echoed on the floor and the sun shining on the lowered blinds cast a pale green hue across the room. Sarah could hear the muffled sounds of village life continuing outside and felt as though she had been suddenly cut off from everything normal in her existence. Somehow that seemed appropriate. After all, nothing would ever be the same again.

'Has Miss Briar been able to collect the money Noah allocated to her?' Ewart asked and Sarah nodded.

'Yes. She went to Otterly a few days ago.'

'Good.' Ewart gave a tight smile. 'I am sure she will have need of it, especially in the coming weeks. It cannot be an easy time for her.'

'No.' Sarah looked at him in surprise. Hepzi's baby was due very soon and it was no wonder that Ewart had noticed her condition.

It was obvious to all now. What was remarkable, however, was that Ewart continued to treat Hepzi with such respect and kindness. He had always seemed so concerned with duty and doing right that Sarah would have expected him to be more judgemental. His quiet acceptance of the situation made him rise in her esteem and she wondered how she could ever once have thought of him as disagreeable.

'Of course, this is also a very difficult time for you. I know you were very close to your grandmother.'

'Yes, I will miss her very much. Everyone who knew her will.' She knew it wasn't considered polite to show her emotions in front of a visitor but she couldn't stop her tears this time. 'I don't know what I'll do without her.'

'Dearest Sarah.' Ewart came to stand directly in front of her and caught hold of her hand. 'I cannot bear to see you so unhappy. What can I do to ease your burden?'

'Nothing,' she sobbed. No one could take away the pain in her heart but as she gratefully accepted the handkerchief Ewart pulled from his waistcoat pocket she couldn't help thinking that he and his brother were more alike than she had previously thought. Race would have thought nothing of making such a spontaneous gesture but she had never imagined Ewart doing so.

'Come now.' He was still speaking. 'There must be something. Although the war is over it may be some weeks yet before your father returns and you will need some support in the meantime. Perhaps I could send William Hogg to assist you again.' He paused and frowned slightly before he spoke again. 'This is a delicate matter but if there is any problem with the tenancy of the shop or the cottage and you have need of money to resolve it, you have only to ask and I will settle matters for you.'

His words brought Sarah's tears to an abrupt halt and she looked up at him in disbelief. How could she have been so stupid yet again? This man was the owner of a large estate and one of the local gentry. He wasn't acting out of friendship but because he pitied a poor village shop girl and he seemed to think throwing her a few coins from his abundance would make everything in her life all right again. There was no difference between Ewart making this offer and Constance taking jelly to those she considered to be in need. She withdrew her hand from his grasp and took a step away from him.

'Thank you, but I have no need of charity.' She saw him start but didn't allow him to interrupt her. 'We have all we need for the moment and I am sure we can manage until Papa returns.'

'We?' Ewart's eyes narrowed. 'Of course. Forgive me, Miss Penghalion, I had forgotten that Mr Eden will be providing for you shortly.'

He strode from the room before she realized that he still thought she was engaged to Albert and long before she had gathered her wits enough to tell him he was mistaken. That hadn't been what she meant at all.

*　　*　　*

When evening fell, Sarah found herself alone in the tiny kitchen. Lucy had gone home to prepare Henry's dinner and Hepzi, who had looked pale and strained all day, had gone to bed early. Sarah was exhausted as well but didn't think she could sleep. She sat in the rocking chair by the fire and stroked Bosun who lay in her lap purring.

'At least you're still happy,' she said softly. 'I envy you that.'

A heavy knock on the back door disturbed her mournful thoughts. It was late for a caller. Still, this was hardly a normal day. She laid the protesting cat down on the hearth rug and went to open the door.

'Sarah.' It was Albert and he came into the small hallway before she had a chance to invite him. 'I'm sorry to call so late. I would have come sooner but I was collecting Mrs Yates from her sister's in Honiton. I've only just heard the news.'

'It's kind of you to call.' It occurred to her

that he would be tired after such a long drive and he'd no doubt had to attend to the horses as soon as he returned to the rectory. 'I was about to make some cocoa and there's some bread and cheese left. We can have supper together, if you'd like.'

'Oh yes, thank you.' He smiled at her. 'I'd like that very much.'

As she prepared the simple meal, Sarah was aware that Albert was watching her every move and it made her feel a slightly uncomfortable.

'Reverend Yates said he's to bury your Grandma on Friday.'

'Yes.' Sarah's hand trembled and a little of the milk she was pouring into a mug spilt and hissed on the hot stove top. She didn't want to think about the coming Friday and it was hard to hear Albert speak of it in such a matter-of-fact way.

'I'll sit with you in the church, if you like. That'll let the village see how things are with us.'

'Thank you, but John will be here and I'll sit with him.' She knew that dear, kind John would comfort his sisters in their grief. Albert had made no attempt to offer her any sympathy since he'd arrived and she thought his suggestion was presumptuous when she hadn't yet given her response to his proposal.

'Of course.' Albert sat chewing on a piece of bread for some minutes and Sarah found she was glad of the silence. However, it didn't last long.

'What do you intend to do about the shop now? You can't run it alone for ever.'

'I won't have to. The war is over. Papa will be home soon.'

'I know, but he's hardly in his prime any more, is he?' Albert seemed blissfully unaware of the distress his comment caused Sarah. 'What you need is someone young with the energy and commitment to make a good go of things. In the right hands, it could turn a good profit.'

'Albert, please, I don't want to talk about such matters tonight.' Ewart might have insulted her with his offer of charity but even he had been more sensitive to her feelings than Albert was being at this moment.

'You may not want to, but the simple fact is that they must be settled. That's the way of business. I understand these things. That's why I'd be the best man to marry you and take things on.' He rose from his place at the table and, before she knew what was happening, his arms were around her waist. 'What do you say, Sarah? I know we can't be wed while you're mourning but six weeks is a decent enough period for that. We could post the banns this Sunday and be wed by harvest time.'

'What?' Sarah gasped. Albert bent forward as though to kiss her and she struggled to release herself from his grasp. She knew now

212

that Grandma had been right. She'd said Sarah's heart knew if he was the man for her or not and now it was telling her that he most definitely wasn't. How could she ever love someone who showed so little care for her feelings at a time like this? She even doubted whether it was her that Albert truly loved. The only time she ever heard passion in his voice was when he was speaking about his plans for the shop.

'Let me go.' She twisted out of his embrace. It was time to tell him that she had no intention of marrying him either within six weeks or at any date in the future. 'I think you should leave.'

'But Sarah—' He looked as though he was about to reach for her again and she was just considering whether she should pick up a wooden spoon to fend him off when a brisk rap on the door interrupted them.

'Who's calling on you at this hour?' Albert looked suspicious.

'I don't know.' For one breathless moment she found herself hoping it would be Ewart and that she could ask him to make Albert leave. Then, as she went to open the door, rationality set in again. He wouldn't be likely to call so late and besides he would hardly wish to be cast in the role of her protector.

'Is this where the Penghalions bide?' The woman standing on the doorstep spoke before Sarah could.

'Yes.'

The visitor had grey hair and wore a grimy apron over a print dress that had seen better days. She looked older than her years and Sarah thought there was something strangely familiar about her. Then the woman spoke again and she realized why.

'I'm Ida Briar, and I've come to get my Hepzi.'

CHAPTER NINE

'It'll just go and see if there's any sign of Jake's cart yet.' John tried to sound nonchalant as he left the shop but Sarah wasn't fooled for a moment. It was the fifth time her brother had gone out on that errand in less than an hour and she'd never known him to sort the mail in his best clothes before. She smiled to herself. It was good to see him looking so eager. The past few days had been hard for them all, although it had been touching to see almost the entire village as well as people from surrounding farms come to pay their last respects at Anne's funeral.

Now they were awaiting visitors. Dan was bringing Lydia and Daisy from Otterly station and John had spent the entire morning wishing away the hours until he was reunited with his sweetheart.

'Are they here yet?' Shortly after John had left, Lucy arrived in the shop with her children. Daisy was going to stay in her cottage and she'd spent the day before making preparations for her guest.

Not yet.' Sarah grinned. 'But John's maintaining so careful a watch that there'll be no danger of us missing them.'

'He does seem smitten,' Lucy agreed. 'I reckon we'll have a wedding in the family before too long.'

'Only if John manages to find another job.' It was good to have their brother at home but Lucy and Sarah both knew he would have to try and find employment again soon if he could. Sarah knew he was worried about that. The harvest holidays had already started in some places and most school boards had made their appointments for the coming term.

'They're here!' The door burst open and John rushed over to catch hold of his sisters' hands. 'Come and meet them.'

In his enthusiasm he seemed to have forgotten that Sarah had already been introduced to both ladies. She hoped this meeting would be more genial than their initial one had been. Her main memory of Lydia, the woman who was to share her home for some weeks, was of a door being slammed in her face. If the actress behaved so rudely here then her visit could be trying. The very idea of an actress staying in the cottage was a strange one. Grandma would have had a fit. Sarah smiled but at once the sadness that accompanied any thought of Anne washed over her. She still missed her grandmother every moment of every day. However, for John's sake, she did her best to look cheerful as she went out to meet the cart.

The ladies were both riding on the front board with Dan. Their smart dresses and parasols must have impressed the wagon driver as Sarah knew he expected most passengers from the station to balance on the letter sacks in the back.

'Dearest Daisy.' John was bold enough to kiss the younger woman's hand as he helped her down. 'Welcome to Borthwick.'

'I'm happy to be here.' Without her stage makeup and finery on, Daisy looked much younger and sweeter. There were no sulks marring her pretty features on this occasion, and she even went as far as giving Sarah a shy smile when she saw her.

In contrast, Sarah thought Lydia looked older than she did on the stage. There were thin lines around her eyes and a few strands of grey peppered through her dark hair. However, she too smiled as she accepted John's hand and climbed down from the cart.

'Thank you for the use of your cart, Mr Gregory. It was a very enjoyable journey.'

'No problem at all, Miss.' Sarah couldn't be sure of it but she thought Dan blushed a little as he replied. Lydia had certainly charmed him even if she probably wasn't being entirely truthful. Sarah had been out in Dan's cart many times in the past and she knew how every tiny hole in the road felt like a chasm when the wheels passed over it.

'Lucy!' Lydia had hurried forward to take hold of her hand. 'I would have known you anywhere.'

'How could you?' Lucy looked a little bemused. 'You've never seen me before.'

For a second Lydia seemed to falter but she soon smiled again. 'Why, from John's wonderful descriptions, of course. He has told me so much about you that I feel I already know you.'

'And me too?' Isaac couldn't bear to be left out of the excitement any longer.

'Oh, of course.' Lydia was certainly much more gracious than she had seemed in Exeter and Sarah thought the way she bent right down to Isaac's level as she spoke to him was kind. 'You are Master Isaac who never means to cause mischief but somehow just can't help it.'

The little boy laughed and Lydia straightened up before turning to Sarah.

'You don't know how very happy I am to see you again.' She laid a hand on Sarah's arm. 'And I'm so grateful to you for your hospitality. It's my fervent hope that we can become good friends.'

'You're very welcome to stay here for as long as you wish.' Sarah was touched and yet a little taken aback by Lydia's demonstrative greeting. She hadn't expected the woman to be so intimate with her but then perhaps the long journey had made her feel emotional. The dust on the road had clearly affected her eyes and they looked watery.

'I'm sure you must be tired and hungry,' she said to both women. 'Come inside and Lucy will make you some tea while I see to the mail.'

'I'll fetch your bags.' John went to the back of the cart and then laughed. 'There are certainly enough of them.'

'We wanted to be prepared for any eventualities and you know how unpredictable the weather has been this year.' Lydia was laughing too. 'Come along, Daisy, we can take our own hat boxes or poor John will collapse under the strain.'

'I can help too.' Sarah went to relieve her brother of some of his burden while Isaac decided that he would try to lift a bag that was almost as big as him and made everyone laugh.

They were all too busy to notice the cottage door open and Hepzi come out with a small cloth bundle in her hand. She paused to watch the lively scene by the cart for a moment and bit on her lower lip. When a tear started to trickle down her cheek, she wiped it off with an angry dash of her hand, then turned and

218

slipped away down the lane.

*   *   *

Later that afternoon, Sarah left John in charge of the shop and went in search of Hepzi. Despite the fact that she could write short sentences now, the girl had left no word of where she'd gone and, as the hours had passed, Sarah had become increasingly anxious. Hepzi enjoyed walking on warm days like this but she had never stayed out for so long before. What if she'd been taken ill or fallen? Perhaps she'd gone into labour and was alone somewhere, unable to walk. Sarah quickened her pace. If only she could be sure she was going in the right direction.

A landau pulled by four almost identical bay horses came along the road towards her. As it drew closer Sarah stepped up onto the grass verge to let it pass and saw Constance sitting in the back beside another woman whom she guessed to be her mother. They were both holding lace edged parasols over their heads but Constance turned and saw Sarah as they drove past.

'Stop!' she called out to the coachman and the carriage came to a halt with a jangle of harnesses.

'Sarah! Mama said that as it was such a warm day we should take a short drive around the countryside.' Constance leaned out over

219

the side of the landau to speak to her. 'Are you out enjoying this glorious weather as well?'

'No, I'm looking for Hepzi.' Constance's mother had slowly turned her head to glare at Sarah and this made her feel uncomfortable as she spoke. 'She's been missing since this morning and I'm worried.'

'Oh there's no need to be, she's fine. I saw her helping with the harvest when we drove past a field a little way back.' Constance suddenly looked at the expression on Sarah's face. 'Didn't you know she was going there?'

'No.' This information troubled Sarah more than Hepzi's disappearance had. 'I knew her family had returned. She's been to see them a few times lately but she said nothing about working with them.' She frowned. 'She shouldn't be tiring herself when her baby's due in a matter of days. She might be ill again.'

'I fail to see what business this is of ours.' Constance's mother gave an impatient sigh. 'Can we drive on now, Constance?'

'In a moment, Mama.' Constance had already opened the carriage door and was negotiating the step. 'I want to talk to Sarah first. You can drive a little further on if you like and I'll walk on to join you.'

'I'll do nothing of the sort,' Her mother retorted sharply. 'It's bad enough that you choose to associate with the lower classes. You certainly aren't about to start tramping round the countryside like one of them as well.' Her haughty gaze was focused on Sarah as she spoke and Sarah knew the words had been intended to slight her.

'Don't mind Mama,' Constance said quietly as she linked her arm through Sarah's and led her a short distance away from the carriage. 'She's terribly old-fashioned about such things.'

The assurance didn't make Sarah feel any better. She felt as if she'd been carrying far too heavy a burden lately and Hepzi's strange behaviour was almost too much to bear.

'Oh Sarah, don't cry.' Constance looked at her in concern. 'I'll make Mama apologize.'

'It's not that I'm crying for.' Sarah fumbled in her pocket for her handkerchief. 'I still miss Grandma so much. Everything's been going wrong and she would have known what to do about it.'

'What's been going wrong?' Constance asked gently. 'Perhaps we can think of solutions between us.'

'It's nothing you should have to trouble yourself about,' Sarah protested. 'I'm probably just tired.'

'You have been working very long hours in the shop ever since Mrs Penghalion became ill.' Constance still looked worried. 'I thought your brother was going to help until your papa got home.'

'He has been.' Sarah dabbed at her eyes. 'And he's been wonderful but he can't stay. He had to resign from his teaching post to come home for Grandma's funeral and if he doesn't return to the city soon he may not find another position. I don't know how he'll manage if he can't.'

'I'm sure he will find a position.' Constance sounded certain of the fact and Sarah wished she could share in her confidence. 'And didn't Ewart offer the services of Mr Hogg to help you in the shop. He said he was going to.'

'I didn't accept his offer.' Sarah sighed. 'And I'm afraid I was very rude to Ewart and have offended him. He hasn't returned to Borthwick since that day.' Sarah's cheeks flushed as they so often did when she thought of Ewart now. She regretted the way she had spoken to him and, although she wasn't prepared to admit it to anyone, she found that she had missed his visits.

'Oh come, you must be used to Ewart's manner by now,' Constance giggled. 'He may have seemed offended but he looks like that when he's happy as well. What makes you think you were rude to him?'

'On the day of Grandma's death he offered me financial support and I told him I didn't want his charity. I was still upset and may have been too sharp.'

'Oh Sarah, I'm sure he understood, and Ewart isn't one to sulk,' she paused and laughed again. 'Well, not for more than a day or two anyway. He's been very busy overseeing the harvest on his own estate. I'm sure that's why he hasn't called.'

'Constance, how much longer must I sit here?' Her mother's voice was fractious and Constance gave a heavy sigh.

'I had better go or Mama will be in an ill humour for the rest of the evening.' She gently squeezed one of Sarah's hands. 'Try not to worry about Hepzi too much and I'm sure Ewart bears you no grudge. You should go home and take some rest.' She gave an awkward frown. 'I would offer to take you in the landau but Mama—' Her voice tailed away.

'I understand.' Sarah had no desire to hear more of the older woman's insults anyway. She watched as the carriage pulled away and then started walking again but she had no intention of going home as Constance had suggested. She knew she couldn't rest until she'd seen Hepzi and established that she really was well enough to be working.

*   *   *

'I really can't imagine why you want to associate with a person like that,' Lady Hawley said as she and Constance were driven on towards Borthwick. 'And I'm sure Hugh wouldn't either.'

'Sarah is my friend, Mama.' Constance hoped her mother didn't intend to spend the remainder of the outing complaining about her behaviour. She was feeling uncomfortable in the heat and she wanted to sit quietly and think about how she could best help Sarah.

'She is an acquaintance. You do not make friends outwith your social class and while we are on that matter I do not think you should encourage her to use Mr Davenport's Christian name either.' Lady Hawley sniffed. 'If you ask me, that young woman is in danger of getting ideas that are well above her station.'

*   *   *

The rhythmic rattle and hiss of a steam threshing machine at work told Sarah she was close to the field that was being harvested. When she reached it, she stopped in the gateway and looked for Hepzi among the crowd of people working there but it was hard to spot her. The men were working their way across the fields with scythes while the women and children followed behind, gathering up sheaves of the cut wheat and carrying it to the thresher. All the women were wearing smocks and brightly coloured head scarves which made them indistinguishable at a distance and Sarah wondered how Constance had managed to recognize Hepzi. Then she saw her and wondered how she had managed to miss her.

Hepzi was working on the edge of the field.

Her flame-coloured hair was sticking out from under her scarf and when she straightened up with a sheaf in her arms it was easy to see the roundness of her stomach beneath her smock. She had fallen a little way behind the other women in the row and Sarah was sure she must be struggling to keep up.

Sarah had seen enough and she began to pick her way through the stubble to where Hepzi had just bent to gather another armful.

'Hepzi?' At the sound of her voice the girl started and turned.

'Miss Sarah, what are you doing here?'

'Looking for you. We've all been very worried. You didn't tell me you were going.'

'I didn't think you'd be minding.' Hepzi wiped a fine sheen of sweat from her forehead and left a grimy trail of dust in its wake. 'You're busy enough with your grand visitors from Exeter now.'

'But surely you didn't think you weren't wanted now.' Sarah was appalled. 'That's your home.'

'No it ain't.' Hepzi gave a firm shake of her head. 'You and Missis Anne were right good to me and I'm thankful for it but this is where I rightly belong.'

'But you're going to have a child in a few days,' Sarah protested. 'You shouldn't be labouring in the fields in your condition.'

'Plenty of others do.' Hepzi tilted her head proudly. 'It's the way things are among my kind.'

'But it doesn't have to be for you.' Sarah thought Hepzi looked pale and the idea of leaving her here to exhaust herself was insufferable. 'Please come back with me at least until after your child is born.'

'I can't.' Hepzi's jaw was set in an obstinate line. 'My family needs me. That's why my Ma came looking for me.' She jerked her head in the direction of the threshing machine. 'You see that clattering monster. It can be doing in one day what it used to take us three days to do with flails and less work means less wages.' She shook her head. 'How can my Ma feed all the young 'uns like that? If I'm working too it means there's another few shillings to help her.'

'But you have the money from Noah,' Sarah protested. 'You don't have to work like this.'

'I do.' At the mention of the money she had collected from Otterly a deep rush of colour surged over Hepzi's cheeks and Sarah realized that she no longer had it. The money intended to help Hepzi with her baby had already gone to her family. Sarah recalled the bruises she had once seen on Hepzi's back and wondered if the girl had given it all willingly or whether her father had persuaded her to do so.

'Please come back with me.' Sarah had no more arguments to use and even as she spoke, she knew her efforts were futile.

'No.' Hepzi set her jaw determinedly. 'I'm

226

grateful for all you've done for me, Miss Sarah, but it's time you were getting back to your duties and leaving me to see to mine. If the farmer catches me gabbing like this, I'll have my wages docked.'

She turned away without a word of goodbye and Sarah could only watch helplessly as the slight figure made her way across to the thresher with her burden of wheat. Hepzi had made her decision and there seemed to be nothing she could do about it.

*   *   *

The late afternoon sun cast a pleasant warm glow across the desk in the drawing room where Constance sat writing. Her mother had complained of a headache and taken to her bed shortly after they had returned from their drive and Constance had used the liberty this had given her to attend to matters which had weighed on her mind since her meeting with Sarah. Three letters had been enough to resolve most of Sarah's problems and Constance had just laid a sheet of blotting paper down to dry on the ink on the last of these when the door opened and her mother appeared, apparently in no better humour after her nap.

'Really.' Lady Hawley shook her head disapprovingly and went to lower the blinds, immediately shutting out the light that

Constance had been enjoying. 'How many times must I tell you that sunlight fades your furnishing fabrics? I see you've learned nothing since you left my household.'

Constance thought she would rather have the light than fuss about fabrics but she knew better than to tell her mother that.

'Will I ring for tea?' she asked.

'No, I shall.' Her mother went to pull on the cord that would summon a servant. 'I'm pleased to see you engaged in an appropriate activity for once. Although I'm sure you don't have to write to Hugh so frequently when he'll soon be sailing for home.'

'I like to write to him.' It wasn't a lie but not entirely honest either. Constance was glad the blotter was still over the last letter and that her mother couldn't see who it was addressed to.

Dear Sarah,
I have given a great deal of thought to the anxieties you confided in me earlier today and I feel it is my duty as Hugh's wife and as your friend to do what I can to help. I hope you will not be offended by my presumption and understand that nothing more than a genuine urge to be of assistance has prompted me in my actions.

By the time you receive this short missive, Ewart will also have received one regarding Hepzi. As he continues to have links with the Lancers and was once

Noah's employer I believe he will do what he can to aid Hepzi at this most delicate time for her.

I have made no allusion to your disagreement with him as I feel it would not be right for me to comment on such a personal matter but I repeat that I am sure you are mistaken in your impression that he has taken offence with you.

As regards John, I am not in a position to make any comment at this time but I am confident of a speedy resolution to his predicament.

I trust the contents of this letter will help to put your mind at rest and that you will be able to find some solace in the midst of your grief. I remain your friend,
Constance Weston.

The first letter she had written was already in an envelope addressed to Ewart and the second was to be sent to Reverend Yates.

Dear Sir,
I regret I will unable to attend the next meeting of the Borthwick School Board but I wish to take this opportunity to heartily recommend Mr John Penghalion to the vacant position of schoolmaster. The gentleman in question is of good character and an experienced teacher. I am sure he will be able to provide excellent references

229

and I will personally vouch for the good name of his family.
Lady Constance Weston.

Her mother had settled at the far side of the room and was occupied with a piece of embroidery so Constance was able to finish off her correspondence and by the time the maid came in with the tea tray, she was ready to hand the three letters to her.

'Please ask Matthews to see to it that these are delivered immediately,' she said quietly enough to keep her mother, who was already occupied with the tea pot, from overhearing.

'Yes, My Lady.' The maid carried the letters away and Constance went to join her mother at tea, content in the knowledge that she had done what she could. The rest would be down to Ewart and she was sure he wouldn't fail her.

*   *   *

Ewart was preparing to make a journey. His usually tidy bedroom was in a state of disarray and his personal appearance was, to his mother's mind, little better. A small pile of clothing lay on the bed beside an open valise while Ewart, dressed only in an open shirt and trousers, rinsed the last of the shaving soap from his face, towelled his skin dry and then began to attend to his packing.

'I don't understand why your valet couldn't

do this for you,' his mother said as he folded a white linen shirt and placed it in the bag.

'I've sent him into Otterly to attend to some business for me and, as you consider my errand to be of such urgency, I thought it best not to delay my packing until he returned.' The loving yet faintly teasing smile Ewart gave his mother was in contrast to the brusqueness of his words. He knew she was worried even though he thought she had little reason to be.

'If I'd known I would have lent you the services of my maid,' she said and this time he laughed aloud.

'And find my case full of feminine froufrou when I arrive in London? I hardly think so.' He swiftly placed the remaining clothes in the bag, closed it and then pulled on a waistcoat before picking up his cravat.

'Here, let me tie that for you.' His mother held out her hand to take it and he gave her an amused smile.

'I am quite capable of dressing myself, Mama.'

'I know you are, dear, but I like to think I can still do something for my boys every now and again.'

'Very well.' The last time his mother had helped him to tie his cravat Ewart had been shorter than her but now he had to stoop low so she could reach to place the square of silk round his neck.

'There, you see. I haven't forgotten how to

knot it properly.' His mother smiled softly and then looked up into his eyes with unshed tears shining in hers. 'You will find him, won't you?'

'I won't return until I have.' His jaw settled into a hard line. 'Although it may take some time to search every gaming room and house of ill repute in the city.'

'Oh Ewart.' His mother looked hurt. 'Why must you always believe the worst of your brother? He went looking for work.'

'Then why hasn't he sent as much as one line of correspondence to tell you of his progress?'

'That's why I'm so worried.' He could hear the anguish in her voice. 'He may be ill or in some kind of danger.' Her voice broke on a sob. 'For all we know he may be dead.'

'I'm sure he isn't or we would've had word for sure.' At that moment Ewart hated Race for the agony he was putting their mother through. 'You are distressing yourself for nothing. Race will return when he's run out of money. He always does.'

'I would rather know for sure that he is safe.'

'I know.' Ewart went to sit on the edge of his bed and began to pull on his black leather boots. 'That is why I intend to find him for you.'

'You're such a good son.' His mother rewarded him with a tender smile and he acknowledged it with a terse one of his own.

He knew that despite all the heartache Race had caused his mother over the years she would always forgive him and always have a special place in her heart for him as her baby. Over the years, Ewart had learned to accept that loyalty and devotion to the family could never win him as great a share of her affections as Race enjoyed.

When his carriage was ready Ewart made his way out onto the front steps of the house and then turned to speak to his mother one last time.

'Now remember what I have said and try not to worry. I will return within a few days.'

'With Edwin?'

'Or at least with word of him.' Ewart wasn't prepared to promise more than that. He was only too well aware that Race might not be amenable to the idea of returning to Bishopston.

'God's speed, my dear.' His mother waved as he climbed up into the carriage and signalled the coachman to drive on. As the horses rose to a trot and the carriage bowled down the driveway, Ewart fixed his eyes on the road ahead of him and wondered what situation awaited him in London. He didn't look back and didn't see the rider approach the house from the opposite direction.

The horse stopped in front of the house and the boy slid down from the saddle.

'Begging your pardon, madam, but I've a

letter for Mr Ewart Davenport from Lady Constance Weston.'

'Mr Davenport has left for London. You've just missed him.' Ewart's mother shielded her eyes against the sun and peered down the driveway where a cloud of dust indicated that the carriage hadn't gone too far. If the boy pushed his horse to a gallop he might still catch it before it reached the main road. She was about to suggest this but then she hesitated. If the letter was from Constance then it could contain word of something Hugh wanted Ewart to do for him. Ewart might have to delay his trip and then even longer would pass before she knew if her dearest Edwin was safe.

She held out her hand.

'Give it to me. I'll see that Mr Davenport receives it as soon as he returns.'

CHAPTER TEN

The sweet smell of tea leaves filled the air as Sarah watched Lydia carefully pour a large scoop of them into a small bag on the scales. 'That's right,' she said. 'Keep going until the scale shifts. We don't want to sell short measures.'

'I'll do my best.' Lydia's brow was creased with concentration. Sarah hadn't expected her guest to want to assist in the shop but Lydia had spent every day since her arrival in there and seemed keen to do what she could to help. On her part, Sarah had found that she enjoyed Lydia's company. Her cheerful outlook had helped Sarah to cope better with the loss of Anne while her ready wit and cheery smiles had already made her popular with the customers. Everyone would miss her when she returned to Exeter.

'Is that it?' The scales moved so that the bag of tea was level with the weight on the other side.

'Yes, that's perfect.' Sarah picked the bag up and twisted the top tightly. 'Now we take a piece of string and fasten it up like this.'

'I don't think I can do it quite like that.' Lydia gave a doubtful laugh as she watched Sarah's fingers dexterously tie a tight knot round the top of the bag. 'And I certainly can't be that quick about it.'

'You haven't had the practice I have.' Sarah smiled. 'I was all fingers and thumbs when I was a girl and Grandpa first showed me how to do it. He said that before long it would come as naturally as blinking and he was right.'

'Did you help him often?' Lydia asked and Sarah nodded.

'Whenever I could. Lucy was happier in the kitchen with Grandma and John always had his head in a book but I loved being here in the shop with Grandpa. I came every day as soon as school was over and on Saturday mornings too. Grandpa called me his assistant and Grandma made a little calico apron just like his to fit me.'

'Your grandparents must have loved you very much,' Lydia said and Sarah smiled wistfully.

'As much as I loved them. They were so kind to the three of us and were all the family we knew for a long time. Of course I love Papa too but when I was little he was away so often with his regiment that sometimes I was quite shy with him when he came home. Grandpa used to tease me about it.'

'And what about your mother?' Lydia asked. 'Didn't anyone ever tell you about her?'

'Not really. She died when I was born and Papa's never wanted to talk about her.' Sarah frowned. 'He must have loved her very much because the very mention of her still grieves him.'

'Do you think he really did?' Lydia's voice was little more than a whisper.

'I'm sure of it. Why else would her memory continue to make him become so sombre to this day?' Sarah gave a slight shake of head and then sighed. 'Anyway, I'm sure you don't want to hear such gloomy talk and there's plenty of work to occupy us today. Are you happy to fill the rest of these bags with tea while I attend to the mail?'

'Of course.' Lydia's smile was wan and

Sarah noticed that her hand shook slightly when she picked the scoop up again.

'Would you prefer to go and rest for a while? I forget that this work must be a good deal heavier than you're used to.'

'Oh no.' Lydia's feeble smile stretched out into a grin again. 'I'm enjoying this much more than the theatre and besides, I like being here with you.'

'And I like having you here.' Sarah smiled back. Lydia was so easy to get along with. In some ways Sarah felt as though she'd known her for years.

She'd felt the same way about Hepzi too. Sarah tried to concentrate on sorting the post before Jake arrived but she couldn't help wondering how the gypsy girl was faring. She hadn't seen her since the day in the field and she'd looked so frail then.

'You're thinking about your friend again, aren't you?' Sarah didn't realize how heavy her sigh had been until Lydia spoke.

'Yes,' she admitted. 'When Constance wrote to say she'd written to Mr Davenport about the matter I truly believed it would be quickly resolved but he hasn't responded at all.'

'Perhaps he's busy,' Lydia suggested.

'Perhaps.' Sarah didn't sound convinced. Ewart would have received the letter some days ago and yet he didn't seem to have acted on it. He obviously hadn't forgiven her for insulting him and no longer wanted to trouble himself in her affairs. She wished now that she hadn't been so sharp with him on the night of her grandmother's death. No matter how misguided his offer might have been, he had only been trying to help and she must have offended him deeply with her curt response.

The sound of a cart stopping outside made her look up and in spite of her worries, she couldn't help smiling.

'Oh, it's Riley. I'd forgotten it was about time for him to call by.' She turned to Lydia. 'You'll like Riley. Everyone does. He was in the Lancers with Papa and they were such great friends that Riley stood as groomsman when Papa married Mama. They would probably still be serving together if Riley hadn't been injured at Sebastopol. He took work as a peddler and says that it's a better life than soldiering ever was. Last time he was here I bought some lace collars from him. They were so pretty that I'd sold them all within the week. I wonder if he'll have more.'

'I have to go out for a while.' Lydia had left her place at the scales and was already hurrying towards the door that led to the cottage. 'I'd almost forgotten. I promised to help Daisy trim a bonnet today and she'll be most vexed if I don't go.'

'Can't you wait for a moment?' Sarah was eager to introduce Lydia to the old family friend but Lydia suddenly looked as distant and aloof as she had the first time Sarah had

238

met her in the theatre.

No,' she said abruptly. 'I must go right away.'

Sarah gave a puzzled frown as she watched the door close behind Lydia. Whatever had caused her to suddenly react like that? It was almost as if she'd taken fright at the idea of meeting Riley and yet she hadn't been shy with anyone else in the shop. What was it about a simple purveyor of ribbons and fancy goods that would alarm her?

'Why, Miss Sarah Penghalion, I do declare you grow prettier by the day!' The door burst open as Riley's booming voice, long red beard and robust figure seemed to fill the room. Sarah put Lydia's strange behaviour firmly from her mind and went to greet her father's old friend.

*   *   *

As the cab Ewart had hired passed through street after street in London he sat forward in his seat and peered out of the window. He was relieved to see that he wasn't in one of the more disreputable parts of the city but this district wasn't one favoured by fashionable members of society and a thinly veiled air of poverty seemed to hang in the air. The road wasn't cobbled and a combination of recent rainfall and heavy traffic had reduced its surface to a series of muddy ruts that made the cab bounce and jolt along its way. The cab turned into another, narrower road where the buildings rose up steeply on either side of the pathways and a number of small workshops stood open to the road. A row of small shops was busy with the morning trade while barrow boys shouted loudly, trying to entice the shoppers to savour their wares. The cab trundled on for a few seconds more and then stopped as the driver banged on the roof. Ewart opened the door. It seemed he had reached his destination.

'Please wait here.' He was aware that several people had abandoned their tasks and were watching curiously as he handed a few coins to the driver and began to search for the address he had been given.

'Is this Bishop's Walk?' he asked a boy who came past carrying a newspaper-wrapped parcel of fish.

'Yes, sir.' Then it was the right place. The name was ill matched to the area. With its muddy roadway, poorly maintained buildings and the smell from the river, it was hard to believe that any high-ranking cleric would ever have chosen to roam there.

'I'm looking for number twenty-two.'

'Down there.' The lad pointed to an alley that ran between the workshops of a boat builder and a wheelwright. 'At the back and up the steps.'

'Thank you.' He rewarded the boy with a

shilling for his helpfulness and then set off in the direction he had been shown. The staircase at the end of the alleyway was built of well-worn wood and shook in places as Ewart climbed it with a degree of caution. A number scratched on the black door at the top of the stairs told him that he had indeed found number twenty-two and, in the absence of a knocker, he used his fist to pound on the door.

There was no reply. Ewart cursed under his breath. To have come so far for nothing was infuriating. He knocked again, and after another fruitless pause, was just about to turn away in frustration when he thought he heard a noise inside.

'Race!' he called out. 'Are you there?'

There was another muffled noise, followed by the scrape of a bolt being drawn back. Ewart waited until the door finally opened and he was face to face with a pale shadow of his brother.

'Ewart!' Race's pinched cheeks stretched into a smile. 'How did you know where to find me?'

'It wasn't easy.' As he entered the room his brother had been occupying, Ewart was unsure which shocked him most; Race's poor physical appearance or his squalid accommodation. 'No one at your club seemed to know where you'd gone. Eventually I was assisted by a . . . lady called Polly although even she was very reluctant to speak until she was satisfied that we were related.'

'Good old Poll,' Race said softly. 'She's a treasure.'

'Who was happy to take five guineas for providing the information,' Ewart added dryly. He looked at his brother again. 'Have you been ill?'

'No more than a mild fever. I'm better now.'

'Mama has been worried.' Ewart was now prepared to concede that she'd been right to be. 'She wants me to bring you back to Bishopston. I assume that you are not in employment and can leave at once.'

'I couldn't find a suitable job.' Race glanced at his brother's disapproving expression. 'Whether you choose to believe it or not I did try but it seems I'm not qualified for much.'

'And why did you choose to live here instead of at the club?'

'I didn't,' Race told him. 'Well, not at first, anyway. I've had some bad luck of late and circumstances aren't quite what they should be. Polly knew of this place.'

'Luck?' Ewart's suspicions were immediately aroused. 'At the gaming tables?'

'Oh come now, Ewart, don't sound so censorious.' Race's brash manner was quickly returning as he pulled on his coat. 'Let's set out now and I'll tell you all once we're well on the way home.' He paused. 'I'm afraid I'll have to ask you to pay my fare as I'm a little short for the moment.'

'There's a cab waiting outside,' Ewart said. 'I suggest we return to my hotel where you can freshen up and borrow some of my clothes before travelling. That will spare Mama the distress of seeing you like this.'

'You're a good brother.' Race had pulled his bag out from beneath the iron bedstead and was throwing what remained of his belongings into it. 'But I'm keen to be home so let's not delay too long. We could still make the afternoon train if we hurry.'

'An early return would suit me too,' Ewart said as they headed towards the door. 'I've already wasted several days when I should have been overseeing the harvest. Perhaps when you've had a chance to regain your strength you could assist in—'

Just as Ewart was about to put his hand on the door handle, the door suddenly burst open and a Goliath of a man stood blocking their exit. He glowered at the bag in Race's hand and took a menacing step forward.

'Why Mr Davenport?' he growled. 'I trust you wasn't about to scarper without settling the small matter of my rent, was you?'

'Of course not,' Race took a small step back and attempted to soothe the giant with one of his most convincing smiles. 'I was just on my way to you with the money.' He turned to his brother. 'Ewart, could you let my good friend, Mr Turnham, have five pounds?'

'Five pounds and six shillings,' the man said

roughly as Ewart reached inside his waistcoat for the money.

'I trust this will suffice.'

'It will.' When the money was tightly clutched in his fist, the man turned his attention back to Race with an amiable smile but a heavy threat in his voice. 'I'm glad we was able to resolve this matter so civilized like. It wouldn't 'ave been good for your health to try and do a runner.'

'That was a close thing.' Race slumped back against the seat of the cab when they were safely under way. 'It's as well you had the means to settle up.'

'But you intended to leave without paying your dues if you could.' Ewart stared at his brother disapprovingly. 'How could you have contemplated behaving in such a dishonourable way?'

'Oh Ewart, you saw the man.' Race sounded defiant. 'He was hardly a gentleman so what does it matter?'

'Everyone is entitled to be treated with respect and to receive what is rightfully theirs,' Ewart said sharply. 'It was wrong of you to try and cheat Mr Turnham. Didn't it occur to you that he might have relied on your rent money to feed his family?'

'Men like that don't have families.' Race passed a hand over his eyes. 'Please don't lecture me any more, Ewart. I'm still weak from the fever and need to rest.'

Ewart continued to look irritated but didn't say any more and Race allowed his eyes to close with an overwhelming sense of relief. For the first time in weeks he didn't have to fear for his safety. Thanks to Ewart's timely intervention, he would soon be on the train back to Devon. No one would know where he was. Now all the threats from his creditors and the bailiffs they sent after him would count for nothing. He frowned slightly as he recalled that Ewart had called his behaviour dishonourable. If a trifling sum like five pounds had made him react so harshly, then it was perhaps as well that he didn't know the full extent of his brother's gambling debts.

* * *

The weather had taken a turn for the worse and ominously dark clouds hung low over the sea as Sarah set out early in the morning. A harsh wind was blowing the menacing storm inland and she drew her shawl up over her head as she headed out of the village.

Two more days had passed and there'd been no word from Ewart; no hint that he was prepared to do anything to help Hepzi. Sarah had endured the agony of waiting for as long as she could and then decided that she must try to do something by herself. John and Lydia were taking care of the shop and she'd promised herself she wouldn't return until

245

she'd found Hepzi and done all she could to make her return to the warmth and comfort of the cottage.

It was strangely quiet in the lanes. No birdsong rose up from the hedgerows and it seemed to Sarah that the world was holding its breath in anticipation of the first thunderclap. That came as she passed the empty field where Hepzi had been working a few days earlier and was immediately followed by heavy rain that soaked through the shawl and made her skirt heavy around her legs. She could barely see through the gloom of downpour but she struggled on. If Hepzi was out in this then there was all the more reason to find her.

There was no sign of life in any of the fields Sarah passed and, as the rain streaming down the road reduced the surface to a slippery quagmire, her progress became slower. Water was seeping in through her boots and even her chemise was so wet that it was sticking to her skin. A small voice inside her head told her the task was hopeless and that she should turn back but she refused to listen to it. She would find Hepzi and at least, she told herself in a desperate attempt to salvage some relief from the situation, she couldn't get any wetter than she already was.

The rain had begun to ease a little when she finally found a small group of people picking potatoes. Thick dark mud oozed over Sarah's boots as she began to pick her way along one of the furrows but she barely noticed. She had seen the person she was looking for.

'Hepzi!' She called out to her as soon as she was within earshot.

'Miss Sarah?' The girl looked shocked. 'You shouldn't be out on a day like this.'

'Nor should you.' Sarah felt like weeping when she saw Hepzi's thin shawl and her bare feet in the mud.

'I'm used to it. You ain't. You shouldn't have come out.'

'I wanted to.' Sarah pushed the dripping hair out of her eyes. 'I've brought news for you. The Lancers have set sail. Noah is on his way back.'

'At last.' Hepzi's smile transformed her drawn features. 'And you'll be having your da back as well.'

'Yes.' Sarah hoped the good news would make Hepzi more amenable to her suggestion. 'Will you come home with me now, to wait for Noah?'

'He's really coming,' Hepzi breathed. A soft glow of happiness was shining in her eyes and Sarah was sure she was about to agree to come back when a man suddenly stumbled up and pushed Hepzi aside.

'What's going on?'

'It's all right, Da!' Hepzi spoke before Sarah could. 'Miss Sarah came to tell me something.'

'I didn't ask you to open your mouth.' Hepzi's father rounded on his daughter and then turned back to glare at Sarah. 'You're not wanted or welcome here.'

'I'm free to go where I wish.' Sarah had seen the way Hepzi shrank back from her father and remembered the bruises there had once been on her back. This man wasn't going to bully her in the same way.

'You're sticking your nose in where it ain't wanted.' He took a step towards her but, despite his intimidating posture and her instinctive urge to do so, Sarah didn't move back or reveal her fear. Instead, she tried to speak in a more placatory tone.

'Mr Briar, please, I consider myself to be a friend of Hepzi's and I've only come out of concern. She looks so tired. Let her come back with me so she can rest.'

'How she looks is nothing to you and she's going nowhere.' His expression was obdurate but Sarah found she could be equally stubborn.

'I don't believe you are really so unfeeling,' she cried. 'At least think of your grandchild.'

She knew at once that it had been the wrong thing to say. Hepzi's eyes widened in alarm and her father's hands closed into fists.

'Hepzi already knows what I think of that,' he snarled. 'Now why don't you take your prissy ways back to Borthwick before I make you.'

He raised his arm and this time Sarah did step back in alarm. Was he really going to strike her?

'Drop your arm, Abel.' The horse seemed to come out of nowhere and stopped in front of Sarah as though shielding her from Hepzi's father. She looked up and felt relief rush over her when she realized Ewart was on its back.

'Mr Davenport, sir.' Abel Briar immediately lost his belligerent air. 'I didn't expect to see you here.'

'Evidently.' Ewart's voice was crisp as he leapt from the saddle and turned to Sarah. 'You are not harmed?'

'No.' And yet she so easily could have been. Ewart couldn't know how happy she was to see him at that moment or how much that momentary flash of concern in his eyes meant to her. Was she forgiven, after all?

'I've just arrived from London and received Constance's letter.' He was busy securing his horse but turned to look at her with a rueful smile. 'I should have known you wouldn't be content to await my return.'

'I didn't know you were away,' she stammered. 'I thought you were still angry.'

'Angry?' She saw his dark eyes narrow as if he were perplexed. 'Why would I be angry with you, Sarah?'

'Over the way I spoke when we last met. I had no right to be so rude in the face of your charity.'

'I don't understand. What charity?' His frown deepened and then eased into a smile as if he suddenly understood something. 'Surely you didn't think—?' he laughed and shook his head. 'We must clear up this misapprehension soon but I think there is a more pressing matter for the moment.' He turned to address Hepzi's father. 'Abel, I came in search of you. There's a vacant cottage at Bishopston and it comes with an offer of work throughout the year if you wish to take it. You won't have to move about or rely on hiring fairs any more. Your family can have security.'

'What's the catch?' Abel sounded suspicious.

'There is none. One of my workers has moved on and I've seen how well you work.'

'I suppose we could offer you our services.' The eager glint in Abel's eye belied the reluctance in his voice. 'But we won't get paid if we leave here early and I don't think we can afford to be doing that.'

'I'll see to it that you receive adequate remuneration from the last quarter day onwards,' Ewart told him. 'Now, are we in agreement?'

'I reckon we are, Mr Davenport.' Abel finally grinned.

'And now that you have no further need of Hepzi's wage she is free to return to Borthwick with Miss Penghalion?' Although Ewart phrased the words as a question, a hard edge in his voice made it clear he wasn't expecting any argument.

'I reckon so.' Abel looked less pleased to have to concede this but he turned to Hepzi. 'Go on then, get away with yer. One less mouth to feed, I suppose.' He picked up the basket she'd been filling with potatoes and began to carry it across to the cart they were to be loaded into. 'We'll be with you by morning, Mr Davenport.'

Sarah was shocked by the apparent lack of affection in Abel's farewell to his daughter, but Hepzi didn't seem upset by it.

'I'm grateful to you for giving them the house, Mr Davenport,' Hepzi said with a shy smile.

'I hope it will prove to be to our mutual benefit. I've never been displeased with your family's work. And now I think you ladies should return to Borthwick before we all get any wetter than we are.' Ewart turned his horse. 'Let me help you mount, Hepzi.'

'I can walk, Mr Davenport,' Hepzi protested.

'But nonetheless you will ride today.' There was the same resolute tone in his voice that there had been when he settled Hepzi's affairs, and a few seconds later the girl was on the horse's back.

Ewart turned to Sarah.

'And now you, Miss Penghalion. He can easily carry two at a walk.'

'Oh I couldn't.' Sarah felt colour rush into her cheeks. How could she sit on Ewart's horse while he was forced to walk beside it?

'You've already walked far enough for one day and besides the exercise will give me an appetite for luncheon.' His lips curled into an almost impish smile. 'Perhaps it will also convince you that I'm not angry.'

He placed his hands on her waist and for an instant, just before he lifted her, their eyes met. Any lingering doubts that Sarah had about having offended him were washed away in that moment. His gaze wasn't that of a man who had been slighted. It was pensive but considerate. She could see nothing of the boorish individual she'd once thought him to be. Indeed, now that she came to think on it, she couldn't imagine why she had ever disliked Ewart Davenport in the first place.

*   *   *

The message for John had come shortly after Sarah had gone in search of Hepzi. He was asked to attend a meeting of Borthwick School Board later that morning.

'They don't believe in giving a lot of notice,' Lydia had observed as he stared at the note in bewilderment.

'I can't understand what they want.'

'Well, you won't find out if you stand there and scratch your head.' Lydia had come out from behind the counter and almost chased him out of the shop. 'Go and get yourself

252

smartened up then see what they have to say.'

What they'd had to say had been beyond John's wildest dreams. He'd entered the Rectory in a state of unemployment and left it, a little later, as the new schoolmaster of Borthwick with a house and a very generous salary. John knew he was grinning inanely as he hurried off to find Daisy but he didn't care. This was a grand day and if she said yes to the question now burning in his mind, it would be the most wonderful one of his life.

Lucy chuckled when she opened the door to him.

'Ah, it seems no time since Henry used to beam like that when he came to visit me.'

'Is Daisy there?' John was bursting to tell his sister his news but he wanted Daisy to be the first to hear.

'No. As soon as the storm passed she went to take some air. I think she was going to walk down by stream.'

'Thank you.' John was half way down the cottage path before Lucy had finished speaking and she smiled to herself as she closed the door. Young love was a grand thing.

John didn't care how many puddles he landed in as he ran in search of Daisy. All that mattered was sharing his joy with her and seeing her sweet face light up as he asked her to be his.

He heard the voices before he saw Daisy. She was standing underneath the oak tree near

253

the church and she wasn't alone. John stopped abruptly. She was with Race Davenport.

'Oh really,' he heard her say with a giggle. 'You're such a card, Race. You know I couldn't.'

'But you could.' Race's voice was full of persuasion. 'You have the talent and you're much prettier than any of the actresses in London. You'd be a star there and who knows what could follow? Paris or perhaps even Rome.'

John felt his elation die away leaving a gnawing ache in the pit of his stomach. Was Race going to take Daisy to London? Of course she would want to go. She was used to the glamour of the stage and he'd been insane to think she'd be happy to be the wife of a dull old schoolmaster. Suddenly his future seemed as black as the skies above him. John turned his back on the pair and began to trudge away, not even looking back when he heard Daisy call his name.

'John!' She was almost right behind him now. He could hear the breathlessness in her voice and realized she must have run to catch up. 'John, wait!'

He stopped. Better to know the truth now than postpone it.

'Why did you turn away?' There was indignation in Daisy's voice. 'Weren't you coming to see me?'

'I was,' he admitted sullenly. 'But I saw you

had other company.'

'Only Race. He's no reason to snub me.'

'Isn't he?' John felt irritation begin to pierce the gloomy cloud around him. It wasn't fair of her to lead him on like this. 'I heard what you were talking about. Why did you let me think you had some affection for me when you've been planning to go to London all along?'

'London?' Daisy stared at him in confusion. 'Why on earth would I want to go to there?'

'To sing, of course. No doubt the great Race Davenport could get you into one of the best theatres and be happy to escort you about town.'

'You're jealous!' Daisy started to laugh and piqued John's anger even more.

'Why shouldn't I be?' he cried. 'It's easy to see why you run after him. He has money and friends in high places. He can give you anything you want and all I have to offer is a schoolhouse and a hundred pounds a year.'

'He can't give me everything.' Daisy's cheeks went red. 'Race is amusing for a time but he cares for no one but himself. He can't give me what I really want and besides I wouldn't want him to.'

'And what is it that you really want?' John wasn't to be easily pacified and Daisy shook her head tenderly at him.

'Don't you know by now? I want the love of a good man. The kind of good man I see standing before me right now.'

'Me?' John was finally silenced and Daisy smiled as she nodded.

'You, John Penghalion. What more can I do to show how much I love you? And why would I want to go to London when all I'll ever need in my life is right here in Borthwick?'

'Oh Daisy.' He caught both her hands in his. 'Do you mean it? Will you really be happy to stay here and be my wife?'

'Of course I would, my silly dearest John, but I was beginning to worry that you'd never ask.' She went eagerly into his arms and it was only as their kiss finally ended that she raised her head to look at him enquiringly. 'By the way, my darling, what was that about a schoolhouse?'

*   *   *

'Both of you sit there by the fire and don't move until I've fetched you some dry clothes.' As soon as she laid eyes on Sarah and Hepzi, Lydia had declared that the world wouldn't end if the shop was closed for a few minutes and had locked the door while she fussed over the two girls. 'A dog shouldn't have been on the roads in that rain this morning.'

'We'll soon be dry,' Sarah assured her. 'And we're not as muddy as we would have been if Ewart hadn't given us a ride home. It was very kind of him, wasn't it, Hepzi?'

'Yes.' Hepzi's reply was barely audible and

256

Sarah looked at her in concern. In the firelight she looked even paler than she had in the field and she'd said very little since her return to the cottage.

'Are you all right?'

'I don't know,' Hepzi began uncertainly. 'I'm feeling a bit—'

'We have the best news!' John suddenly burst into the room almost pulling Daisy in by the hand. 'We're to be married.'

'Oh that's wonderful.' Lydia hurried over to kiss them both but Sarah had leapt up to be at Hepzi's side. The girl had doubled over and let out a worrying groan.

'What's wrong?' Her anxious cry brought Lydia over. She bent to look at Hepzi and then laid a hand on her stomach.

'Ah, so that's how it is.' She straightened up again with a brisk air. 'Sarah, put the kettle on to boil and John, run for the midwife. It seems we'll have double cause for celebration today. There's a baby on its way.'

CHAPTER ELEVEN

Dear Constance,
Hepzi has asked me to write on her behalf to thank you for the shawl you so kindly sent for little Samuel. He is a beautiful and very contented baby although it must be

257

said that if he continues to grow at his present rate he will not be 'little' Samuel for much longer. Hepzi says she will wrap him in the shawl when we set out to see the Lancers return tomorrow. She wants him to look his very best when he meets his papa for the first time.

Isn't it wonderful to think that in just a few more hours we will be reunited with our loved ones again? Lydia has kindly offered to watch the shop so we can all go to meet Papa together. We're very excited and I'm sure that you must be too.

Constance sighed and dropped her letter from Sarah down onto the table beside her. At that precise moment she was anything but excited. She was frustrated, she was indignant and she was so angry that she wanted to scream and throw things. However, she had been raised to believe that a lady never behaved in such a way so she was forced to sit sedately on a sofa and vent her rage on a piece of embroidery; stabbing her needle into the fabric with a lot more force than was necessary and tugging on the threads so viciously it was a wonder they didn't snap. It wasn't fair. She should be mistress in her own household and yet her mother still contrived to treat her like a petulant child.

It had all started over dinner the night before when Constance had announced her intention to take the carriage to Otterly and meet Hugh.

'I hardly think so.' Lady Hawley hadn't even looked up from her consommé as she spoke. 'You're the wife of a gentleman, not some tawdry camp follower. I'm sure Hugh would prefer you to greet him here with some decorum rather than making a scene on the quayside.'

'I have no intention of making a scene,' Constance said with more composure than she was feeling. 'I will stay in the carriage and send Boyer to fetch Hugh. I'm sure he'd be pleased to see me there.'

'He would be happier to see that his wife knows how to conduct herself properly. Your place is here in his home where you should ensure that everything is ready for his return and then welcome him in a seemly fashion.'

'But I can have everything ready before I leave,' Constance pointed out. Hugh had been content for her to travel to Otterly with him on the day he left. She was sure he would be just as happy to see her there when he returned.

'Don't argue with me, child.' Her mother frowned. 'I must say that I find the contrary attitude you have adopted of late very tiresome. Marriage has made you quite disagreeable.'

'I have no wish to be disagreeable, Mama.' Constance made an effort not to lose her temper but being called a child had irked her and made her all the more determined to carry out her plan. 'However, I am mistress of this house and it is my intention to take the carriage into Otterly tomorrow.'

Lady Hawley had sharply sucked in her breath at what she no doubt perceived as her daughter's insolence but she hadn't argued. The remainder of the meal had been conducted in an awkward silence but Constance was sure she had won the battle. Until she had woken that morning to discover that her mother had breakfasted early and sent for the carriage. According to Matthews, Her Ladyship intended to spend the day at Bishopston with Mrs Davenport and would not return until after tea time.

The carriage was gone. Constance's initial, angry reaction was that she would ride or, if need be, even walk to Otterly rather than let her mother get the better of her. However, in the next moment she recollected her condition and was forced to accept that she had no choice other than to stay at home.

Now she tried to imagine what her reunion with Hugh would have been like if she'd been able to travel to Otterly. Would he have hurried to the carriage to be at her side again? Would he have been bold enough to kiss her there and then? She was sure he would have smiled at her in the way that always made her feel as if she was the luckiest woman alive to have him. Suddenly her needle stopped and her eyebrows gathered into a troubled frown. What did that smile look like? She tried to concentrate on summoning up Hugh's image in her mind but the best she could achieve was a hazy outline of someone tall in uniform. It had been so long since she'd seen him that her memory simply couldn't supply the finer details of his appearance. She had a portrait of him, of course, but she had never considered it to be a very good likeness and besides, a painting wasn't animated. It didn't know how to smile or how to laugh lovingly at her initial, disastrous attempts to run a household. How naive and foolish she had been as a young bride and how long ago those first happy weeks of their marriage seemed. So much had happened since Hugh went away and she had changed so much. Her frown deepened. Their courtship had been swift and the time they'd spent together since their marriage even briefer. She knew she missed Hugh and she was quite sure that she was in love with him but did she really know him? How would he react to the changes she had instigated in the household and the role she had established for herself in his absence? He had married childlike, fearful Constance Hawley. Who was to say that he would love or even like the confident, forthright and able young woman Lady Constance Weston had become?

* * *

'Are you quite sure you don't mind being left alone for the day?' Sarah had carried a mug of tea through to the shop where Lydia had just finished serving her first customer of the morning.

'I wouldn't have offered to watch the place if I did,' Lydia assured her. 'Besides, I've only a Wednesday half day to contend with and I've watched you sort the post so many times now that I'm sure I can do it.'

'Well, we're very grateful to you. It means so much to be able to go and meet Papa all together like this.' Sarah smiled at the older woman. 'Try and have a rest when you close up for the afternoon. There may not be too much peace when we all come back for supper. I can't recall a time when so many people will have squeezed round the kitchen table at once.'

'I'm sure it will be a grand party.' Lydia turned away from Sarah's eager smile. While the rest of the household were in such high spirits she felt as if her heart was breaking. This wonderful time with her precious daughter and her stepchildren had to end today. Her bags were already packed and, as soon as she locked the shop door at one o'clock, she would have to slip away before George returned and denounced her as Betsy Penghalion, his runaway wife. She didn't dare to imagine what Sarah would think of her if that happened.

The bell above the shop door tinkled as Daisy entered, closely followed by Lucy and her children.

'Ah there you are.' Sarah greeted them with a smile. 'John will be pleased. He's eager to be on the road.'

'I want to go and see Grandpa!' Isaac wailed and Sarah looked at him in surprise.

'But you are going. We all are.'

'I don't think he should,' Lucy said anxiously. 'He's been up half the night coughing and I swear there's a touch of mild fever on his brow. I know it's likely to be little more than a cold but the journey won't be good for him.'

'That's true.' Sarah gave her nephew a sympathetic smile. 'It might be better if you stayed at the forge with your papa, Isaac. You can still have supper with Grandpa tonight.'

'I don't want to stay.' Isaac burst into tears and was promptly overcome by another coughing fit which destroyed any chance he might have had of changing his mother's mind.

'The trouble is that he can't stay at the forge today,' Lucy said with a sigh. 'Henry's gone to shoe the horses at Netherlea Grange and won't be back until after noon. Do you think he might stay here with you, Lydia? I'm sure he won't be any trouble.'

'He never is.' The kindly smile Lydia gave Isaac betrayed nothing of the way her thoughts were racing as she spoke. How could she agree to care for Isaac when she had to leave the village in just a few hours time? Then again, how could she refuse to do so without arousing suspicion? Lucy had said that Henry would get home sometime after noon. Perhaps that was the answer. When it was time for her to depart she could take Isaac back to the forge and leave him in Henry's care before starting out on her journey. If she left her bags behind the currant bushes in Lucy's garden, Henry wouldn't notice anything was amiss.

'Of course he can stay with me,' she said and Lucy hugged her. 'Thank you. It means so much to know he'll be safe with you.'

'We should head off.' John was looking at his pocket watch as he and Hepzi came through to join them.

Lucy bent to kiss Isaac. 'Be a good boy and I'll bring you back a treat.'

Isaac wasn't to be so easily appeased, however. He twisted out of his mother's embrace and went to stand morosely by the window.

'Goodbye, Lydia.' Daisy waved to her friend. 'We'll see you tonight.'

The lump in Lydia's throat made it impossible for her to reply. In a few seconds all the people she cared for most would leave and she would never see them again. She knew she should be grateful to have had these weeks with her daughter. It was more than she deserved but that made the parting no easier. She couldn't even say a proper goodbye. Tears filled her eyes but she quickly turned away and pretended to be busy with an order before anyone could see them. She heard the shop door open, then close and knew she was alone. From now on she always would be.

*   *   *

It seemed that half the county had turned out to see the Lancers' ship dock. Otterly was busier than it was on market day and indeed a few of the more enterprising merchants had set up their stalls in order to tempt the visitors with mutton pies, stewed eels or hot potatoes.

While the rest of her family strolled around the docks enjoying the entertainment provided by stilt dancers, acrobats and puppet shows, Sarah decided to rest for a time in a quieter spot outside a nearby church. A gig pulled by a grey horse was standing in the road outside and, from the way its tail and mane were plaited and dressed with flowers, Sarah guessed a wedding must be taking place inside. She smiled. Soon there would be two weddings in Borthwick church to look forward to. There was sure to be a great celebration when John and Daisy became man and wife and it would be a happy day when Noah and Hepzi were finally able to marry and leave behind all the problems that had beset their lives together so

265

far.

'Good day, Sarah.' A familiar voice made her turn and she was aware of a slight flutter in her heart when she saw its owner walking towards her.

'Good morning, Mr Davenport. Have you come to see the Lancers ashore too?'

'Yes. It seems I am incapable of completely severing my connections with them.' Ewart turned his gaze towards the quayside where the ship was being slowly brought about into a docking position. 'This is a slow process. It will be some time before they disembark.'

'It would seem so and yet my brother was sure we would be late when we set out this morning. At least the weather is fair.' Sarah remembered that it hadn't been the last time she and Ewart met. 'I haven't yet thanked you for your intervention with Mr Briar and for taking us home afterwards.'

'There is no need to. I was glad to be of assistance. And I heard from Mrs Briar that Hepzi was safely delivered of a son that night.'

'Yes, little Samuel. She has brought him with her today.'

'Noah will be glad to see them both,' Ewart said. 'And now that he has a career in the army he'll be in a good position to support a family.'

'The Lancers have been good to them. I know Hepzi was glad to have some of his pay when she and her family needed it.'

'I only regret that I didn't think to make

266

arrangements for her earlier than I did.' Ewart frowned slightly. 'The Lancers maintain a voluntary fund to assist their dependants in times of need. Hepzi could have received a payment from that had I fully comprehended her situation.' He stopped and looked at Sarah for a moment before continuing. 'It was this fund that I referred to when I asked if you required financial assistance on the night of your grandmother's death. After all the years of devoted service your father has given to the regiment you had more reason than most to be entitled to it. After all, he has willingly contributed to it throughout his career.'

'Oh.' This information took Sarah by surprise. 'I didn't know what you meant. I thought—' She stumbled over the words. 'I thought—'

'You thought I was being high handed enough to toss you a few alms from my bounty,' he finished the sentence for her, then laughed and wagged a finger at her. 'Don't try to deny it now, Miss Sarah Penghalion. Your guilty expression tells me I am right and under the circumstances you had every right to dismiss me as angrily as you did.'

'I should have been slower to take offence.' Sarah could feel her cheeks turning pink enough to make the bright flowers on her new hat seem faded.

'And I should have realized that my intentions could have been misinterpreted.'

He paused again. 'I hope you see now that I only had your welfare in mind. I wouldn't wish to think of you suffering any kind of hardship, Sarah.'

'You are very kind.' Something in Ewart's voice made Sarah feel suddenly shy and she was glad when the church doors opened providing her with a distraction. 'Oh look, the bridal party are emerging.'

The bride was in a white satin gown that must have been especially made for her wedding. She wore a veiled bonnet and a smile that left no one watching in any doubt of her joy that day. It was impossible not to share in such obvious happiness and at first Sarah smiled but then she gave a surprised gasp. She had recognized the groom.

'Oh, it's Albert!'

'Mr Eden?' Ewart sounded equally shocked. 'But I understood . . . that is, I thought he was betrothed to you.'

'He wished everyone to think he was but I had never accepted his proposal.' Even so Sarah couldn't help feeling a little slighted by the speed with which Albert had embarked upon another courtship. 'I recognize the lady he has married. Her father owns a draper's shop here in Otterly. Albert must be well pleased with his lot. He often spoke of his desire to have an interest in a business.' A faint sigh escaped from her lips. 'Indeed, if I were to be honest, I think he cared more for

268

the idea of our shop than he ever did for me.'

'Then he's a bigger fool than I took him for.'

Ewart had been so pleasant to her just moments ago that now the sharpness in his voice took Sarah by surprise. She glanced round to see if she could ascertain what had irritated him and found that he had already left her side without a word of farewell. Now he was striding back towards the crowds on the quayside in what appeared to be a high temper and Sarah was left with the uneasy feeling that she was somehow responsible for his anger.

*   *   *

By the time the troops eventually began to disembark from the ship, almost another two hours had passed and everyone had been glad of the impromptu picnic John had purchased from the stalls around them. Now, as a band on the decks of the ship struck up 'Rule Britannia', the family had joined everyone else who was trying to get as close to the ship as possible in order to catch the first sight of their loved ones.

'There's Papa!' Lucy pointed excitedly at a figure on the gang plank 'It's him, I know it is.'

'And his hat is brown just as he said in his letters,' Sarah said.

'Papa!' Lucy waved and shouted despite the fact that it would have been impossible for their father to hear above the clamour.

'Let's go and see him.' John caught hold of Daisy's hand and, with Lucy and Sarah following on, began to ease a path through the crowds to the spot where George had disembarked.

Papa.' This time he did hear Lucy's eager shout and he turned to greet his family with a broad smile that lifted the ends of his moustache

'What a joy it is to see you all again. Lucy, Sarah.' He kissed each of his daughters in turn. 'And even John all the way from Exeter.'

'Not from Exeter any more,' John informed him proudly. 'I've so much to tell you.'

'But I think our news can wait until Papa has had a chance to catch his breath.' Sarah could see deep lines of weariness etched into her father's features and was afraid that if everyone tried to talk to him at once it would overwhelm him.

'It has been a long voyage.' George acknowledged his daughter's intervention with a grateful wink. 'But at least tell me if you are all well. And Ma? Is she recovering?'

Then her letter hadn't reached him. Sarah felt the mood of her brother and sister shift at once and knew her father had noticed it too. He looked at her with the unspoken question in his eyes and she nodded sombrely, unable to say the words.

'I see.' George lowered his eyes and Sarah

reached out to take his hand. Their father would need his time to grieve.

'Have you told your family that they've got a proper hero in their midst now, Lieutenant Penghalion?' One of George's comrades jostled his way into the small family group, oblivious to their sorrow.

'Not yet, Harry.' George spoke quietly and Sarah noticed that he endeavoured to conceal his distress from the man.

'Well, be sure you get him to tell you.' Harry reached out to clap George on the shoulder. 'Braver than any other man on the field that day, he was, and he's to get a medal to prove it. If you ask me they should have promoted him to general instead of lieutenant.'

'There'll be time enough for stories later.' With characteristic modesty, George seemed unwilling to have his exploits related so openly. 'For now I want nothing more than the warmth of my own hearth and the chance to sit quietly with my children round me.'

'Then we should head for home.' It had been a long day and Sarah was ready to return to the peace of Borthwick as well.

'Miss Sarah.' Someone plucked at her sleeve and Sarah turned to find Hepzi, standing looking troubled. 'Miss Sarah, everyone's ashore now but I can't find Noah.'

'Are you sure you haven't simply missed him in the crowds?' It was so busy and the Lancers' uniforms made them all look very similar from

271

a distance.

'I'm being certain of it.' Hepzi sounded tearful. 'I watched them all come off and I've searched the quay. He isn't to be seen. Oh Miss Sarah, what do you think's become of him?'

'There's sure to be a good reason why he hasn't disembarked yet. Perhaps he's helping with the horses.' Sarah refused to even consider that there might be a more sinister reason for Noah's absence. Not now, when Hepzi had overcome so much. She was about to ask her father if he knew where the boy was but then thought better of it. He had just learned of his mother's death. He didn't need to be troubled by anything else.

'Start for home,' she told her family. 'I'll catch up a little later but I have to speak to someone first.'

She had seen the person who could assist her standing in conversation with some of the officers. After his earlier outburst she wasn't sure how Ewart would react to her request for help, but for Hepzi's sake she was prepared to find out.

*   *   *

When she had locked the door behind the last customer of the day, Lydia took off her apron and hung it up for the final time.

'Come along, Isaac. We'll take a bite to eat

and then I'll take you back to your papa.'

There was no reply and no sign of Isaac, either. Earlier, he'd been sitting by the window playing with Bosun but now only the cat was there, curled up on an old piece of sacking. Lydia couldn't help feeling exasperated. She knew Isaac loved to play hide and seek but there wasn't time for that now.

'Isaac, where are you? Come out and I'll give you a piece of fudge.' Her words echoed around the empty room and it occurred to her that the shop was too quiet. If Isaac was hiding close by she was sure she would hear some tiny movement or a stifled giggle. 'Isaac?'

He was gone. She'd searched the shop and the cottage and there was no trace of him. He must have slipped out of the shop when she wasn't looking. When had that been? It had been so busy in the later part of the morning that she couldn't recall exactly when she had last seen him. He might have been missing for hours.

Lydia glanced at her bags which now sat in the corner of the kitchen. If she didn't leave soon it would be dark before she found somewhere to spend her first night on the road. Isaac's naughtiness was very vexing. No doubt he had become tired of waiting and decided to go home by himself. He was probably already in the forge watching Henry at work.

Well, she didn't have time to fret about him

any more. Lydia picked up her bags but then paused. What if Isaac hadn't gone home? He'd been so set on going to Otterly. Was it possible he'd decided to make his own way there? Only a few hours earlier Lucy had thanked her for taking care of him yet she had failed to do so. She thought of the three children she had abandoned in this very house so many years ago. She had failed them as well. At least they had been in the care of their grandparents, but she didn't even know where Isaac was. Could she leave without knowing he was safe? She gave the matter less than a moment's thought, then dropped her bags and hurried out in search of the boy.

*   *   *

Did men really endure such conditions at sea? Was this how her father had been forced to live? The space beneath the decks of the ship was cramped and dirty while the air was heavy with the stale odours of sweat, horseflesh and illness. Half a dozen injured men lay on straw mattresses on the deck and, as Sarah looked at their pitiable conditions, she felt tears of pity prick at her eyes.

'Perhaps you should have remained on deck as I suggested,' Ewart said quietly. 'I warned you this wouldn't be a pleasant experience.'

'And I told you that I wouldn't leave Hepzi when she might need me most.' Sarah made an

274

effort to conceal her horror of the squalid scene. 'I am made of stronger stuff than you might think.'

'I've never had any reason to doubt your fortitude.' Ewart's eyebrows lifted slightly and Sarah suspected he might have smiled under different circumstances, but not here. No one could move amidst such misery and find any reason to smile.

If Sarah hadn't been so concerned on Hepzi's behalf she would have been greatly cheered by the way Ewart had responded when she told him of Hepzi's plight. His earlier ill humour seemed to have completely dissipated and he had immediately gone in search of someone who might know where Noah was.

He had been away for no more than a few minutes but Sarah guessed that every one of those must have seemed like an hour to Hepzi as she rocked Samuel in her arms and waited anxiously for word. When Ewart had returned and informed them that Noah was still on the ship, Hepzi had burst into tears of relief but something in the grave set of Ewart's lips told Sarah that Hepzi's trials weren't over yet and his next words had confirmed this.

'I will take you to him but I'm afraid you should prepare yourself. He has been injured.'

Sarah had decided at that moment that she would stay with Hepzi for as long as she was needed, but she knew that under these circumstances there was little more she could do to alleviate the girl's suffering.

'Noah!' Hepzi gave a cry and dropped to her knees beside a pallet. The boy lying there was pale and gaunt but he managed to reach out to clasp her hand.

'Dearest Hepzi. I thought I'd never see you again.'

There was something familiar about the boy's voice and his deep blue eyes. Sarah took a moment to think what it could be and then remembered. He was the young soldier she had met when she was looking for Isaac on the day the Lancers sailed. He was late because he'd gone looking for his sweetheart—for Hepzi. At last they were together again but what would the future hold for them now. She turned to Ewart.

'You said his injuries were serious?'

'Yes.' Ewart was watching as Hepzi held Samuel out to his father. 'The wheel on a gun carriage gave way over rocky terrain. Noah pushed another lad out of danger but wasn't quick enough to save himself as well. The lower part of his leg was crushed beneath the gun and couldn't be saved.' There was deep sympathy in Ewart's eyes. 'He'll be crippled for the rest of his life.'

'Oh no.' Sarah turned away from the tender scene in front of her. It was so unfair. If anyone deserved to have some happiness at last, it was Hepzi. 'What will happen to them?'

'I've sent for a carriage to take them to Bishopston. I'm sure my gardener and his wife will offer Noah shelter again and Hepzi has her family to care for her. Beyond that, I don't know.' Ewart shook his head ruefully. 'I thought the lad had years of army service ahead of him and wouldn't be back. His position on the estate has been filled and I gave the Briars possession of the last empty cottage. Even if Noah is able to work again I've no job to offer him and no home for them, either.'

'You had no way of predicting the future.' Ewart wasn't to blame for the situation and Sarah didn't like to hear him reproach himself. 'Besides, you spoke earlier of the Lancers' charitable fund. Won't that offer them some support?'

'Yes, but I fear its benefits will be limited. There will be widows and other injured men in need of its assistance as well.'

'Oh.' Then Hepzi and Noah's future looked bleak. Sarah bit down on her lower lip. She wouldn't cry. Tears wouldn't help Hepzi.

'I won't see them destitute.' Ewart laid a hand on her arm and spoke with quiet determination. 'I give you my word on that, Sarah. You have been a true friend to Hepzi in the past. Will you trust me to care for her now?'

Sarah raised her head and found herself looking directly into Ewart's steady, concerned gaze. 'Yes.' She could trust him with this. She suddenly felt that she could trust him with anything and he would never disappoint her.

*   *   *

It was almost dusk when Sarah reached the outskirts of Borthwick. She had seen Hepzi and Noah safely on their way to Bishopston and had promised that she would come and see them as soon as she could.

It was strange that Constance hadn't come into town. Sarah had expected to see her carriage on the quayside but Sir Hugh had set out for Farleigh Park alone on horseback. Perhaps Constance had decided that the journey would be too much in her condition. Sarah hoped that was all it was. She toyed with the idea of sending a short note to enquire after her health but then thought better of it. Lady Hawley had already made her disapproval of their relationship abundantly clear and now Sir Hugh was home. Constance wouldn't want to be bothered by a lowly postmistress any more.

There were no lights shining in the windows of the cottage as she approached and Sarah frowned. She would have expected her family to be in the kitchen ready to sit down to the large cured ham she'd bought as a celebratory meal. Instead, both the shop and the cottage looked dark and deserted.

278

There was someone at home though. She heard voices as soon as she opened the back door. Angry, discordant voices and what sounded very much like someone in a state of great distress. The scene that greeted her in the kitchen was quite unlike anything she had expected. Lucy was in the armchair looking pale and cradling a sobbing Isaac in her arms. Daisy and John were standing by the fireplace with shocked expressions on their faces and her father was in the middle of the room, resting his hands on the kitchen table and glaring across it at Lydia who stood shaking and crying as if she would never stop.

'What's going on?'

Her father turned at the sound of her voice and at once she could see he was angry, angrier than she could ever remember him being.

'Ah Sarah, there you are at last.' The words bristled in his mouth as he thrust his hand towards her. 'Come and meet your mother!'

CHAPTER TWELVE

'Will you take more tea, Hugh?' Lady Hawley smiled at her son-in-law across the breakfast table. 'Of course you should eat some more as well. You need feeding up after the ordeal you've been through.'

'Thank you.' Constance watched as her husband accepted the cup with a tight smile. He'd been very quiet since his return three days earlier and she wondered if he was merely tired from the journey or whether something more worrying lay behind his reticence.

'It's a shame your best silver was stolen. This set isn't of the same quality at all.' Her mother, on the other hand, barely stopped talking. It didn't seem to have occurred to her that the young couple might have appreciated some time alone together, and she had been a constant presence since Hugh's return. Now here she was presiding over a meal as if she were in her own home. Normally this would have irritated Constance but today she had other things on her mind.

Before breakfast she'd overheard two maids talking as they swept out the fire in the drawing room, and hadn't been able to resist eavesdropping when one of them mentioned Sarah.

'Who'd have thought it? After all these years thinking her mother's dead, she not only finds out she's alive and well but also that she's nothing more than some common music hall turn. I don't know how she can bear it.'

'I heard as how there was a right rumpus anyhow,' the other added. 'She had no idea who was living with her until her pa showed up and threw the hussy out, bags and all. My sister lives a few doors down and she says he was shouting loud enough to rouse the devil. Called her a faithless Jezebel, he did.'

'Oooh, it must've been a right sight,' the first girl sounded as if she was hanging on every word. 'I s'pose she cleared off after that.'

'Well, any decent person would've but, no, she's still in the village. It seems John's intended came over all tearful and begged him to help her friend, so he's taken her in to live in the schoolhouse until she finds somewhere to go. Apparently he took to the news with the least trouble. Mrs Croft was in the shop and heard him tell Sarah that a lot of things made sense to him now.'

'I'll wager Sergeant George won't be happy about her staying, though.' The first maid laughed.

'Lieutenant George now,' the other girl corrected her. 'Either way, I don't suppose he is. He'll be the talk of the village. Sarah, too, for that matter.'

'Constance, have you listened to one word I've been saying?' Her mother's voice brought her thoughts sharply back to the present.

'Sorry, Mama. I was thinking about the menus for this week. Cook will wish to receive them this morning.' If the maids were right, the entire village was gossiping about the uproar in the Penghalion family and Constance had no intention of spreading the story any further, especially as her mother would probably take great delight in hearing

281

that Sarah was embroiled in a scandal.

'I was telling Hugh that it's becoming imperative that you engage a monthly nurse and, more importantly, a nursemaid as soon as possible. It isn't a matter you can continue to ignore for much longer.' Lady Hawley turned back to Hugh. 'Mrs Fotheringham recommended a very competent girl some time ago but Constance didn't even write to take references.'

Constance bit lightly on her lower lip. She knew her mother was right. The time left to find a nursemaid was growing shorter with every passing day and she ought to take some action but she was loathe to do so. The idea of a stranger from London caring for her baby made her feel uncomfortable and yet there were no suitable local girls available for the post, so it seemed she had little choice in the matter. She looked up and found that Hugh was watching her with the strange, unreadable expression that had been on his face so often since his return. She wished he would smile the way he used to. This new solemn look suggested that he was displeased with something and she was sure it must be her. His reserve was worrying but perhaps matters would be worse if he did tell her what was troubling him. It might be that he disapproved of the part she had been playing in local affairs and that he expected her to devote her energies solely to him and his household. Now that she had experienced a taste of freedom, she didn't know if she could do that.

*　　*　　*

'It does a man's heart good to see so much greenery again.' George briefly stopped walking to stand and gaze at the heavy green leaves of a horse chestnut tree. 'Even when all that rain was falling in Africa, the landscape never looked this fresh.'

It was early evening and he and Sarah were strolling along the path that led to Bluebell Wood. They had often enjoyed walks like this in the past but tonight Sarah was aware of a sense of uneasiness between them. They had yet to properly discuss the events of the past few days and she guessed this was why her father had suggested this outing—so that they could speak openly, well out of the hearing of the village women whose frequent visits to the shop had so obviously been attempts to garner salacious gossip rather than buy provisions. Every pantry in Borthwick had to be overflowing, judging by the number of shopping trips made by their owners in the course of the past few days.

'I'm sorry you came home to such a shock.' She saw little point in prevarication. Pretending that the crisis in their family didn't exist wouldn't make it go away.

'It wasn't your fault, lass.' Her father's voice

283

was gruff. 'You had no way of knowing who she was or that she was using a charade to take advantage of your good nature.'

Sarah released a troubled sigh. Even now that she knew the truth, she found it hard to believe the worst of the woman who had become such a good friend.

'I'm sure she didn't mean to do that and she didn't mean to cause you so much upset either. She would've left before you got home but then Isaac went missing. She could have gone anyway but she didn't. She went out and searched all along the road until she found him half way to Otterly. Lydia—' She still couldn't quite bring herself to call her Mama. 'Lydia's not a bad person.'

'Lydia!' George gave an angry snort. 'Just the sort of highfalutin' name she would choose. Plain Betsy wasn't good enough for her.' The indignation in his voice abruptly faded, leaving behind a tone that sounded regretful. 'Any more than I was, I suppose.'

'Oh Papa.' He had been living with the pain of this rejection for so many years and now, when he was already grieving for his mother, the wound had been reopened. Sarah reached out to take her father's hand. She hated to see him suffer like this.

'You were named for her, you know.' He spoke briskly as though trying not to let his emotions get the better of him. 'It was your Grandma's idea to pretend all three of you had the same mother and she changed your name when Betsy ran off the way she—' He fell silent, his gaze suddenly fixed on the path a little way ahead. Sarah looked up and saw the object of their conversation walking towards them.

'Strutting about the place like a duchess,' George muttered under his breath but Sarah felt his grip on her hand tighten momentarily and guessed that he was concealing apprehension beneath his show of contempt.

Betsy Penghalion was nothing like glamorous actress Lydia Prescott had been when Sarah first encountered her in Exeter. Tonight she was wearing a plain grey dress that her alter ego would have condemned as 'dowdy' and had a black shawl draped over her shoulders. Her dark hair was drawn up into a simple knot and, judging by her drawn expression and tear-reddened eyes, she was suffering just as much as her estranged husband.

'Good evening.' When Betsy spoke her voice shook so much that Sarah was sure she would have been happier to scramble through a hedge and take flight across the fields rather than stay and face them.

'It was.' George gave her a hostile glare and her hands trembled as she drew the shawl more tightly around her as if it could offer some kind of protection from his resentment.

'I know you've a right to hate me.' She

raised her eyes to cast a beseeching, penitent glance at Sarah. 'You both do, and I don't blame you for it, but please let me explain why I've acted as I did in these past few months.'

'It's more than a few months that you owe an explanation for and I'm not sure that I'm ready to hear it yet. I'm not sure as I ever will be.' Dropping Sarah's hand, George turned abruptly and began to stomp back down the path to the village while Sarah watched in silent amazement. She had been expecting an angry showdown but instead her father, the veteran of so many battles and a medal-winning hero of Ulundi, was fleeing like a hare that had caught the scent of hounds. She could hardly believe it unless . . . Suddenly she thought she understood. Betsy Penghalion scared him much more than any Prussian or Zulu onslaught ever had. They had threatened his body with guns and spears but she had done something far worse. She had broken his heart. The minor injuries he had sustained in battle had always healed but perhaps this deeper wound hadn't. What if all his angry blustering was no more than an act? He was, after all, a career soldier, trained never to show the enemy any signs of weakness and he had seemed more anxious than angry when Betsy had first appeared. Was it possible that he still had deep feelings for his wife and had been afraid to stay just in case he let them show, just in case he weakened and gave her a

286

chance to hurt him all over again?

'Do you want to go too?' Betsy asked in a hushed voice.

Sarah hesitated for a moment. If she hurried she could still catch up with her father and try to offer him some solace but the woman standing in front of her was evidently in need of support too and she was her friend. No, she was more than that. She was her mother.

'No,' she said quietly. 'I'll stay.'

That relief seemed too much for the older woman to take and she suddenly burst into uncontrollable sobs.

'Oh Sarah, I didn't mean to deceive you, I swear I didn't. The day after we met I wrote a letter telling you who I was but I was too frightened to send it. Then John and Daisy wanted me to come here as a chaperone and I couldn't resist the chance to get to know you, my dearest daughter. In all the years we were apart not a day went by when I didn't think of you. I never wanted to leave you like I did but I thought it was best for you. I couldn't care for you the way I should've. Please don't despise me for what I've done.'

'I don't.' Sarah felt nothing but compassion as she put her arms around her mother and held her until she became a little calmer. 'I don't believe Papa does either. He's shocked and upset now, but I'm sure he can't hate you.'

'Your grandma did,' Betsy whispered. 'She

never approved of me or what I did. Having an actress in the family was nothing but a disgrace in her eyes.' She sniffed. 'Of course, she's not the only one to think that way. There are plenty of decent folk who'll shun you when they find out your mother was on the stage. I should never have come here.'

'Don't say that,' Sarah told her. 'I'm glad I've met you and I wouldn't wish to continue an acquaintance with anyone who behaved in such a way. You're my mother. I want to make up for all the years we've lost and I won't disown you because of tittle-tattle.' Sarah was certain of her feelings but as she was speaking, she suddenly and inexplicably saw Ewart's image in her mind. Lately she had almost dared to hope that their friendship had transcended the difference in their classes but how would he react when he learned the truth about her past? For some reason, she feared the possibility of his disapproval more than anyone else's.

*　　　*　　　*

A fine veil of cloud passed over the full moon as Abel Briar and his oldest son crept through the undergrowth in the grounds of Farleigh Park.

'I'm dead beat, Pa,' the boy whined. 'Why we'd have to walk all this way anyhow? There's plenty of pickings to be 'ad at Bishopston.'

'Haven't I taught you nothing, Davy?' His father made a halfhearted swipe at the lad's ear but missed in the dark 'It don't do to go upsetting those as keeps the bread on yer table. Now, Mister Ewart is fine and fair as far as gentry goes but there's no point risking the roof over our heads for the sake of a few rabbits. If he finds snares on his land we'll be prime suspects for poaching, whereas Sir Hugh wouldn't even think to look in our direction. Now shut yer mouth and go and check the traps we set last night. We'll 'ave to be away before dawn and time's passing.'

'Yes, Da.' The boy stumbled off into the darkness and returned a short time later with a rabbit in his hand and an anxious look on his face.

'Da,' he hissed. 'There's someone else out here. I saw a light over by the house. Bobbing about it were like it were dancing. D'ye reckon it's the little people?'

'I'll give you little people if you don't hand over that rabbit and keep yer mind on the job.' Abel stuffed the carcass into the sack he had in his hand. 'Seeing things, you are, and it had better not be because you've been a-swigging at my cider jug or this rabbit won't be the only thing getting skinned tonight.'

'I haven't, Da, I swear it.' The boy pointed in the direction of the house. 'Look, there it is again. I tell you there's someone there.'

'You might be right, after all.' Abel peered

into the darkness. 'I don't reckon it's anyone from the house, though. It's almost as if whoever it is don't want to be seen any more than we do.' He scowled. 'I'll wager it's someone who's come across our snares and thinks they'll 'elp themselves to the rightful rewards of our labour. Well, we'll see about that. Come on, lad. We'll go round and take them from behind.'

*   *   *

Constance couldn't sleep. The baby had been kicking vigorously for the better part of half an hour and although it had finally stilled again, her troubled thoughts continued to keep her awake.

Hugh had been like a stranger since his return. It wasn't that his character had completely changed. He was still a true gentleman and had been almost too solicitous about her welfare, but he seemed to have acquired an air of detachment while he'd been at war and she missed the loving, good-natured husband who had sailed away from her all those months ago. Perhaps her condition was to blame. She had heard that impending fatherhood could sometimes have a strange effect on a man but in his letters from Africa Hugh had sounded so pleased at her news that she found it hard to believe this lay behind his mood. That made it more likely that she was somehow responsible for it and that, equally, she had to find a way to win back his affections, if that was possible.

For a moment she considered slipping through the door that connected his bedchamber to hers, waking him and asking him to tell her what the trouble was. They had lain in each other's arms and talked late into the night on many occasions in the early weeks of their marriage and the intimacy of the darkness had made it easy to share some of their deepest secrets with each other. That was how a man and wife ought to be. Constance sighed. Such closeness seemed like a distant dream now and Hugh might not appreciate being woken at such an hour.

She punched at her pillow, settled into as comfortable a position as her advanced pregnancy permitted and hoped that sleep would come. Perhaps there would be a chance to speak with him in the morning . . . if only Mama wasn't always there.

She was almost asleep when something pulled her sharply back into wakefulness. A noise! It had sounded like a muffled cry outside her window. She lay still and tried to reason away her fears. Ever since the robbery she'd been too easily alarmed by every creak and groan the old house made at night. This had probably been nothing more than an owl, or perhaps a fox barking at the moon. Wasn't that said to sound like human cries? A fox couldn't speak, though, and the next sound she heard was quite definitely a word, albeit one that no one in polite society would ever use. There were people right outside the house. Without any further misgiving about how Hugh might react, she hurried into his room, bent over his bed and shook him by the shoulder until he groaned and opened his eyes.

'Wake up! I think we're being robbed again.'

*   *   *

'Hold yours fast, Davy. This pair aren't going nowhere 'til they hand over what's justly ours.' The man Abel had pinned to the ground was struggling but unable to escape from the gypsy's firm grasp. 'Now give us what's in them bags. I know you've robbed us of it.'

'I haven't robbed you of nowt,' his prisoner protested. 'Now let us go afore you rouse the whole household and they see who has been robbed.'

'You're going nowhere 'til I gets my rabbits,' Abel argued. He made a grab for the rough Hessian sack in the man's hand. His fingers closed over something inside it and he grinned but then was surprised to discover that it was solid, not like the soft fur of a rabbit at all.

'What's going on here?' The front door of the house suddenly flew open and three lanterns carried by Hugh and two of his footmen flooded the area with light. Abel

292

noticed the pistol in Hugh's hand first and then the silver goblet lying on the ground where his captive's sack had fallen open during the scuffle. He quickly reassessed his evaluation of the situation and realized that although he was in trouble he could turn matters to his advantage yet.

'Sir Hugh.' He quickly pulled the other man to his feet and pushed him forward. 'I'm 'appy to say I 'ave apprehended these brigands as had done mischief and robbery in your house. It's lucky for you that Davy and me was about here when we was, to stop 'em making off.'

'What nonsense!' A woman's shrill voice rang out from somewhere just inside the house. 'It's apparent they're in collusion with each other and we're lucky we weren't murdered in our beds. You have a gun, Hugh, use it.'

'That won't be necessary.' Hugh regarded the scene before him for a moment and Abel felt sweat break out on his brow as he awaited his judgement. At least Davy still had the other villain down on the ground and it was clear that a fight had been taking place.

'Peters, Smith, lock the two who have been detained in the coal cellar and then send someone for the constable.' Hugh gave instructions to the footmen who hastened to obey. 'And Matthews, gather up the contents of those bags.'

'Yes, sir.' The butler set about his task with

as much dignity as if he was wearing his frock coat rather than a striped nightshirt and tasselled hat.

'Glad I've been able to be of assistance, Sir.' Abel tugged at the peak of his cap, grabbed Davy's arm and began to back away, but Hugh hadn't finished with him yet.

'Wait.' It never did to disobey a man with a gun in his hand and besides, it was just possible there might be a reward for his efforts. Abel stopped at once.

'Yes, sir.'

'I am grateful for your intervention in this matter but I am curious as to how you came to be in my grounds at this hour and why there is a rabbit in your bag.'

'A what?' Abel looked down. It was too late to try and deny it. In the scuffle the contents of his sack had been jostled and now there were a pair of long furry ears sticking out of the top in full view.

'Ah that.' For the first time that night Abel was lost for words. He struggled to provide a valid explanation. 'Well, you see, me and the lad here were on our way to Borthwick to take this rabbit to the young lady who was kind enough to look after my Hepzi not so long back, only we lost our path in the dark and—'

'You're Hepzi's father?' A younger woman, with a cloak wrapped over her nightgown, stepped into the light, ignoring the insistent cries of the older one that she should 'come inside at once'.

'Yes, ma'am.' Here was another chance to put himself into a good light. He affected the look of a concerned parent. 'We're doing what we can for 'er on account of 'er betrothed losing his leg in Africa. He can't earn a wage until he gets fixed up with a wooden one and they'd be facing the workhouse if not for us.'

'How dreadful, poor Hepzi.' He'd made a good job of the tale judging by the way she pressed her fingertips against her lips.

'Do you know the girl he's speaking of?' Hugh asked.

'Against my better judgement,' the older woman interjected and Abel wished she would keep her nose out.

'Yes, and she doesn't deserve such hardship.' The young woman laid a hand on Hugh's arm. 'We must do something to help her.'

'And having her father arrested for poaching wouldn't be beneficial.' Abel was relieved to see an indulgent smile on Hugh's face as he spoke to her. With such a pretty little thing pleading his cause he might be all right. However the smile faded as Hugh turned back to address him and for a moment Abel felt his confidence falter.

'I don't believe a word of your story and I'm sure a walk round my grounds in the morning will reveal the presence of illegal snares. However, for the sake of my wife and in recognition of the service you have done for us tonight, I am prepared to overlook the matter on this occasion, although I warn you, I will not be so lenient in future.' He frowned. 'Now go before the constable arrives.'

'Yes, sir.' It was going to be all right after all. Abel assumed a suitably humble stance as he and Davy retreated 'It won't 'appen again, sir. Thank you, sir.'

'Hugh, have you completely lost your senses?' Lady Hawley demanded as soon as they were all inside again. 'You've let a common thief go free. You may as well hang a notice in all the local towns stating that poachers and pillagers are welcome here.'

'The man saved our valuables.' Hugh's voice was weary. 'He deserved some clemency for that.'

'And will no doubt be the next to try to rob you.' Lady Hawley wasn't to be easily placated. 'You've been a fool!'

'Perhaps I have, but it's a choice that's mine to make.' Hugh rounded on her in an unexpected angry outburst. 'Madam, you are Constance's mother and as such are always welcome in my home but you should remember that you are a guest here. If you could bear that in mind and try to behave accordingly, we would all be happier.'

'Well!' Lady Hawley's cheeks were crimson as she stared at her son-in-law. Constance waited for her to lash out with an outburst of her own but for once it seemed her mother was completely lost for words. She sucked in one affronted breath, then turned and stamped up the stairs.

'Oh dear.' As his temper abated, Hugh gave his wife a rueful look. 'Forgive me, my dear. I know I ought to have held my peace but I simply couldn't for a moment longer. I'm afraid she's been driving me to distraction ever since I returned.'

'She has? But I thought—' Constance thought she saw a hint of impish humour lurking behind Hugh's penitent expression and found the confidence to speak. 'Then it isn't me? You don't regret marrying me?'

'Regret—?' He looked at her as if he was unable to believe what she had said and then strode across the room to take her into his arms. 'Dearest Constance, how could you think that? I love you more than I ever did and I'm so proud of all you've achieved in my absence. Now why does that make you cry?'

'Because I'm so happy,' she smiled up at her husband through her tears. 'I truly thought you were angry with me.'

'I've been angry at having no time with you. We're never alone.' He reached out to brush a tear from her cheek with a tender smile. 'Of course, we could be now. Do you remember how we used to lie and talk late at night?'

'Oh yes, Hugh.' She smiled as he took her hand and led her up the staircase. 'I've missed those talks so much and besides, I've had an idea and you must tell me what you think of it.'

*　　　*　　　*

A few days after her conversation with Betsy, Sarah was surprised when Ewart walked into the shop just as she was about to close up for the day. She hadn't seen him since the day of the Lancers' return but now the faint glow of pleasure she felt in his presence was tempered by the fear that he might have heard the gossip about her family. However, whether he had or not, there was only one question she wanted to ask him.

'How is Hepzi?'

'Very well.' His smile was as warm as it had been when they last met. 'Indeed, she's the reason I'm here. I've news of her.' He glanced briefly towards the door. 'It's a lovely evening. Perhaps we could take a short walk down to the harbour while I relate it.'

'It would be nice to take some air. I haven't had a chance of any all day but Mrs Thomas says there's a storm building and she's never wrong, so it might not do to stay out for too long.' Sarah realized she was covering up her anxiety by gabbling like a giddy schoolgirl and forced herself to stop talking. At this rate Ewart would regret making the offer before they'd stepped out into the street.

'I'll bear that in mind.' There, she knew it.

Ewart looked as if he was trying not to laugh at her ridiculous chatter. 'Why don't you fetch your bonnet and I'll wait for you outside.'

It was a time when most villagers were preparing or partaking of their evening meal and the main street was quiet as they strolled down towards the harbour wall where the waves of high tide were lapping against the stones.

'You said you had news of Hepzi?' This was the only subject Sarah felt comfortable discussing. She certainly didn't want Ewart asking too many questions about her father's homecoming.

'Indeed. I know you've been concerned about her and would have come to tell you earlier but I wanted to be sure everything was settled first and now it is.' Ewart gave a satisfied smile. 'Miss Hepzi Briar, or Mrs Noah Kettley as she will be four weeks hence, has been engaged by Lady Constance Weston as a nursery maid.'

'Then she's to live with Constance?' Sarah was pleased to hear Hepzi's future was secure. 'But what of Noah?'

'Hugh has recently discovered that he has need of a gamekeeper.' Ewart's lips twitched as if he was enjoying some private joke. 'Noah is already getting about well on a crutch and, with a stick, will be almost as mobile as any man when he's able to use a wooden limb, so Hugh has offered him the post.'

299

'That is excellent news, and did you say that a date has been set for their wedding?'

'Exactly four weeks from today here in Borthwick church. I'm sure Hepzi will want you to be there.'

'And I wouldn't miss it.' Sarah gave a contented sigh but in the next moment Ewart spoke again and her joy immediately vanished.

'Sarah, may I ask you something?' He looked troubled now. Had he heard the stories after all?

'Yes.' Her lips had gone dry and she had to force the word out through them.

'It is a matter of some delicacy.' His frown deepened and he seemed unwilling to continue. 'Although perhaps it would be better to be forthright.' Sarah realized she was holding her breath as he turned to her. 'Has Race called on you in recent weeks?'

'Race?' It was the last question she had expected to hear and she'd been so busy trying to compose answers to any question he might ask about her family that it flustered her more than it normally would 'No.' Though it was true that he had once been a frequent visitor. She blushed as she recalled how she had almost fallen for his charming, flirtatious behaviour.

'I'm sorry. I see I have embarrassed you.' Ewart turned away before she had recovered her composure. 'I only asked because I am concerned about him and thought he may have confided in you. I believe he may be in some kind of trouble.'

'Why?' Sarah asked with a worried frown. For all his faults, she was still fond of the spirited young man.

'There is no hard evidence for my suspicions and sometimes I wonder if I am simply imagining it.' He shook his head slightly. 'Since our return from London, Race has been more subdued than usual. He rode here with me this evening but it's the first time in many days that he has ventured out of the house. That's most unlike him. Then a few days ago when I entered a room he was bent over the fireplace. He said he was merely warming his hands but the flames were higher than usual and I believe he may have been burning something.'

'He is lucky to have such a caring brother in you.' As Sarah spoke, a sudden squally gust of wind blew in from the sea and made her clutch at her hat for fear it would be blown off. The storm was approaching. 'I'm sure you have no reason to worry about Race. He seems to have a knack for escaping from all kinds of trouble.'

'Perhaps you are right.' A high wave broke over the harbour wall and splashed down onto the cobbles just in front of them. 'The weather is turning fast. We should head back.'

'Yes.' The sea, which had been placid such a short time ago, was now choppy and unpredictable. Sarah turned to glance at the ever-growing waves and then gasped. 'There's a boat out there.'

'Where?'

'There.' She pointed it out and saw the colour drain from Ewart's face.

'It's Race. I'd know that red waistcoat anywhere. What the devil is he playing at?'

Sarah couldn't answer that question but she knew enough of the sea to know that the boat was in terrible trouble.

'The sail is set wrong for the wind. He'll capsize.'

'And he can't swim.' Ewart suddenly began to run down the jetty and, as he pulled off his coat, Sarah realized what he intended to do.

'Wait!' She chased after him and caught at his arm just as he was about to jump into the water. 'You can't swim out there. The currents are too strong. We'll take Ned's boat.'

'I will.' He tried to shake off her hand. 'You're not going out there.'

'But you need me!' The idea of Ewart rowing into such danger alone filled her with a cold horror. 'I know where the rocks are and how the currents run.' She could still see opposition in his eyes and made a last desperate plea. 'Besides, two can row faster than one. You won't make it out to Race in time without me.'

Ewart looked as if he was about to protest but that moment the tiny boat upended and Race was thrown into the water. There was no more time to argue.

'Quickly, it's this way.' She snatched hold of his hand and they hurried to the place where Ned's little fishing boat was moored. Far offshore, Race had disappeared under the waves and, as Ewart frantically worked the mooring rope loose, Sarah prayed they would be able to reach him before it was too late.

CHAPTER THIRTEEN

Sarah's arm muscles burned with pain but as she sat beside Ewart and pulled on her oar she knew she couldn't rest even for a moment. They had to reach Race before the sea claimed him. A flash of lightning ripped across the sky as another high wave crashed over the prow and icy water soaked through her already sodden clothes but she was so intent on her task that she barely noticed.

'Can you see him?' she shouted out above the roar of the wind. It was as dark as night beneath the clouds and the rain hampered her vision even further. How could they have been rowing for so long and yet still seem so far from Race?

'Yes.' Ewart sounded equally exhausted. 'He's clinging to the side of his boat.' He didn't say any more but they both knew that a strong wave could loosen Race's tenuous grip on the hull at any moment. That thought renewed Sarah's resolve. She ignored the sting of the blisters rising on her hands and rowed as hard as she could until they finally drew level with the half-sunken remains of Race's vessel.

'Try to hold us steady.' Ewart gave her his oar before crawling back to the stern where he reached out to his brother. 'Race! Catch hold of my hand. I'll pull you aboard.'

Race was wide-eyed with fear and seemed unwilling to relinquish his grasp on the only thing keeping him afloat but, at Ewart's further urging, he tentatively stretched out one hand. Both men's fingers strained to close the short distance between them but they were still too far apart. The force of the currents made the oars jerk about in Sarah's grasp but she used every last ounce of her strength to try to inch the boat a little nearer. They were so close now. Ewart would have hold of him at any moment.

The sudden high wave caught them all unawares. The boat was almost swamped and, when the water died down, Race was gone.

'No!' Ewart lunged forward. Sarah was terrified that he was about to plunge into the water behind his brother but he braced himself and she saw determination harden every muscle in his face as he started to pull at something. He had managed to catch hold of Race's wrist.

Minutes seemed like hours as Ewart

engaged in a deadly battle against the sea to win back his brother. His efforts made the boat rock so violently that Sarah could do little to steady it and was afraid that they might all be thrown into the water. Eventually, however, Race's torso appeared over the top of the stern. Ewart gave one last pull and both men landed in a heap in the bottom of the boat.

'Thank the Lord.' Sarah slumped with relief but Ewart still looked tense as he edged back to his place beside her.

'None of us are safe until we make it back to shore and Race is in no fit state to aid us. Can you be strong for a little longer?'

'Yes.' There was blood smeared on the oar that she handed back to Ewart. She saw him glance at her smarting hands but had no intention of giving into weakness now. She would do what he had asked of her and be strong.

'What was that?' After another gruelling struggle against the tide they had almost reached the safety of the harbour when a dull boom echoed off the buildings behind them and Ewart looked up at a bright white light that flared up overhead.

'A maroon to summon the lifeboat crew,' Sarah explained. 'Someone must have seen us.'

'We scarcely need rescue now.' Despite his evident fatigue, Ewart managed a grim smile. 'It's a pity no one fired it earlier.'

'They might not have reached Race in time.'

'That's true.' As he spoke, Ewart looked down at his brother who was lying in a puddle of water at their feet. He had been ominously still since he was hauled aboard and Ewart's next quiet words sent a chill through Sarah. 'I pray that we have.'

A small crowd had gathered round the harbour and members of the lifeboat crew hurried down the jetty to help pull the boat back to a secure mooring. They were safe. Other hands were towing the boat along. She didn't have to do any more. There was so much bustling activity around her and yet she suddenly felt oddly detached from it all as if it was all some kind of a dream. She saw the anxiety on Ewart's face as he helped the men who were lifting Race's limp body ashore. Then watched his expression transform into one of relief as Race coughed and suggested that a brandy might be more beneficial than the blanket someone had wrapped round him.

'Sarah.' The voice seemed to come from a long way off. 'Sarah, it's all right you can let go of this now.' Ewart was in front of her, his hands gently easing her fingers out of their locked position on the oar.

'I thought I heard him speak.'

'You did. He's going to be all right but now you need care as well.'

'You're so wet.' It seemed absurd to giggle at such a time but she couldn't help it. There was the dignified Ewart Davenport with dripping hair plastered down against his head and a saturated cravat hanging limply against his wet shirt.

'I fear that you're no better and you've lost your hat.' With a gentle smile he reached out to tuck a tendril of soaked hair back behind her ear and then put his hands under her elbows to help her rise. 'Come along, we need to find you a warm fireside.'

Her legs felt as if they were no longer under her control. She managed to stand but when she tried to take a step they buckled. She stumbled. Ewart put his arms out to catch her and, before she knew it, he was holding her in an awkward embrace.

'I'm sorry.' She looked up, almost expecting to see irritation at her clumsiness but encountered an altogether different expression on his face.

'Don't be.'

The sudden warmth of his lips against hers made the icy chill of the sea seem like a distant memory and she couldn't help but respond to the kiss. His arms grew tighter around her and she felt as if she was where she truly belonged. Except that she wasn't. This was wrong. He was a gentleman and she was a postmistress. There could never be anything between them.

'Don't.' Pushing him away was the hardest thing she had ever done.

'Forgive me.' Colour surged across Ewart's cheeks and he released her so abruptly that she almost fell again. 'I shouldn't have done that.' He sounded angry and Sarah couldn't be sure if he was annoyed at himself for stooping to such a thing or at her for having the audacity to rebuff him. He would undoubtedly find out soon enough that she had acted in his best interests. Kissing an actress's daughter would be disastrous for his reputation.

He barely looked at her as he helped her out of the boat and it occurred to her that her actions had been in her best interests too. If she had allowed the kiss to last for a moment longer she would have been in danger of completely losing her heart to this wonderful man and that could only have led to it being broken.

'Sarah!' With his usual indefatigability, Race had already recovered from his ordeal and hurried across to her. 'You saved my life. How can I ever thank you?'

Before she could reply, he threw his arms round her and landed an enthusiastic kiss on her lips. Sarah was too surprised to react as swiftly as she had to Ewart's kiss and, when Race finally released her, she found that Ewart was watching the scene with narrowed eyes.

'Now that you are quite done with your expressions of gratitude, Race, perhaps you would care to tell us why you behaved in such a foolhardy way in the first place.'

'I believe he was trying to escape from me.' A burly man in a bowler hat pushed his way to the front of the small crowd and glowered at Race. 'It's about time you realized that you can't, Mr Davenport.'

'And who are you?' Ewart glared at him.

'My name is Fulcher, sir.' The man pulled a sheet of paper out of an inner pocket of his coat and handed it to Ewart. 'As you can see, I have been engaged to act on behalf of parties that Mr Davenport owes a considerable amount of money to. Money which he seems . . . unwilling to repay.'

'More debts?' Ewart's shoulders slumped as he read the document and then crumpled it in his hand. 'Call at Bishopston tomorrow morning, Mr Fulcher,' he said wearily. 'I will see to it that all my brother's creditors are satisfied.'

'Sarah, dearest, I heard the maroon and then someone said it was you in peril.' Lucy hurried up with a blanket that she wrapped around her sister's shoulders. 'My, but you're chilled to the bone. No wonder you're shivering so. You should be inside.'

Sarah allowed Lucy to lead her away but she couldn't help glancing back to see someone taking Race and Ewan into the inn to dry off. She lightly touched her fingertips to her lips. They were still pulsing from the pressure of Race's kiss but she knew that it was the memory of his brother's much gentler, tender caress that would stay with her for ever.

'My dear Mrs Davenport, I came as soon as I heard the news.' Lady Hawley burst into the drawing room at Bishopston and started speaking before she had even unbuttoned her gloves. 'Of course I can understand why Race feels he can't show his face in the district but what foolish notion has made him decide to go to America of all places?'

'Lady Hawley, what an unexpected pleasure.' A pale circle appeared on each of Mrs Davenport's cheeks as she rose to greet her guest. 'Won't you take some tea?'

'Thank you, but I won't. My dear Constance's confinement is imminent now and I daren't linger away from the house for too long but I just had to come and sympathize over the loss of your son.'

'He isn't to be lost to me.' The circles on Mrs Davenport's cheeks grew a little larger. 'He is simply going to seek a new life overseas. There will be letters and he may return one day.'

'Of course.' Lady Hawley didn't sound as if she believed that for a moment. 'But even so, you must be heartbroken. I couldn't bear to think of my Constance being so far away. She's such a loving daughter and I do declare that Hugh fusses over me as if I were his own mother and Farleigh Park my own home.' She had the grace to flush a little as she said this.

The truth was that since Hugh's outburst she had been obliged to remember that she wasn't at home and to adjust her behaviour accordingly. She felt tolerated rather than wanted and had already decided that she would return to London and her own circle of friends, who no doubt missed her counsel a great deal, as soon as Constance's baby was born.

'I will miss Edwin,' Mrs Davenport conceded. 'But I must console myself with the knowledge that Ewart will still be here. He's a truly caring son and such a comfort to me.'

'Indeed.' Lady Hawley sniffed. 'There's no denying that he's of a better character than his brother but in my opinion he needs to exercise a little more discretion over the company he keeps. I've heard that he was walking out with Miss Penghalion when he was obliged to rush to Race's aid.'

'I don't believe he is courting her.' An edge had crept into Mrs Davenport's voice. 'However, I would not be displeased if he were. I've met Miss Penghalion and found her to be a very charming and perfectly respectable young lady.'

'I'm sure she is. It's just such a pity that the same can't be said of her mother.' Lady Hawley's smile was venomous. 'I heard of the scandal only yesterday. Did you know that the woman abandoned Sarah and her siblings for a life of debauchery and corruption on the stage?' She released an exaggerated sigh and pressed a hand to her chest. 'I was never blessed with a son but if I had been I would be most concerned to think he was consorting with the daughter of such a woman.'

*　　　*　　　*

Sarah laid aside the book she was trying to read and went to gaze out of the window. It was the kind of mellow autumnal day that would have gladdened her heart once but now not even the sight of the sun shining on the reddening leaves could cheer her. It seemed that nothing could.

After Race's rescue, her father had insisted that she needed some time to recuperate. To that end, he had taken on the running of the shop and issued strict orders that she wasn't to work again until her spirits had lifted after what had, he acknowledged, been an arduous year for her. She had protested but he'd been adamant and she couldn't explain that having nothing to do only made her sense of melancholy worse. She needed to work, to do any task that would keep her thoughts fixed on anything other than Ewart Davenport.

It was as if he was haunting her. She saw his face in her dreams and heard his voice in her head. When she tried to concentrate on her sewing or on a book, she found herself reliving conversations with him or recalling his kindness to Hepzi or, most frequently, thinking of the tenderness she'd seen in his gaze just before he kissed her. She tried to remind herself that she'd once considered him ill-mannered and arrogant but she hadn't believed that of him for a long time. He was neither of those things, although she almost wished he was. That might make it easier to cope with the fact that she was probably never going to see him again. There had been no word from him since she had left him at the harbour, and when a shiny round box from the best milliners in Otterly had been delivered to the cottage, the card accompanying the exquisite hat inside had only contained Race's signature. She didn't know if she had offended him by rejecting his kiss or whether he had learned the truth about her parentage but, whatever his reasons, Ewart had made it plain that he wanted nothing more to do with her.

The clock on the landing chimed the hour and she tried to focus on happier thoughts as she went downstairs. The shop would be closed now and Papa would want her company. It wouldn't do to mope in front of him.

Her father was already sitting at the kitchen table with a mug of tea when she entered the room and, to her astonishment, he wasn't alone. Her mother was sitting opposite him.

'Come on in, lass.' If George had noticed her startled expression, he chose to ignore it.

'We're just having some tea.' Beneath his moustache it was hard to be sure but had he really just smiled briefly at his guest? 'Betsy came in to see how you were faring after your adventure. She didn't expect to find me behind the counter but when she saw how rushed off my feet I was, she put an apron on and stayed to help. She's a grand assistant.'

'I was well trained.' Betsy smiled up at Sarah. 'How are you feeling, my dear?'

'Very well, thank you.'

'Are you sure?' Even after being absent for so many years it seemed that Betsy hadn't lost a mother's instinctive knowledge that all wasn't right with her child, and now she frowned. 'You look troubled by something.'

'Not at all.' Sarah didn't meet her gaze as she sat down. 'How is John?'

'Busy making preparations for his wedding.' Betsy smiled a little sadly. 'I wish I could be here to see it.'

'Why wouldn't you be?' Sarah asked.

'Because it wouldn't be fair to John and Daisy. They say I'm welcome to stay for as long as I wish but newlyweds don't want someone else under their roof. Besides, it's time I was earning a living again.'

'So you'll go back to the theatre?' Sarah tried to hide her dismay at the idea of Betsy's departure.

'No.' Betsy shook her head. 'I hope I might find something in another shop. I have no taste for acting any more and besides, an audience wants to see young pretty faces, not old crones like me.'

'You're still pretty as far as I can see,' George said abruptly before flushing as if he hadn't intended the words to come out. Sarah noticed that Betsy's cheeks had gone pink too and she wondered just what had passed between her parents in the shop that afternoon. She knew it would take a good deal more than one day of working together to heal the divisions between them but it was good to see that Papa had managed to overcome his initial animosity towards his wife. Who could say how matters might have progressed, if only Betsy didn't intend to leave so soon.

*　　　*　　　*

Although it was a bright morning the wind blowing across the platform at Otterly station was a chilly one and Ewart stamped his feet to warm them.

'You don't have to stay.' Race was sitting on his trunk and seemed unaffected by the cold. 'The train will be here soon enough.'

'Of course I'll stay.' Ewart looked at his brother. It was hard to believe that this was the last time he would see him for what might be many years. They'd had their differences of late but he would miss Race's constant optimism and good-natured humour. 'You will remember to write when you reach Boston, won't you? Mama will be waiting eagerly for word.' He swallowed down the lump that had unexpectedly formed in his throat. 'We both will.'

'Of course, but I warn you I'll be too busy finding a suitable profession to write every day.' Race stood up as if to add emphasis to his declaration. 'I'm a reformed character, Brother. Just wait until you see how successful I become.'

'See to it that you do.' Ewart's sharp tone was belied by his affectionate smile. 'I can't come and bring you home this time.'

'You won't have to.'

They were both silent for some time. Race glanced at the front page of the newspaper he was carrying and Ewart stood staring at the railway tracks in front them, longing to ask the question that was burning in his mind and yet almost dreading to hear the answer. Hearing the cold facts would be painful but he decided eventually that he would rather know the truth.

'When do you intend to send for Miss Penghalion to join you?'

'Sarah?' Race folded the paper again and looked at his brother with a confused frown. 'Why would I send for Sarah?'

'Because you love her, just as she loves you.' Ewart pulled his watch out of his pocket and made a pretence of studying it so Race couldn't see his pained expression. 'I know you received a letter from her only yesterday. I saw how you kissed her that day in Borthwick and how she had reacted earlier when I mentioned your name.'

'Oh, and how did she react?' Race was grinning and it was almost too much to bear.

'She blushed and seemed quite disconcerted.'

The sound of an engine whistle made them both look up. The train was coming.

'Did it occur to you that she might have blushed because she didn't want to discuss me when she was walking with you?' Race shook his head and his grin grew broader. 'Did it not once occur to you that perhaps she loves you . . . just as you love her?'

'What?' Ewart started and this time Race laughed.

'I kissed her in the heat of the moment and out of gratitude. What lay behind the sweet moment I witnessed when you were in the boat with her? You seemed a good deal more . . . grateful than I was. Then, of course, there's the matter of the hat, which her letter was to thank me for. Why would a man take as long as you did to select just the right one for a girl if he didn't love her? I would have bought the first one the milliner showed us. You had us there for almost an hour but then refused to admit your part in it. Oh, but of course.' Race clapped his hand to his forehead as understanding dawned. 'You wouldn't sign that card because you thought that I, her beloved, should take all the credit for it. You love her and yet you would have stood aside for me.' He laid a hand on Ewart's arm. 'You're a better brother than I have ever deserved even if you have been sorely mistaken. I admit she was pretty enough to tempt me when I met her but she was far too sensible to let someone like me turn her head. There's nothing between us, so you no longer have to worry about my sensibilities. Go and declare your feelings to her.'

'Why do that when she's made it clear that she doesn't want me to?' Ewart muttered as the train pulled into the station in a rush of smoke and hissing steam.

'I think you're mistaken about that as well.' Race shook his head.

'Here, will you help me see this trunk safely into the guard's van?' When the trunk was safely stowed away, Race walked back to the first-class carriage but turned to face Ewart before he boarded. 'Goodbye. Kiss Mama for me.'

'Take care of yourself.' Ewart reached out to take his brother into a warm embrace. 'And please try to stay out of trouble.'

'Why, Brother, you shouldn't take on so.' Race's smile was at its most engaging as he climbed aboard. 'You should know by now that I lead a charmed life. I never come to any harm.'

The guard slammed the door shut but Race pulled the window down and Ewart stepped up to him as the train started to edge forwards.

'Promise me that you'll come home one day, Race.'

'I will—when I have made my fortune.' Race raised his hand in farewell, then seemed struck by a sudden thought and stuck his head out of the window. 'Promise me something too.'

'What is it?' The train was gaining speed and Ewart had to run along the platform in order to hear his brother's final words.

'That for once in your life you'll take a risk. Open your heart to the woman you love. You might be pleasantly surprised if you do.'

*　　*　　*

The day of Hepzi's wedding dawned with a pale pink glow of sunlight in the sky and the promise of fair weather ahead. Sarah rose early and went out into the garden to gather the last of the dahlias and chrysanthemums blooming there before walking up to the church. She wanted to decorate the altar where her friend would make her vows but intended to stop somewhere else first.

Her grandmother's grave was in a sheltered spot shaded by the branches of a rowan tree. It was just the kind of place where Anne might have been happy to sit and rest on a hot afternoon, and Sarah found great comfort in going there.

'I wish you could be here to see Hepzi happy at last,' she said as she laid three of the blooms from her bouquet down on the dew-soaked grass. 'And I hope you understand that finding my mother and growing to love her doesn't mean that I could ever love you any less.' She straightened up. A slight breeze rustled the branches above her and a blackbird, perched high overhead, started to sing. Somehow she was sure that Grandma was giving her and Betsy her blessing and, as she walked along the path to the church, she felt that nothing could disturb her peace. Until she turned a corner and saw who was standing by the lychgate. Why hadn't it occurred to her that Ewart might attend the wedding? Of course, he had every right to but she had convinced herself he would never come to Borthwick again. Her heart had begun to race and her thoughts tumbled about in a barely coherent muddle. She couldn't face him. Not now when it was likely that every word she uttered, every look she gave him and even every breath she took would betray her feelings for him. If she turned back she could retrace her steps and slip into the church by the side door. He need never know that she had been there.

'Sarah?' At the sound of his voice, she stood

rooted to the spot. He had seen her. She couldn't run away now and besides, she didn't know if she could trust her legs to carry her anywhere. All she could do was stand and watch helplessly as he walked towards her. 'I was about to come down to the shop in search of you. I had hoped—' As he approached, his voice tailed away and a smile momentarily transformed his tense expression, lightening his handsome features and making her pulse jump about even more erratically. 'I knew that hat would look well on you. It brings out the roses in your cheeks.'

'I wrote to thank Race for it.' She was quite sure that the raging colour in her cheeks at that moment had nothing to do with the hat. 'I hope he received the letter before he sailed.' If only he would stop staring at her quite like that. It was so very disconcerting.

'He did. I wish he could have seen how very beautiful you look in it.'

'Mr Davenport!' If he had the slightest idea of how his words were affecting her, he surely wouldn't torment her so.

'What? Am I Ewart no longer? I had hoped you might still regard me as your friend.'

'I do. That is I—' What did she think and how could she accept mere friendship from a man she loved so much and always would?

'That isn't true.' Ewart didn't seem to have heard her stammering reply. 'I don't want to be your friend, Sarah.' She saw him clench one

321

of his hands into a fist and pass the other rapidly over his mouth before he spoke again. 'I hope for so much more than that. If it cannot be; if you cannot begin to care for me with even a fraction of the love that I feel for you then please tell me now so that I can leave with some remnant of my pride intact even if my heart is not.'

They were words she had dreamed of hearing him say. In her dreams, this was the moment when she would go willingly into his arms, but in reality there were still so many reasons why she couldn't.

'You don't know what you are saying,' she murmured. 'There is so much to impede any chance of happiness we might have.'

'Tell me that your heart isn't set on another.' He took a step closer. 'I stood aside when I thought you wanted Albert Eden and then Race but I'll be damned if I'll let another man steal you from me now.'

'There is no one else.' She resisted the almost overwhelming temptation to reach out and touch his cheek. 'There never has been, but you must consider our positions. You own Bishopston. You move in exalted circles and I am merely the—'

'The daughter of an officer in the same regiment that I served in,' he interrupted her. 'I see no impediment there and besides, I wouldn't care if you were a scullery maid. I would still love you just as passionately.' He reached out to encircle her waist with his arm. 'Marry me, Sarah. End the misery I've been living in for so many weeks.'

'I can't.' She shook her head violently. 'There is something else. Something you don't know that would scandalize society if I was your wife and it came to light.'

'I see.' He studied her for a moment and she was sure he must be reconsidering his rash proposal, but then he spoke again. 'I assume you're about to confess that your mother is one of the actresses that Race used to dine with in Exeter.'

'You know?' She looked up at him in disbelief. How could he know that and still speak of marrying her?

'I came into the room shortly after Lady Hawley had taken great delight in acquainting my mother with the fact. Therefore I was present to witness Mama telling her unwelcome guest to leave at once. I don't believe I have ever seen Mama become quite so enraged. She and I are in agreement that no one who treats you with anything other than the utmost respect will ever be welcome at Bishopston.' He drew her closer. 'Now that you know this, will you consent to be my wife?'

'I hardly know what to say.' A thousand emotions were whirling round in Sarah's head. 'You can't begin to know how hard I have tried to teach myself not to love you in recent weeks.

'Ah, so you admit that you have loved me. This is progress.' Ewart sounded triumphant as he traced the outline of her lips with one finger. 'Dearest Sarah, are you quite sure you couldn't teach yourself to love me again?'

'I believe I might.' She looked up into his eyes and finally permitted the joy bubbling up inside her to express itself in a radiant smile. 'In fact, now that I have given the matter some consideration, I'm quite sure that it will be a simple process.'

'I'm glad.' He smiled down at her. 'Are those flowers for Hepzi?'

'Yes.'

'Then give them to me.'

'Why?'

'Because if I don't lay them safely on the ground they will be completely crushed by the time I finish doing what I am about to do, and Hepzi deserves better than that.'

Sarah permitted him to relieve her of the flowers and then, just as she had done so many times in her dreams, went willingly into the arms of the man she loved.

*   *   *

The bells of Borthwick church rang out as Noah and Hepzi Kettley stepped out into the sunshine to be greeted by their friends and family. The radiant bride who stood smiling at her husband's side was nothing like the scared

324

girl who had asked for help writing a letter so many months earlier. Noah walked with the aid of a stick and his limp was noticeable but he held himself with pride. He had a position in life and the means to support his family.

'I'm glad it turned out so well.' Sarah turned to Lucy who was dabbing at her eyes with a handkerchief as she watched the bridal party.

'It's beautiful,' she sniffed. 'And to think it will be John and Daisy standing there before we know it.' She looked across the path to where that young couple stood hand in hand, no doubt dreaming of their own forthcoming nuptials. 'I love a wedding so much.'

'Then I think you have much to look forward to.' Sarah stifled joyful laughter. She couldn't share her happy news yet. Even love couldn't make Ewart completely abandon his sense of propriety and he'd been insistent that he must speak to her father first.

'I heard that Betsy is helping Papa in the shop again this morning.' Lucy turned to look enquiringly at her sister. 'Do you think they might yet be reconciled after all this time?'

'They certainly seem to take some pleasure from each other's company.' Sarah frowned. 'But I don't see how they can be reunited when Bet . . . Mama intends to leave again.'

'Oh but she doesn't.' Lucy shook her head. 'Sarah, what has made you so preoccupied of late? Didn't you know that John has persuaded her stay, at least until after his wedding?'

'No, I didn't, but I'm glad to hear it.' Sarah suspected that her father might be equally pleased about the news.

'Miss Penghalion?' A voice at her side made her turn and she recognized the man who had approached her.

'Sir Hugh, how nice to meet you again.'

'I wondered if I might draw you away for a moment. Constance is in the carriage and she is most anxious to see you.'

'Oh but of course.' Sarah followed Hugh to where his wife sat in the open carriage looking pale but happy. 'Constance, I didn't expect to see you out so soon after your confinement.'

'I really shouldn't be,' Constance confessed with a smile. 'And I have no doubt the very idea of such a thing would have given Mama a fit of the vapours if she was still here but I was determined to see Hepzi wed and to show you Isabella.' She drew the edge of the white shawl back from the face of the baby in her arms. 'Isn't she delightful?'

'She's beautiful.'

'Hugh has given me his word that her education won't be confined to needlework and music. We intend to encourage her to study all she can and to think independently.' Constance gently covered the baby up again. 'You will come and visit me sometimes, won't you, Sarah? I'll miss you if you don't.'

'I'm quite sure that I will.' Once again Sarah

had to keep her secret although she longed to tell Constance that very soon she would invite her visit her at Bishopston. She imagined how her friend would gasp and was still smiling over this as she made her way back into the churchyard.

'I trust it's the thought of me that makes you blush so prettily.' Ewart was standing watching for her return.

'As I've been unable to think of anything else all morning, it must be.' She gasped as he caught her into his arms again. 'Ewart! People will see.'

'They are all too busy throwing rice and I swear I can't go another moment without a kiss from you. Surely you wouldn't deny me that?'

'No.' She laughed as his lips drew close to hers. 'I could not deny you a thousand kisses.'

No one seemed to have noticed her absence or the fact that her cheeks were glowing when she slipped back to join the bridal party a few minutes later but not everyone had been throwing rice and when Ewart reappeared some time after her, Isaac pointed at him and shouted out in a voice that no one could fail to hear.

'I just saw that man kissing my Aunt Sarah.'

*   *   *

'It wasn't quite how I envisioned telling

everyone that we were to be married,' Sarah admitted that evening as she and the man that she was now formally engaged to strolled, arm in arm, down to the shore.

'No,' Ewart agreed. 'But it certainly made everyone laugh.'

'Including you.' Sarah turned to look at him. 'When I first met you I was convinced that you never laughed.'

'I rarely did and Race frequently took me to task over it. He was forever telling me that I should learn to enjoy life.'

'And have you?' she asked with a coy smile.

'I believe I have begun to now.' He stopped walking and put his arms around her waist, drawing her close to him. 'Of course, now that Race is gone I'll need someone else to see to it that I don't become too dull again.'

'I think I am equal to that task.' Sarah reached up to let her lips brush against his cheek. 'Although I'm not sure I can promise to make life as exciting as Race did.'

'I'm relieved to hear that,' Ewart said with a soft laugh. 'I think we've both had all the excitement we need for some time.'

'Quite.' Sarah let her head rest against her fiancé's shoulder as they stood and watched the sun set. The past few months had certainly been eventful and she knew it would be naïve of her to think that the years ahead would be completely free of troubles. This time, however, she wouldn't face them alone. She and Ewart would be together forever, supported by their love for each other and ready to embark on whatever adventures the future might hold.